International Acclaim for Venson Jordan's The Rebel Marcus Madison

Here's What Real People Think

A great novel, Venson Jordan took a real life problem and fictionalized it for public consumption.
---Masayori Miyazaki
Osaka Japan

As a black woman who raised two sons in this country, this story touched me deeply. Beneath this novel's compelling story is a real picture of life and hope for the forgotten people in America and the rest of the world.
---Glenda Campbell Roberts,
Takoma Park, Md. USA

A tender story that hits a hard spot in many people. It is a well written book that opens the mind to a world view of law enforcement that may contradict our own.
Sewonuku Komla,
---Kadjebi Ghana

This is an excellent novel. In the growing age of Trumpism, Venson Jordan proves that the pen is still mightier than the sword.
--- George Thompson,
Gary Indiana. USA

This book was a joy to read. The writing is exciting and rich. The story is current, life like and educational.
--- Jalegat Tallam,
Nairobi Kenya

The Rebel Marcus Madison references contemporary issues to knit a thought provoking story. The book is entertaining, revolutionary and transformative. It is a great read,
---Hilary Banks
Popular talk show host on BCfm radio, Bristol UK

Few Things Are More Powerful Than The Love Between A Man And His Mother

THE REBEL
MARCUS MADISON

Venson Jordan

CHIOMA
PUBLISHING

CHIOMA PUBLISHING
Since 2013
Cranston, Rhode Island

ISBN-13: 978-1718955158

ISBN-10: 1718955154

DEDICATION

My dedication will always begin with my family, they manage to love me in spite of my hermitic nature.
Chontell, this book would not have happened without your support. To Tristan and Shakeelah thanks again for your patience.
Keisha, and my high-end grandchildren Justin and Jordan, thank you.
Karen, I love you.
And
Natalie, with you in my life everything is possible.
.

CONTENTS

A Few Short Quotes From

Frederick Douglass

1818-1895

Social reformer, abolitionist, orator, writer, and statesman. He was a man so powerful that white people found it hard to believe he was once a slave.

Find out just what any people will quietly submit to and you have the exact measure of the injustice and wrong which will be imposed on them.

It is easier to build strong children than to repair broken men.

If there is no struggle, there is no progress.

Power concedes nothing without a demand. It never did and it never will.

Those who profess to favor freedom, and yet depreciate agitation, are men who want crops without plowing up the ground.

I prefer to be true to myself, even at the hazard of incurring the ridicule of others, rather than to be false, and to incur my own abhorrence.

At a time like this, scorching irony, not convincing argument, is needed.

It is not light that we need, but fire; it is not the gentle shower, but thunder. We need the storm, the whirlwind, and the earthquake.

I prayed for twenty years but received no answer until I prayed with my legs.

ACKNOWLEDGMENTS

For encouraging me to undertake this project and supporting it with their talents or finances, I would like to thank Nasik Immanuel Ben Yehudah, Patricia Silva Franklin, Rodney Jordan, Linnell Williams, Adina and the team of Kohane Habakkuk Ben Levy and Tirzah Baht Yosef (Madeleine Gray).
I am always grateful for the continued support of
Mrs. Lucille Hester.
Thank you.

A special thanks to the fans, friends and loyal professionals in the literary community who helped me grow as a writer.

PROLGUE

Marcus Madison was a college student, home for a weekend to celebrate twenty years of a happy life together with his parents Gerald and Lisa Madison. They were wealthy owners of the most popular restaurant in the city and two of the most law abiding civic leaders in the country. An hour after their twenty year wedding anniversary celebration, tragedy strikes when their luxury car was stopped by the police.

Following the officers' precise instructions, Gerald Madison slowly reached into his breast pocket to retrieve his identification. His wife Lisa moved and the officers opened fire through the windows; riddling the high-end interior with glass and bullets.

Riding in the back seat, Marcus was badly wounded, but his parents, the pillars of his stability, were dead. For months he recuperated but he would never flush the face of his mangled mother from his mind. After the community outrage and political pressure was exhausted the actions of the officers were deemed justifiable, and criminal charges were never filed. It was a double blow of injustice to a peaceful young man resulting in a psychic trauma set with nightmares, grief, and overwhelming guilt. Struggling to fight the looping memory, young Marcus withdrew to a state of near-sanity and discovered an anger he never knew. With the help of his girlfriend Tatyana, he recovered and conjured a persona based on a favorite comic hero. Now armed with a new confidence and training, he vowed to avenge the death of his parents.

The ultra-intelligent, emotionally traumatized Marcus Madison became an avenging vigilante dedicated to the abolition of police corruption. Fighting for justice against those sworn to protect it, his mysterious ability to digitally confound and overwhelm the common worries of those who wear and protect the blue shield stokes a hidden flame of fear within the American justice system.

1 CHAPTER
We Are In It Together

And the Lord looked and was displeased that there was no justice... He saw that there was no one, he was appalled that there was no one to intervene; so his own arm achieved salvation for him, and his own righteousness sustained him. Isaiah 59:16

"Hello America. I regret this interruption of your evening program, but this is important. My fellow Americans, the most beautiful thing about us is that we are a country of laws. As such, we cannot allow anyone to take the law into their own hands. There exists among us a serious threat to our democracy and at this time we cannot identify the culprit. Someone out there knows who it is. If you know this person, do the right thing and turn 'em in. Our society cannot stand under vigilante rule. No matter what you think of these officers they were acquitted in a court of law; and no one is above the law.

No one has the right to ignore a jury's verdict and punish people. I know there are some sick minds out there who see this as payback. But let's call it what it is, "terrorism." A deliberate attempt to intimidate law enforcement. People, if law enforcement is under attack, who will protect you? When the forces of evil turn on you who will be there? No one. Please hear me, if you know something, say something, and turn 'em in."

"Wow, not again. Eric, is it me or does it seem like the president is on TV every week making this kind of announcement?"

"Yeah Mike, I noticed that."

"Look, now CCN just reported another cop is missing. Apparently this guy was very careful and didn't go to the bathroom without his guard dog and a gun. But the reporter said that the dog is dead and the investigators can't find a trace of the cop."

"Wow, pretty soon they'll be posting photos in the supermarkets of these guys, like Amber alerts."

And someone barked, "That's pretty disrespectful." It was a bear of a man who towered over everything in the small shop. He stood no more than six feet away from Eric and Mike. It was Jason Henley, a former US Marine and physical educator with a passion for teaching high school wrestling. Like most people in Sarah's Donut and Coffee that evening, Jason was rushing through to grab a hot glazed one and move on. But the line was moving slower than normal, partially because everyone in the line gave a bit of their attention to the national alert being announced by the president. Eric and Mike didn't expect a third voice to enter their conversation, and their reflexed response to the comment merely echoed what he said. "Disrespectful," they replied, and quickly spun around to see the face that uttered the word.

But the big voice of Jason wasn't finished. "You guys seem to see this as a joke. Good men and women die every day to keep us safe, and you stand here, in the comfort and security they provide, and you mock them." His heavy voice shook at the edge of every angry word. "Whatever you think happened, you didn't see all the evidence." He pointed his beefy finger at the flat screen mounted on the wall above the busy workers behind the counter. "The jury has to weigh more than a few YouTube videos," he said. "They did that and made a decision. These missing police officers have been acquitted in a court of law. Look, I admit our justice system ain't perfect but it's the best the world has to offer, that's for sure. Life is like wrestling. If you lose the match on points, you accept it, shake hands and try to do better next time, that's it. But this kind of thing undermines our way of life."

"Who's way of life are you talking about?" Eric's scratchy voice injected. Eric made every face and polite gesture he could think of, working hard to resist the force of thoughts that took control of his tongue. When Jason paused he added, "Dude, you and this president live in la-la land. For me, this life ain't like wrestling. There has never been reliable justice for Black and Brown people in America. That's your way of life - our life is not that way. For us, we get justice in the next life. In this one, there's Just-Us.

The way I see it, things easily rise to the level of terrorism when people do sh** to the police. But the police have been terrorizing our asses for a few hundred years and it barely makes the news. Why is that? Hell, if I knew who it was I wouldn't give him up, I'd give him a hug. The president can call my mind sick all he wants. My mind may be sick, but my ass feels safer knowing that someone is out there keeping the police in check."

Everyone in the slow-moving line had an opinion but few wanted to wade into the growing heat of the discussion. Spontaneous discussions about this kind of thing are usually fraught with more emotion than logic. The facts are almost always a luxury item because they center on a re-occurring nightmare America refuses to directly address; and that is, America now has, and has always had, a race problem.

For most White people the issue of racial animus looms over the country like a unicorn standing on the American flag. But from the perspective of many Black people, the racial divide in America is so large that White people can't see it. Until something like this happens the majority of White Americans avoid the issue all together, presumably because it's not an important factor in their daily doings. Generally speaking, when in mixed company Americans lock their thoughts safely behind their eyes, smile and bare it. But in this case, a woman standing directly in front of Jason reluctantly entered the discussion. "I think the police are afraid. And whenever that happens, things for our minority communities get worse, not better. This is not about race," she insisted. "This is about fairness."

"Ma'am," Mike injected, "Have you seen these police? I don't know about your neighborhood, but in mine, they roll up like combat warriors. What are they afraid of? Al-Qaida ain't in the hood. And the people they are killing are not armed people. About two years ago a prominent family in this town was shot up by the police. They were on their way home from a party, in their own car. No one in that car had a gun. They were pillars of the Black community less than a hundred yards from their home and the police cut them down like weeds in the garden; and those cops weren't even charged with a crime. Fortunately their son survived, but barely. Lady, they are already killing us. How much worse can things get? It's easy for you to characterize a problem when it doesn't affect you."

She snapped back. "What do you mean it doesn't affect me? I am an American. This system is supposed to protect all of us. The wrongful death of any American affects me because I am a human being just like they are. We are all connected." Mike strained to force a wrinkled smile to the corner of his lips. To him, she was one of those well-meaning middle class liberal types who never ate a donut in her life, and here she stands in a donut shop, wearing yoga pants. Struggling to take her seriously he responded, "No disrespect ma'am, but only a few days ago the police choked a man to death in broad daylight." Mike worked hard to restrain the frustration that ultimately took over his tone. "Three cops held the man down while one guy choked the man to death," he said. "He couldn't breathe, and bystanders witnessed it. The man was helpless, begging them to stop. So many people stood around too afraid of the police to jump in and help. We had innocent Americans scared of being killed themselves; scared of being prosecuted for helping him. That is a tragedy in itself - that's the real terrorism. When the citizens are so intimidated by their own public servants that they are willing to stand by and watch them strangle a man in broad daylight, something is really wrong with that connection you spoke about. There's a video of the whole thing. Let's see if the president interrupts prime time TV to have a frank discussion with America about that."

"I saw that video. It was sad," she responded. "I believe it was wrong and I'm against violence in general. I'm a pacifist. I know we have to do something but some mysterious Black man out there roaming the country killing police, doesn't help that situation. And it doesn't bring the dead people back."
Until then, Eric had been content to listen to Big Mike banter back and forth with the woman, but something she just said made his ears perk up. Before she could start another sentence, Eric erupted and his steaming thoughts splashed all over the conversation.

"Who said it was a Black man?" he sniped. "The president and the FBI said they didn't know who it was. The FBI chief specifically said be vigilant because it could be anyone. But you seem to know it's a Black man. The chief also said the cops are missing, he didn't say they were dead. But you concluded that the cops are dead and a mysterious Black man killed them. Yeah," he said sarcastically, "This ain't about race."

Each pair of eyes in the line were forced to share the same uncomfortable moment and the silence was so loud no one dared to break it. Eric and Mike slid from the conversation and were quietly leaving the shop, but Eric thought it was important to leave a parting comment. "Yeah Mike," he said loudly, "The biggest difference between the White liberals and White conservatives, is that the conservatives openly acknowledge that the primary responsibility of the police is to protect them; but the liberals like to pretend that those protections extend to the rest of us." Mike nodded his head in agreement, swallowed a piece of his donut and said. "You got that right." The open smell of coffee faded as the glass door slowly closed behind them.

A Tale In Two Cities

One year and ten months earlier, in another city, on the evening of their twenty-fifth wedding anniversary, Gerald and Lisa Madison were driving home from a party. Their only child Marcus was in the back seat and his college antics filled the car with joy and nostalgia. He was twenty-one years old, a senior in college, and neither of his parents ever suspected a thing. Their son had a secret that would change the mood, and he was finally ready to come out with it.

"Well, I wanted to wait until you two were stress free to tell you this," he said. "Today being your twenty-fifth wedding anniversary and all, I thought it would be perfect." His voice no longer held the humor it did only minutes ago. Now it was slow and cautious, and he kept playing with his fingers. "I know you both have such high hopes for me after college. Well, in a few weeks I'll be done. I just need you to know how I really feel on the inside about things and stuff. I

am…well, how do I say it?"
"What is it Marcus? You're making me nervous." His mother spoke in that I'm concerned high pitched tone all children find annoying.
"I'm trying to tell you Mom, but you keep interrupting me. How can I say what's on my mind if you keep interrupting me?"

"Well, stop making me nervous," she blurted. "Just say it. It doesn't matter what you say, we love you. That will never change." Her eyes started to swell with water, her lips trembled, and she repeatedly tapped that open space in the middle of her chest all mothers touch when they can't stop crying. "I just want you to be happy and OK Marcus." And she took another deep breath.
"Well, mom, dad… I know you won't agree with this life-style at this time in my life but…
"Marcus… are you gay?" she sharply interrupted. "I mean if that's who you are, you know I still…"
"What!" he shouted. "No mom… That's crazy. Of course I'm not gay. Wait a minute, why would you think that?"
"Well, I didn't think so," she said honestly, "But your generation - you can't tell by looking. You know Tina's son told her he was gay and he's a football player. I just wanted you to know if you were, I wouldn't love you any less."
"Ahh, mom… I know somehow you mean that in the most loving way possible but please don't ever think that way about me again."

"OK. I thought you were kind of into the young lady you brought to the party this evening anyway."
"Well, how could you think… never mind. Anyway, she is what I want to talk to you about.
I waited for this day, the day of your anniversary to ask her… to ask her to marry me. So I did. That's the big secret. We wanted you to be the first to know. Our plan is to live together for two years and then have a small wedding.

Something that she and I could pay for on our own. Tomorrow we would like to have lunch with you two and talk more. What do you think?"
"Marcus!" she screamed. "Marcus that is beautiful." She couldn't stop wiping tears from her eyes.
Mr. Madison, clearly an intelligent man, understood the fine arts of parenting. He had mastered the manual on marital discourse, so he well knew the two chapters addressing how to be silent when a Black woman was having an emotional moment with her son.

Quietly, he kept both hands on the wheel and maintained good driving posture. With his eyes on the road, he waited for the appropriate time and he asked a question.
"Do you love her son?"
"Yeah dad, I do."
"Well, I'm glad to hear that," and he smiled. "When we spoke to her at the party your mother did notice the way she looked at you."
"Really?" Marcus replied.
"Yep, and she leaned over to me and said I think she's in love with our son."
"Really?"
"Yep."
"So you already knew something was up."
"Yep."
"Well, why did you let me go through all of this then if you knew?"

"We didn't know. Your mother could sense something from her - I didn't. I never pick up on that kind of thing but, I'm glad you told us son. She seems like a nice young woman. I heard an accent, but I didn't want to be rude and ask her about it. What is her country of origin?"
"She's Russian, Gerald. She's a post-graduate fellow with the Harvard-Howard partnership program for African American culture. She studied cyber-engineering and technology at Saint

Petersburg State University. It's one of the oldest and largest universities in Russia, established in 1724. Before the USSR broke up it was called Leningrad State University. She's twenty-one years old."
After his mother's grand interruption, Marcus and his father laughed. They tried to look at each other but his dad was still driving.

"Jesus Christ mom, how do you know all that?"
"Well, I spoke to her," she said unabashedly.
"You just met her mom," he chuckled. "Sounds like you interrogated her. Did you ask her shoe size too?"
"No Marcus, of course not. But she did say one of her ancestors came from the US. That was a motivating factor in choosing the fellowship program she did. She's interested in finding out if any of them are still here."
"Dad, are you hearing this? How does she know this stuff?"
"She's your mother Marcus. And she's a woman. They always know."
"You and your dad can make fun of me if you like. But I enjoyed my conversation with, how do I pronounce her name again? Tat-ya-na?"
"Yes mom Tatyana."
"Well I loved her Marcus. We spoke for most of the evening. I think she's adorable and she does have a cute accent."
"Yeah mom, she's pretty cool."
Breaking his silence again, his father said, "You know Marcus, I have never heard a Black woman with a Russian accent before. She's educating me already. I'm glad you're happy son."
"Yeah dad, I am."

His father just smiled and mumbled about her accent, "A Black woman with a Russian accent. Wow, a Black Russian."
"Hey dad, are you speeding?"
"No," he said curiously. "I'm doing the limit." Then he glanced down at the speedometer. "Actually, I'm a little

below."
"Why are they following us then?"
"Who?" he asked, while peeking at the rear-view mirror.
"The police dad."
"Yeah, I see them now. Maybe they're not following us at all. I think they are just trying to overtake us because I'm moving so slowly. I'll change lanes here and let 'em by."
But when he did that the sirens started, and the lights… Blue, red, white - all flashing and spinning at the same time, like a nightmare Christmas; it was disorienting. Then a magnified voice came thundering from the same direction.
"PULL THE CAR OVER… TURN OFF THE ENGINE…AND ROLL DOWN YOUR WINDOW!"

While his father was doing all that the voice ordered him to do, Marcus asked, "What did we do wrong?"
And his mother, who was obviously agitated, confidently said, "We did nothing wrong Marcus. Just relax. Your father will speak to them and clear up this misunderstanding."
Marcus kept spinning his head from the back window to the side and to the back again. No matter how much he squinted he couldn't see through the bright of the flashing lights. A voice appeared from behind another light. This time it was shining in the face of his father.

"I stopped you because you were changing lanes erratically sir." The pace of the voice was slow. It was a deep male voice and he seemed suspicious. "Where are you going?" the voice asked.
"I'm going home. I live only a block from here."
"Have you been drinking?" the officer asked. His eyes darted around the interior of the car and he cast a long pause when he saw Marcus.

"No, I don't drink alcohol, if that's what you are asking me," Mr. Madison said.
At that time another light glared through the passenger side

window. At first it shined on his mother's face… and then it shined on Marcus.

The lights from the police car were blinking, spinning, changing. The white light of the officer was burning the back of Mr. Madison's eyes and the officer on the passenger side of the car was flashing a separate light at his wife and his son. Now disoriented, he asked, "What did you ask me officer? Oh, my name... My name is Gerald Madison. I live…" and the officer interrupted,

"Whose car is this?"

"It's my car of course," Mr. Madison responded. But he felt like the officer didn't believe him. The day was so wonderful when it started; now he was being emasculated in front of his wife and son and he didn't know why. It was all wrong.

"May I see your license and registration sir?" The voice of the officer grew even sharper.

"Ok. It's here in my…"

Again, the officer interrupted, "Don't move!" he shouted.

Mr. Madison was nervously reaching into his breast pocket to retrieve his wallet. The wallet is where he kept his identification.

"Listen to me very carefully!" the officer shouted. "Do you have a gun?"

"No, I do not," he replied fearfully.

"We do not own guns," Mrs. Madison screamed. "Why are you doing this?"

"Sir," the driver side officer repeated to Mr. Madison, "I want you to slowly put your hand in your pocket and slowly pull out your ID and show it to me. Do you understand that?"

Visibly shaking, Mr. Madison answered, "Ye-yes, I understand." The police officer was barking and holding a light in his eyes and a gun in his face. His wife was highly agitated, and his son was in the rear seat too petrified to reach for his cellphone to video anything. The law abiding non-violent Mr. Madison was trying to comply with the officers'

commands, but he was numb with confusion.
Mrs. Madison had had enough. With anger in her voice she shouted, "You have no right to treat us this way! We are lawful people! We have done nothing wrong! This was a happy night until now. I will not sit here and be humiliated!" and she slammed her open hand on her lap.

The passenger side police officer shot first. Seeing her hand near her lap he opened fire, hitting her several times in the face and twice in the throat. Almost every other round in his clip found its way to the center mass of her torso until pieces of her flesh hung from her mangled face and body, like leaves from a tree. Once the shooting started, the driver side officer then shot Mr. Madison in the head and multiple times in the chest. A furious flurry of rounds aimed at Marcus were caught by the body of his father and two of them passed through his tattered mother. When the screaming stopped, Marcus Madison lay slumped over the middle armrest of the car bleeding profusely from the face. He was barely alive; he was completely conscious and his parents, the pillars of his life, were dead.

For two days Tatyana waited beside him in the hospital. All the doctors said he was lucky because the bullets were deflected, and the impact was defused by his parents. They saved him with their death. One of the bullets even passed through the head of his mother and entered Marcus with only enough power to crack a chip from his jaw bone. When Tatyana spoke to the medical staff they were very optimistic about his recovery.

"His body is strong, and it will heal just fine," one of the doctors uttered. The plastic surgeon spoke next. "His face will heal Miss. Everything will function normally. He will keep that U- shaped scar on his cheek, but given the dark hue of his skin it won't be perceptible to anyone - not really. He is a very, very fortunate young man," he said. The psychiatrist chimed in, "He seems OK right now, but we don't know; we can't know. The human mind is a complex thing," she said. "He's been through a lot. It's hard to imagine what's going on in his head right now. And then there's this environment. For a moment, try to imagine yourself in a place where the highest compliment any professional can articulate is, how fortunate you are that your mother's head took a bullet meant for you." She rolled her eyes in an upward sense of disbelief and spoke in a slowing pitch aimed to reprimand her one-dimensional colleagues. "This hospital can be a very insensitive place," she added. "The psychological damage caused by such a traumatic event may dissipate over time or it may never heal completely. We don't know. This is a post traumatic area of study we are learning more about each day. So, let's note the changes in his behavior and hope for the best. Marcus is a very intelligent young man. It can be hard to track the effects of the psychological trauma if he wants to conceal it but in my professional opinion, given what happened to him, there will be emotional damage. What he does with it, I can't know."

Over the months his body recovered, but he was haunted by his thoughts. The media was at his family home hounding him, a community of friends and business associates were stomping with outrage, and those closest to him couldn't understand how this could have happened.

His parents were active civic leaders, they owned one of the most popular restaurants in the city and they were gunned down a stone's throw from their home. It was a tragic circumstance. Something in the system went wrong.

The Final Interview

To close the investigation, two officers requested an interview with Marcus. They met him at the Madison family home, sat in the family room and exchanged all the niceties necessary to ease the inhibitions of a subject. Until this incident, Marcus had no interaction with police and no natural aversion to law-enforcement. He was a rare organism in American society, a fully integrated African American male. His parents were rich, his mom was good looking and he was quite content to finish every day without a controversial thought. Marcus was naïve, but his final interview provoked another change in his perception of reality.

"To begin, I will use a voice recorder and my partner will take written notes. Is that OK sir?"
Marcus nodded yes.
"Your full name is Marcus G. Madison. Is that correct?"
"Yes. That is my name."
"I'm just asking you these questions because we want to establish an official record of what happened on the evening this horrible incident took place. Is that OK?"
"Yeah, that's OK."
"By the way, what does the G stand for?"
"Gerald. It stands for Gerald sir. It was my father's name."
"OK great, thanks. Now again, tell us what happened that night."
"Sir, I have told the police what happened several times already. Why are you asking me the same thing again?"
"Well, we just want it one more time. To compare it to… well, you know…just for comparisons sake. For example, why was the gun kept under the seat, instead of in a safe box as the law required?"
"What gun? No one had a gun."
"You mean you didn't know the gun was under the seat?"
"Sir, there was no gun. Where did a gun come from?"
"Well, are you saying your father never told you he kept his handgun under his seat?"

"What? My father never had a gun! My father was against gun possession in urban environments."
"So, let me write this down correctly. You are saying, your father was OK with keeping his gun under the seat when he was out of the city. Right?"
"No, that's not what I said…"

"Excuse me, Marcus," Tatyana's voice called from across the room. Tatyana was distrustful of the officers when they came unannounced to the home that morning. She hinted to Marcus that maybe an impromptu interview with two detectives wasn't a good idea. When he didn't get that hint, she hinted he should have a lawyer present, but he didn't get that one either. Tatyana had a sense of mistrust for all government enforcement agents. It's an innate quality sown into the personalities of all young Russians. She didn't know the US system, but she heard about it. In Russia they study American hypocrisy in grade school. She had even seen online footage of Black people being eaten by dogs and sprayed with water at high pressure, but she never imagined encountering such a thing so close. In addition to all of that, she was in a post-graduate program to study African American culture and her study materials are riddled with this kind of thing. Tatyana was deeply in love with Marcus, and now she was angry.
"Where I am from things happen," she thought, "but not like this - so open… so blatant. They took his parents from him. Now they are trying to trick his memory while he is still grieving."

She called him again. "Marcus, may I speak with you for a moment please? Now… please?"
He heard her, but it was too difficult for him to break his attention from the officers' impact questions. And they were accumulating at a rapid pace.
"Well, I don't understand Marcus," the first officer said. Before he could respond, came the next question. "So are

you saying that there was a gun or there was no gun?" asked the second officer.
"Excuse me sir!" Tatyana dropped the pretense of being polite. Her body and her voice stood between her fiancé and the two detectives.
"Wait a minute ma'am. This is an important interview. You can't interrupt it."
"I just did," she said sharply.
"Well, can you at least let him finish his response?" the other officer sternly added.
She ignored those words. "Marcus," she stood with her rounded rear in his face, and her angry brown eyes shielding and slicing into every word the blue-eyed officers had to say. "This interview is over."

Her face… so beautiful, so serious, so descriptive, and it told the two men so clearly what to do that her four words were merely a formality.
"You can leave now," she said. And her manicured finger indicated the direction. Reluctantly the two men quietly left the house, entered the unmarked police car and drove away.
As they drove away she felt the rise of anxiety and her heavy heart thumping against her chest. She didn't notice it before because she was too angry to be afraid. She looked at Marcus. "Did you notice what they were trying to do?"
"I didn't at first," he uttered. "But eventually, I got it."
"They are in this together," she said.
"Yep," he said. "And so are we."

2 CHAPTER
Meet The BRO

He was affable. It was father's day and Marcus was standing in his father's wardrobe looking at his father's impeccable taste in clothes thinking about the best word to describe the man he admired so much. Holding a photo of his father, Marcus smiled and said, "You were the kindest man I ever knew." His dad's wardrobe felt like the private fitting room at Gieves & Hawkes and Marcus couldn't help slipping into a few things just to see how he measured up. If one didn't know his dad, one could see the quality of his life reflected in his clothes. Gerald Madison was an inch or two above or below six feet; he had the natural build of an athlete, though he never trained as one. Marcus on the other hand was a short pudgy little boy who grew to become a point guard on his college basketball team and the state judo champion in his weight class three years in a row. Now standing in the mirror he was looking at a replica of his dad and everything fit perfectly. "Interesting," he thought.

The doorbell pinged a few times and Tatyana called him.
There was a guest at the door; a family friend he hadn't seen for many years. The guest and Tatyana were engaged in a pleasant conversation when Marcus arrived. Trying not to interrupt, he eased a seat beside Tatyana and struggled to recognize the casual looking man but he couldn't place the splash of gray on his hairy face, or the raspy jazz in his voice. Seeking to avoid an embarrassing moment, Marcus desperately worked to place at least one physical

characteristic. He didn't want to stare but he couldn't help glaring at his left eye.

"It was the pupils," he thought. Something about the eyes of the man was odd.

Tatyana was about to finish her last word and suddenly he could see the oddity.

"Heterochromia," Marcus quickly blurted. Leaning forward and looking at the man's eye he repeated, "You have "heter-o-chro-mia." His voice slowed with confusion. He knew the eyes… but not the person. Something was wrong, something was off.

The man chuckled, "Hello Marcus," he said.

Tatyana glared at Marcus as if he had picked his nose in public. "Marcus…" It was completely out of character for him to respond in such a rude way. She struggled not to apologize for him and she wondered if this kind of thing was another personality alteration caused by the psychic trauma he suffered.

"I know you," he said. "I'm so sorry. I just can't place your face. You see, there was a horrible incident with my parents." Marcus felt it again. The tightening in his throat…the intense feeling of loss. It was rising. The soft voiced man injected,

"I know Marcus. I can't begin to imagine what you're going through. But your memory is not the problem here. You were very young and I look drastically different than I did when you last saw me. I'm an old friend to your mother. Actually, your mother and I were best friends."

"Really? I do remember my mother had a good friend with one green eye and one brown eye. She taught me how to swim. But I don't remember you."

"That was me Marcus. Your mom and I were sorority sisters. We came in together. And I, well… obviously, I changed."

"Lena?" he shouted. Marcus was astounded. He couldn't see a woman anywhere in his body - even his voice.

"It's Leonard now," he chuckled, "But it's me. Not as you

remember me…but I'm the Lena you remember," he said quietly. "How are you Marcus?" Leonard stood from the sofa, and gently reached across Tatyana to shake the hand of an astonished looking Marcus but Marcus bluntly refused it. Pushing it away he said, "Leonard, the Lena my mother knew would never shake my hand." And he stood taller than Leonard, reached over the still seated Tatyana and bear hugged the fair-skinned black man that used to be his Godmother.

For more than a decade Lena lived as a man. She divorced her husband and underwent several surgical procedures to achieve the physical attributes she felt necessary to live a full life as Leonard. Over the years, Leonard had come through a lot of adversity. He was smart, funny, well connected and wise; but he just had a hard time understanding how Lisa Madison, the gentlest woman God conceived, could produce a young man capable of squeezing people to death when he hugged them. Maintaining his trademarked sense of humor, he wheezed. "So you see Marcus, your memory's not so bad, but you are crushing my ribs."

Marcus recoiled. "I'm sorry," he said. "I'm just so happy to see you." It was a clumsy moment and poor Tatyana was being moved around like a blade of grass. "Tatyana," he said excitedly, "This is my Godmother…I mean my Godfather." Tatyana was laughing too hard to return a comment. Turning back to Leonard Marcus continued, "Did my mother know about your change? She looked for you. I know for a fact she thought you were somewhere in India."

"No Marcus, she didn't know about the change," he said. "After my divorce I stayed in India for a while, that's where I left Lena. Your mother never met this body. I chose to stay away and it's one of those things I will always regret. I'm sorry to hear about what happened to them. The results of that fictional investigation makes a mockery of their lives."

The conversation turned and the rounded words of outrage carried the rest of the discussion.

"Leonard, do you know how I heard about that? I heard it on the radio. In the middle of my jazz program the police chief announced that the officers who slaughtered my parents were cleared of all wrongdoing and will not be charged with a crime. Can you believe that?"

"Yes I can believe it. It happens all the time. One of the reasons I am here is to help you change that. I know what you are planning, and you can't succeed on your own. You will be caught, and you will be killed. And I… well we, won't let that happen. You will need help Marcus."

"How did you know what I…"

"Marcus Madison, were you about to ask me, how did I know what you were thinking?"

"Well, yeah. How did you know?"

"You told me. Hell, you told everyone who cared to know. When you got online and used a conventional search engine to research your ideas, you inadvertently shared your thoughts. At some point you switched to something encrypted. I assume Tatyana was responsible for that."

"You've been watching me?" Marcus replied.

"No, we watch the system. The system was watching you. The American government watches everything it can. The agencies that run this country are all linked to a central database; that database is monitored by three departments.

Each department has a team devoted to two things: detecting and eradicating threats to the system. They haven't detected you yet, but if you stop telling people how upset you are with the outcome, they will. Right now, you're OK. Your anger profile is appropriate."

"What does that mean?"

"Well, your parents were killed by the police and the amount of anger you have shown is acceptable."

"What in the hell does that mean? If it wasn't for Tatyana

taking my keys that night, I would have bought a can of gas and burned the whole damn police station to the ground!"

"Well, I guess we should all thank Tatyana for saving you from yourself because that would be the angry rants of one man. They would label you a black-identity extremist, turn the Black community against you, enlist Black leadership to help hunt you down and make an example of you to kill your memory in the minds of the next generation. They might even give you a trial before they kill you; but your private fiasco will have done nothing to stop law enforcement from terrorizing Black and Brown people. In fact, history shows it would have made it worse. Anger, Marcus… guard yourself against anger. It is a rare friend."

Marcus was sensing something official about Leonard. He seemed CIA like. It was the way he spoke, the candor of his words, the conviction in his tone. He was like an uncle with a background who came to help, but Marcus couldn't resist the college instinct to say what was on his mind so he forced in another two sentences.

"I have to do something Leonard," he said. "We can't continue to live this way."

"You will do more than something Marcus, but you must stop telling people what you think, and tell people what you want them to know. And never, I mean never… make important decisions when you are angry. At this point you have shown them what they expect and it's important that you continue to do that. Give them no reason to believe you are different from their profile of you."

Marcus wiped the angry tears from his eyes and glanced over at Tatyana, who was quietly nodding her head most of the time.

Leonard continued to speak, "There was a nice police detective who helped you in the hospital. Remember her?"

"Of course," Marcus answered, "Her name is Briana. She's about the only decent cop on the force. She's also the one who helped us find the police records the department was hiding from the investigators. Yeah she's OK."

Leonard chuckled, "No she's not. She's the reason investigators knew as much as they did about you. They don't see you as a threat because her report highlights how sheltered and naïve you are. You were too busy looking at her ass to notice her reading your confidential psych records."

Tatyana leaned back in her chair and rolled her eyes to gaze at the ceiling.

"How do you know that Leonard?"

"I read the reports. About two months ago they sent two other detectives to interview you. Their job was to evaluate her conclusions. They confirmed her findings. That's the only reason the government is not closely watching you right now."

"Leonard, the more I learn about this justice system the less I think of it and now you tell me that they think I'm naïve. They think I'm stupid enough to follow the same old patterns? Well, we'll see."

"Yes Marcus, we will see because you are too smart to change that pattern. When your enemy is going in the wrong direction, don't be so willing to help him find his way. America has always underestimated Black people and we will use that to bring these corrupt cops to justice."

"I get it, I'm ready."

"I know you are Marcus, that's why we are here."

"When you say we, are you like ex-CIA or something like that?

"Something like that. When we were in university, your mother and I were young members of BRO. BRO is the Black Resistance Order - a society of working people dedicated to the global defense of Black and Brown people. We were sorors working to support the organization as watchers."

"What's a watcher?" he asked.

"Watchers work everywhere in government and corporate

America. From the unskilled laborer to the most skilled artisan, they keep their eyes and ears open for anything interesting to be pushed to the next level. Nothing more than that. This organization started that way. You see, until lately we have always been information gatherers. For centuries, intelligence agencies around the world have used Black and Brown slaves and servants to collect intel but they have always maintained a counter balance in our ranks. By that I mean there has always been an inside informant keeping watch on the watchers. They always seemed to know what we knew. They would stop any major rebellion before it started.

Every attempt to effect police corruption had been thwarted and we didn't know why. With the help of a few international friends, we changed our methods and now they don't know who we are. They can't tell how we know what we know and most importantly, they don't know what we want. Also, watchers no longer report to anyone. They load intel anonymously on the dark sites on the Dark Web. They are invisible - we are invisible - you will be invisible."

"My plan is sort of like that," Marcus said. "To strike and be like Pancho Villa, everywhere and nowhere."

Tatyana injected, "Pancho Villa was ambushed and killed Marcus. That's not what we want for you."

Leonard laughed, "I agree. He was not invisible Marcus. He couldn't resist the camera or the press, but you will be better. You will be different. When they interviewed you, they saw a Black man and a gentrified one at that. They will never suspect you of anything."

"My Marcus," Tatyana added lovingly, "You will beat these evil people. I will support you, God will support you. These evil police have gotten away with killing and beating Black people for too long, but they are clearly culling the men. Even in my high school biology days, we learned that there are basic things that run in the mind of every animal. The fear of losing one will trigger a fight or flight instinct. I mean, even a well tamed dog will bite if you beat him long enough, but the Black and Brown man in America is expected to comply and not resist conditions even his dog wouldn't accept. These people believe that a few hundred years of fear conditioned him to do something his dog could never do, stay docile. This kind of thinking cannot stand. One day we will have children - we may have sons. If we stay in this country they will not be docile. Yesterday you said when people are more afraid of losing their life than fighting for their freedom, they end up losing both. I think you are right and there is something else here that is too eerie to be a coincidence. Before Leonard rang, I was reading an article about how many American ministers were steered away from the teachings of the prophet Isaiah. I find it very interesting because the prophet Isaiah accurately predicted many things, but he was relentless in his condemnation of the maltreatment and oppression of God's people. His forecast of judgment against the oppressor is not just a warning to ancient Israel, but to every sovereign forever. World history books and biblical scriptures are filled with stories of oppressed people rising like the arm of God to strike down great powers. Whether it is the biblical children delivered from pharaoh or the South African children of apartheid, at some point the fright of oppression will give way and the oppressed will rather die than comply. This is not a coincidence. I am with you Marcus, God is with you Marcus and the time to fight back, is now."

Leonard added, "Looks like we have a team. The Black Resistance Order will be your eyes and ears Marcus, and you will be the tip of a long spear for justice. You will be, like a spook in the night."
"Or by the door," Marcus added, and the three of them laughed at the pun.

The Force of Righteousness

For over a year, Marcus discovered the power of silence. He quietly learned more about himself and his country in this time than he ever thought possible. The green patina of naiveté his parents nurtured to protect him was buffed away by the BRO; and the ultra-intelligent young Marcus was plugged into a worldwide network of evidence he never thought accessible. For him, the constant flow of open sourced information put the uncontrollable truth on a collision course with his expensive western education. Now he realized almost all of his schooling was a socially engineered plan to keep people like him comfortable enough to concentrate on staying comfortable. It was a circle of miseducation that kept him locked in the pursuit of an American dream that never included him. When Marcus finally saw the truth, he realized there was no social buffer between his mind and reality; and it was clear that the global concept of justice was a successful illusion promulgated by a few, to govern their fear of the permanent underclass who make up the many. It was sad for him to learn that his parents believed in social rules that never existed for them, but he knew that they would rest happy knowing that their son was working to make justice a reality for others. Marcus Madison was more than a vigilante. He was a powerful reminder to the corrupt that there now existed an invisible force of righteousness fighting police corruption and a justice system that harbored it.

At the end of a beautiful day of the summer solstice, the sun set at 8:31pm and the horizon was glowing like the sky was on fire. Leonard Hughes arrived at the Madison home. He walked to the back end of the house and found his Godson sitting on the ground in a meditative state, peacefully gazing at the heavens. Leonard quickly assumed a mischievous posture and slowly but quietly crept up behind the motionless Marcus. He was just about to pounce a surprising hug… when Marcus commented. "I am no longer surprised by the beauties of God Leonard. I have learned to just admire them."

Leonard dropped his hands and gasped, "At least you could let me pretend to surprise you Marcus."

"OK, then consider me surprised," he replied with a boyish grin.

"Hello Marcus."

"Leonard, good to see you."

"Congratulations to you and Tatyana. We spoke a little when she let me in. I saw the little bundle. How old is he now?"

Marcus produced a smile that nearly covered his whole face and he answered, "Ten weeks and growing like a piece of bamboo."

"It's good to see you happy Marcus, you deserve it. I am hearing great things about you. Actually, let me say that a better way," and he cast an approving gaze. "It is good that great things are happening, and I have not heard your name associated with them."

Marcus chuckled, "Thank you Leonard. Someone once said even a fool who persists in his folly will become wise."

Marcus Madison always had a reserved demeanor, but the stress of his tragedy produced a growth only the experts could have predicted. Post-traumatic growth, PTG, was a term referring to people who grow stronger and build a more meaningful life after a devastating tragedy. These people didn't just bounce back to normal, they bounced higher. This psychological phenomenon was a perfect description of Marcus. Now he was more than reserved, he was methodical, versatile and his self-deprecating response was a personality trait that marked a modesty in the man his parents hoped he would become. Leonard couldn't be more proud of his Godson, and he said,

"Marcus, I read an interesting description of the leak today. Have you seen the Post?"

"Yes, I saw it."

"The FBI is devastated. They think the Russians hacked their

archives."
"Well," said Marcus, "Nothing is redacted, and the stuff has gone viral."
"They are livid," Leonard added.
"I saw, and they blame the Intercept," Marcus replied.
Leonard continued, "The mainstream media is trying to slow it down, but the web is flooded with raw copies of every page; they can't discredit it, they can't stop it."
One week before, Tatyana realized that someone leaked a cache of post-civil war documents from the US archives. It was an obscure folder among many, but this one was a red stamped photo copy marked FBI, Top Secret. She didn't know it at the time, but she found an old answer to a modern question, a plot that started only a few years after the civil war.
The document titled "The Order of America," code named (TOAMA), systematically explained how several White supremacist organizations colluded to discourage the integration and prevent the rise of the Black and Native American people. To many law makers at that time, the idea of reconstruction was a necessary ploy to pacify the European abolitionists, who refused to resume normal trade activities with the divided states of America. After the war, most of the southern states and many northern communities were desperate to rebuild an economically sustainable way of life but they had to compete with a formally enslaved population.

The free White population couldn't compete as laborers with the slaves. For a few hundred years, slaves had been programmed to work harder, work longer and adapt faster, for much less. The leak was devastating to the FBI because the detailed document chronicled the many fears of the White population across America from the mid 1860's to the late 1990's. To soothe the constant fear that an oppressed people would eventually revolt, one of the most chilling entries was the well documented incrustation of White supremacists in law enforcement and criminal justice. Essentially, the White Nights of Insurrection gradually transformed until the white hooded instrument of oppression, fashioned a national image of crime suppression.

To Marcus, the disclosed documents explained what he already suspected, the American justice system is rigged against Black and Brown people. The people who killed his parents and the ones who adjudicated them were part of the same race-based club; and over a hard-to-determine period of time, they expanded from a southern regional White Hood Club, to a national association, known as the Knights of the Blue Shield.

Leonard was overjoyed about the leak, but he didn't know that Marcus knew the identity of the leaker, and Marcus didn't let on that he did.

"Someone exposed a dangerous secret to the world," Leonard said. "Government considers this leak the highest form of treason because it drastically erodes the thinning trust in the US justice system. Now they are in full damage control status. The primary spin on mainstream media is that the Russians did it, followed by a steady beat of talking heads saying what you see on the internet and social media is fake news. In other words, don't believe what you read on your own. Believe what we say. It's the worse form of solipsism."

"It is crazy. The people deserve the truth Leonard. When the police have done wrong for so long it is impossible to bury it," Marcus added. "Big governments have traditionally buried things like this under a top- secret label in hopes that the following generation will burn it; but you can't bury or burn the truth. I guess that's what William Cullen Bryant meant when he said, 'Truth, crushed to earth, shall rise again'."

3 CHAPTER
Smothered Mate

In the early evening hours of the following day, Marcus patiently waited for his frustrated victim to realize the error of his ways.

"Where did you come from? I can't get out. I can't move. Is that it?"

"Yeah, that's checkmate."

"I don't understand. What happened?"

"It's a smothered mate. See here in the corner? Your white king sits on the h1 square surrounded by protection pieces. I moved my black queen to the g1 square to attack your king, and that's check, right?"

"Yes, I see that."

"Now in your mind maybe you're thinking, Marcus just made a huge mistake. He didn't see my rook sitting there guarding the g1 square. 'Why would he move queen to g1?' you thought. 'Can't he see I'm going to take his queen? It's the most powerful piece he has on the board. Why would he put her in such a dangerous place? How could he make such a blunder? Something must be distracting him because he's a better player than this.' So far, am I close to what you were thinking?"

"Very close," he chuckled.

"Now, when I placed my queen there I knew you would take it. Earlier when you defended your position so heavily, you told me where your weakness was. I attacked g1 because you inadvertently told me where you were vulnerable. Now for you to get out of check, you had to take my queen with your rook. And you did - you won my valuable queen and you were happy. But when I moved the knight to f2, it checked your king again, and once more you had to move it. That's when you realized you had a larger problem. Your rook that took my queen blocked your king from escaping. And because your other pieces were tightly guarding him they couldn't take my knight. Smothered."

"Wow, Marcus. I never saw that coming. I never expected you to sacrifice your most powerful piece."

"She's not the most powerful piece, at least not to me," Marcus replied. "In that situation the knight was most important. He had position, he had stealth. But you didn't see that. You were so dazzled by the prospects of snatching my queen you couldn't see your predicament. I just gave you what you wanted."

"So, what you're saying is… you gave me the queen and you took the game."

Marcus smiled. "Something like that," he replied.

The barber shop was packed with customers. Some quietly waiting around the chess table, others chatting while they sat, many standing while they chatted; and each of the art painted walls had a different theme and a flat screen playing something different. It was a place of comfort for Marcus and his father. Before Marcus was strong enough to get in the chair, Leroy the barber cut his hair. Leroy's barber shop was a cordial mix of class, community and ideology; a friendly place where gossip and the gospel sat, usually at the same time. Open conversations about sports, entertainment, chess, and political change were always in the room. For Marcus, it was a trusted way to keep his ear to the ground of the community.

This was a highly charged evening because a day before, another unarmed Black man was killed by the police. To bypass the government censorship, a few tech-minded regulars rigged the TV to receive relay streamed international programing from the internet. Customers waiting in the barbershop could regularly enjoy news as it happened. The latest officer induced killing was live streamed a day before by a witness from her window. The graphic images clearly showed the man running away and the police shooting him in the back. While he lay dying the officers yelled, "PUT YOUR HANDS WHERE I CAN SEE THEM!" The man didn't move. Then one officer screamed, "STOP RESISTING!" and shot him again. As the video played, the room was without a sound for two of the longest minutes in history. There were a few tears but for the most part, faces in the room were angry and somber. As the man lay on the ground, one of the officers slammed his knee down into the back of the still motionless man. The officer holstered his gun and handcuffed what appeared to be a dead man. The second officer reached over the first one and dropped an object near the body of the handcuffed victim. It was a graphic example of urban policing in America. Marcus scanned the room to see the reaction to the next news report.

He was the only one in that room who knew what was coming. It was still, the hour was late and angry customers were locked in the same set of emotions, but no one could find the words to express them. A small boy broke the silence. "They did it again," he said. As the boy spoke, the broadcast media screen was showing something different. Another reporter was talking. "Turn that one up," a customer shouted.

The reporter was speaking quickly, in an animated tone. She seemed baffled.

"The police are now seeking the whereabouts of the two officers involved with the shooting of an unarmed Black man early yesterday morning," she said. "The two officers were questioned yesterday and were scheduled to be questioned today, but neither of the officers showed up for their interviews. The lawyers of the two said their families were concerned and the FBI is now involved." The screen flipped to a different talking face.

"No," barked an obviously irritated agent. "We do not believe the officers are avoiding their interviews. We believe foul play is involved and we are treating this as an abduction," the FBI woman said. "Anyone with knowledge helpful to this situation please contact the FBI." The report ended.

"Yes!" someone shouted, and the room erupted in applause, high fives and hugs. It was like the OJ verdict all over again. Men in their chairs covered with barbershop blankets pumped their fists because they couldn't stand. It was that kind of moment. In all of American history Black people have rarely been as unified on any issue as this; but it wasn't revenge that ignited the crowded room, it was justice. The people in the room could feel it, and the idea that there was finally someone out there who heard the cry of the underserved communities was enough to rock the American air waves with the sounds of joy and blackness.

While he blended with the joyful noise, Marcus listened intently to the opinions of the people.

"The devil is a lie!" shouted the potbellied deacon standing and bouncing across from Marcus. "The devil is a LIE. I'm sayin' it right now, God done had enough, I know it. I can feel it people. This ain't nothing but an act of God y'all… nuh'in but God." His heavy voice was swiftly overtaken by a lighter one.

"It feels like he sent a Black angel, another Nat Turner don't it?" Pointing to the somber agent on the screen he added, "Look at her face, she finna cry." His eyes were aglow with no concern for her dilemma; but it was common. The response contrast between White Americans and Black Americans was stark. Even the owner of the establishment, Leroy himself, a typically silent man was moved to stutter out a comment.

"She—she wants us to help the FBI? They just put a Black face up there tryin' to make us think we're in this together.

You know what? That's some craziness right there. I-- I ain't sayin' nothin," he stammered. "Even if I knew somethin." His uncharacteristic outburst crippled the room with laughter. Marcus heard it all with a smile; and then the pictures on the screen drained the smile from his face. For many moments, he drifted to the nervous point of the first encounter with the missing subjects. He took each man separately, methodically, but before the first one fell he paused. He imagined the mangled face of his mother, the grey splashes of her delicate brain slowly sliding down the light blue leather of his father's seat. Her warm cheeks, her lifeless eyes gazing back at him, full of fear, full of hope. Fighting back the tears he thought, "Separate your mind from the madness Marcus. The eyes of the enemy are nothing like your own. Quiet your mind," he repeated. And his body became still like the cat but coiled like the Mamba. He didn't move, not even an eyelash.

"See the target as a piece on the board," he thought. He took another breath, deeper this time. Now every heart beat had a purpose, every slow and measured breath had a reason to clear the imperceptible space between his chest and the atmosphere surrounding him. "Find the empty space in your thoughts and leave your anger there," he reasoned; but his piercing eyes never left the target. Slowly, he exhaled the nervous pocket of air from his lungs, and without hesitation he moved quietly, quickly and directly to attack the soft tissue of each target, locked the unsuspecting subject in an inescapable clutch; and then quietly removed them, one at a time. It was over before pain could begin and two evil pieces were off the board. Barely winded he planted himself firmly on the ground and looked to the horizon. "Now it's on," he whispered loudly. "White to move."

It was as if he was sitting in a bubble- so quiet, so pleased, so clear. Every thought insolated him from all sound except the sounds in his head. But even in the silence of a noisy room his daydream was soon interrupted.

"Who is Kondo?" Leroy asked. He was now standing to the right of Marcus who hadn't moved from his seat at the chess board. Marcus had fallen so deep into his memory he never heard Leroy calling him. The jovial atmosphere was a reasonable excuse, so Marcus used it.

"I didn't hear you," he said leaning in to block the shouting in the room.

Leroy expounded, "You said something about somebody named Kondo. You said, Kondo was right."

Moving on, Marcus just smiled and said, "He probably was. Ready for me now Leroy?"

"Yeah Kid, Let's do it. So stay with the Malcom X goatee and a trim, right?"

Reclined in the chair and looking to the ceiling Marcus replied, "Yes. Thanks Leroy." And the evening was good.

A few days later in the old cold wine cellar of the Madison family restaurant, the oversized hands of Marcus struggled for leverage to reverse the devastating position master Kondo put him in. Miyamoto Kondo was younger than any ninety-two year old man should be. Nothing about him looked old, in fact, the only thing about him that was old, was his age. He was built like a fire hydrant, close to the ground and solid. Except for his chin he was hairless, fit, and his mind was full of information that always seemed fresh.

The focused training from master Kondo brought Marcus, the competitive judo champion, into the eclectic world of stealth fighting. Miyamoto Kondo was one of the last surviving Shinobi practitioners who kept the old ways of Ninjitsu or Ninpō. Under the wings of Kondo, Marcus came to embody the Shinobi practice of "Flow." Flow was the ancient concept of mixing all fighting styles and techniques to confound the enemy and achieve success in all things.

Master Kondo was right. The endless hours of planning and practice paid off. On his first encounter, Marcus executed a meticulous maneuver to exact justice and send a strong message to America, that there will now be balance in her unbalanced system.

Master Kondo was sympathetic to Marcus and devoted to helping him find focus and balance in his life. He was younger than Marcus when he violently lost his parents. He understood the struggle to cage the vengeance and what it took to win. From his memory he designed a training space to mimic the one he knew in Nagoya, Japan. It was an old bomb shelter dug at the base of the historic building that housed The Black Diamond, the Madison family restaurant. Together they fashioned it into a World War II bunker-style Dōjō - a place of the way, with no electricity, no windows and no excuses. On the rear wall Master Kondo scratched these words to remember:

"Flow, is not a fighting style. It is a way of life. Every day is training day. This is the way of Flow. All learning is training, either you are training for something in life or life is training you for something. When you recognize this, you are living."

Kondo had been an underground member of the BRO for over fifty years. He firmly believed that the law enforcement arm of the US government was corrupt; it operated largely without honor, and it was foolish to trust any law enforcement power to govern the behavior of itself.

A National Conversation About Race

The United States of America was not united on this issue. Police across the country have expressed outrage at the kinds of open support Black people were giving to the person or persons responsible for these crimes. The ACLU has filed a Freedom of Information Act request asking that the FBI and other government agencies release documents of any sort, pertaining to the top secret files marked: The Order of America, code named (TOAMA). Outbreaks of violence between the police and the average citizen had been forecasted but not realized -at least not yet. The Native American and African American communities generally expressed a sense of vindication about the TOAMA documents, while the government enforcement agencies were divided in their condemnation of them. Some government officials argued that the leak was an act of treason and the files were a record of an America long passed. Others dismissed the documents as fake news and/or propaganda, saying it was yet another Russian ploy to divide and conquer America. The police unions and organizations flooded the air waves with a predictable stream of fear, denial and promises to root out the bad cops with the good ones. But something was different. The underserved communities were not responding as usual. The customary influx of Black members of the law enforcement fraternity recruited to sway public opinion were not persuasive. The traditional army of religious politicians who gradually worked their constituents into a peaceful choir to sing the songs of change and deliverance were ignored. Questions were asked and answers were given but a major problem remained. The cloak of invincibility has fallen, the scent of revolution was in the air and White America was beginning to smell it.

"Tonight the issues and the controversy… a thousand people have gathered here tonight in the prestigious Maverick Hall at Tarvard University for a town meeting with Malcom Ben Carter," pronounced the popular talk show host. "The topic: 'How do we put our past in the past to move forward?' We'll be right back after a few words from our sponsor."
The gigantic hall was more like a very big movie theater. Every seat had a body in it and each of the grand aisles leading to the stage had a long queue of people standing for their opportunity to ask a question.
Malcom Ben Carter, an ordinary Black man, worked his meal truck for ten years until his oldest son was killed by a policeman. The Carter story was internationally viewed when the girlfriend of his son Jason used her cellphone to stream the encounter for the world to see. Malcom Ben Carter became an outspoken opponent of the police and the laws that protect them. His talent for simplifying legal jargon has made him the most recognized voice in America on this issue.

"My son was murdered," he said to the audience before he even sat to start the interview. "The law makers in this country have twisted the laws so that any police officer who feels threatened has a right to use deadly force. Now I ask you, 'How do you measure a feeling?' If you or I feel threatened by an officer there is no law to protect us. What they are saying is this: the life of an officer is more valuable than yours and mine. In the case of my son, he had no weapon. He had no chance. The officer told him to get out of his car. He told the officer he didn't feel safe. He asked the officer to call a supervisor. The officer ordered him to step out of the car. My son refused and asked again for a supervisor. The officer drew his weapon and pointed it at the face of my son. My son put both hands on the steering wheel and begged the man to take the gun out of his face. He shot my boy in the head. The video shows it. Dana was screaming and crying, but I thank God she kept that phone on, or we would never know what happened. They took her phone and broke it, but she had streamed everything to the internet, thank God. But even with all of that, the laws on the books protected the police. The officer simply argued that in his five years of experience and to the best of his judgment, he felt his life was in danger. In the split second fog of the moment, he felt the man was going for a weapon. Now, after carefully watching the video, the D.A. found no reason to charge the officer with a crime. Not even a charge, and they were OK with that. When the D.A. spoke to me, he talked about how tragic it was - how my son had every right to call for a supervisor. Oh, he was very apologetic about the outcome. 'We need to tighten the laws,' he said. But there was no outrage. No urgency. Just sympathetic babble. But now," he paused - and his big voice rose and hovered above the room.

"Now that Officer Friendly is missing, they all want to know if I know something. Some of them want to know if I did something. NO!" he shouted, and the people welcomed his words with strong applause. He slowly sat in the leather chair situated behind him and reached for the glass of cold water on the short table. He had a thought... he quickly took a sip of water and stood again. "But if I did hear something," he added loudly. The audience hushed to a whisper. "There is no law in this universe that would make me tell you anything." And the stately seated audience roared like a crowd in a sports arena. Not everyone in the room appreciated his words. In full uniform, members from the order of the blue shield stoically sat in the front three rows of each segment creating a wall of blue. They perched themselves throughout the room to intimidate, but it didn't work.

The host of the show was Bert Tilden, the most popular talk show host in the country. Bert was a professional. He brought the stadium-like audience to order quickly. "Welcome everyone," he said. "Welcome to 'Change the Nation.' It's an evening with a controversial agent for

change…and you. If you are still in the auditorium I assume you know the program and you know the rules, as the producers have reminded you of them twenty minutes ago.
Our guest this evening is a man who needs no further introduction.
Now, I see the lines are long and the mics are live. If we have an opportunity to take questions, please remember, one question per person and you are under no obligation to state your name before you ask a question."
"OK, let's begin. Mr. Malcom Ben Carter, another week is gone and another cop is missing. What do you say to the man who believes that this guy roaming the country picking off innocent cops is a terrorist? Or that middle American who says he should be caught and shot?"
"I say he is entitled to his opinion."
"But did I hear you say if you knew his whereabouts you wouldn't report him to the police?"
"No Bert, that's not what I said, but it is how I feel."

"How is that moral, Carter? I grant that you have some bad cops, but the average police officer is a human being trying to do their job and go home. They are here to protect us. They work for us. You must see that."
"No, Bert I don't see that. I do see how you can see it that way though."
"See Carter, what I'm trying to get at is this. These are violent acts this person is committing. You're not condoning violence are you?"
"Bert I'm not here to condone anything."
"No, here's what I'm saying Carter. You have a recognizable image. Shouldn't you use that platform to unite people? You have an opportunity to accentuate the positive. Shine the light on our similarities and bring us together, not wallow in our differences that pulls people apart."
Many in the audience jeered. The men and women in blue abandoned maintained their statuesque demeanor.
Carter smiled and waited for the sound to drop. "I find your

comment interesting Bert, because you have the most popular program in the country. Why don't you use your fame and notoriety to help us stop the police from killing Black people? They're right here." And he pointed to the ranks of officers strategically lining the great room. "Also," he waited for the applause to diminish. "Also," he added, "You do remember why I am in this spotlight. Have you forgotten that they killed my son? That's the only reason I am here, you seem to forget that."
An unforgiving sound seemed to accompany clapping hands. Bert was not comfortable with his poor judgment. He just paused another moment.
"Well, Carter, you're right. I didn't mean to offend. I apologize. I'm just thinking about a peaceful way to resolve things on the ground level. There has to be a peaceful way. I guess, officers should be accountable."

"Bert, I'm not a leader of anyone except me. When White Americans see a Black person on TV with an opinion, they assume that's the voice of Black folk. I only speak from my own experience. For Black people, the most effective weapon against injustice has been the partially effective tool of civil disobedience. We have always tried to use a non-violent tactical assault on the cultural conscience of the oppressor. Percy Shelley popularized it with his poem, The Mask of Anarchy. After Gandhi and a few others used it, civil rights leaders found some success with it here in America. By now we all know that the idea is to psychologically arrest the aggressor by fighting violence with pacifism. The aim is to use shame as a weapon against the more powerful opponent until he yields. In short, it's a guilt trip. But what happens when the oppressor doesn't feel guilty? From where I sit, the police don't feel guilty. Now God finally sends someone to help us… and the police want us to find out who it is and give him up.
Yesterday the man who killed my son disappeared… and they want me to feel bad about that. Just this morning detectives

came to my house and questioned me. Look at me. I'm an old man. One officer talked to me about my civic obligation and later he mentioned that there was a cash reward. Amazing, these people. First they tried being nice. Then they offered me money. Now over a hundred of them sit here like a small army trying to intimidate anyone who will let them. Bert, I couldn't buy a call from a detective when I had questions about my son's case. Now they want to talk to me. If this wasn't a live show I would tell them where to go… and I'd tell them what to kiss before they left. I may be old, but they're crazy."

There were a few more than a thousand people in the auditorium and a fair number of them supported law enforcement. The sound that took over that auditorium after Mr. Carter spoke, was loud enough to lift a person out of their seat. No one could scream or applaud louder.
The producers were not able to gain control of the crowd. A few people started tossing things in the direction of the police to provoke a confrontation. The show was abruptly halted and the auditorium was evacuated without incident.

The Issues And The Controversy Go Viral

The day after the action-packed program ended with a bang, the show was on the lips of everyone in every office around America. At times, the riotous fans caught action that was never intended for primetime family viewing. It was miraculous that no one was seriously hurt and the images would last forever. Just when we thought the hysteria could rise no higher, a morning news show broke through with another announcement. Another officer attack. "This time we got him," an excited voice announced. The FBI said a suspect was in custody. Details later. After a minute or so, a calm, authoritative male voice told us, "America is breathing a sigh of relief. The monster in the minds of most Americans is now in the firm hands of the law. The identity of the cop killer has not been officially released to the public, but sources say they are confident they have the right person." The CCN sources confirmed that the cop killer was wounded by the officer he attacked.

"We can confirm that he is a Black man, he appears to be between 21and 30 years of age. The officer who captured the assailant spoke briefly with a CCN reporter ten minutes ago. Here's what he said, 'Well I knew something was up when I saw this strange man hanging around my doctor's office. He looked like the same guy who bumped my cart in the supermarket. As I approached my car, I saw him out of the corner of my eye. He started walking faster, closing on me ya' know? I knew he was up to something. And everybody knows there's someone out there hunting cops, right? Then he screamed, 'Hey … you're that cop who killed that kid.' I backed up, ya know… to create some space. He tried to grab me and like lunged. I had my hand on my pocket you know, so I pulled my gun… shot him right there." He placed the tip of his index finger on the chest of the reporter showing the point of impact.

"Are you OK though?" asked the reporter.

"Yeah, I'm OK. Just thinking. I had to stop him. Anybody

in my position would have done the same thing."

"Well, you acted heroically sir. I know I speak for most Americans when I say, we thank God you're OK," the reporter replied.

Few Black people see this man as a hero. He killed a twelve year old two years before. He was one of two officers responding to a call at the Raymond Housing Project. On June 30th at 1:30pm, 911 operator Judy Spat received a report that a man was waving a gun in the court yard. Security cameras showed the two officers driving up to Adam Anderson, a twelve year old boy playing cops and robbers with a toy gun in front of his house. The footage also showed the officers pull up, take cover behind the car door and thirty seconds later, Anderson was on the ground. After the protest and outrage of the community the government launched a full investigation. They found that only one officer fired. It was Jim C. Daniels who fired six rounds… and five of them found the twelve year old chest of Adam Anderson.

Officer Daniels argued that in the split second fog of the moment he felt his life was in danger. After carefully watching the video and a six month investigation the District Attorney's office could find no reason to charge either officer with a crime.

The Anderson killing was another bitter place in the memories of many in the African American community. Very few if any, saw him as a hero.

Two women standing in the middle of America spoke openly about the controversy.

"It is not some racial victory I feel," Ms. White proclaimed passionately. "I feel all Americans are safer because this man is in custody. If he is willing to go after the police like that, he is a danger to all of us. And let me add this, because we talk like this is a racial issue. It is not a racial issue, all police aren't White. At least two of the officers he killed are Black like him. Every society has rules, laws and people to enforce them. No democracy can work if people ignore the rule of law and do their own thing. We are all Americans now, and we have to live together. A long time ago a lot of stuff happened. When you think about it, every ethnic group in this country has a grievance, but today we are all equal and we need to move forward."

Ms. Brown, an eloquently dressed obviously upscale Black woman, took a moment to touch the side of her hair. She raised an eye-brow before she responded. She seemed to catch one thought, replace it… and then she spoke. "I find your perspective interesting. I mean, well, it's interesting how you view US history. This country has given my people hell since we were dragged to this mother f***er in chains and you somehow believe I should be grateful for that because I'm still here. Then you say, 'We are all Americans now. That stuff was a long time ago. Everyone has historical grievances somewhere in the long chain of American development, let's move forward.' Ms. White, when you speak like that, I know you mean no disrespect, and I feel your words are sincere. But please, try to feel what I am saying to you now. I mean let's go a lot deeper than just hearing me. What I am saying to you is this. Your view of my circumstance is so self-serving that if you could hear yourself from my perspective you wouldn't fix your tongue and lips to utter some dumb sh** like that." She mounted the back of both wrists on the slope of her hips, shifted her weight… and waited.

"There's no need for profanity Ms. Brown. I can understand your position very well without it," White injected. "I'm just saying we have changed and you seem to ignore that. The idea that this country has not come a long way is absurd. The depiction of Black and Brown people in US culture is changing for the better every day. I see Black people in positions we never would have seen forty years ago. And things are happening faster than ever before. Anyone with eyes can see that," she said with a slight dig of sarcasm.

"Obviously we both have eyes Ms. White. We just see things differently. The eyes of White America see many things all the time, but they rarely ever see me. What you see growing is White American fear. America is trying to get in front of what it sees as a long overdue revolt of Black and Brown people. Not only did you enslave and mistreat us, now you want to decide how we respond to it. It's not OK for us to be in full rebellion, but if we want to protest, that's OK. As long as we do it in a way that makes you happy. You want Martin Luther King marches. You prefer something that may threaten your moral reputation…but not your life.

Somebody is snatching police. I don't know who it is. I don't know if this is a man or a woman. I don't even know if the missing people are dead. Some of us imagine it is a modern day John Brown, Nat Turner, Juda Maccabee or someone like that. I do know that this situation scares the hell out of the police because they don't know who it is. All they do know for sure is, it's coming for them." Finishing that sentence, she turned her attention to the wind and kindly walked away.

"Well," White added. "Thank God they caught him. Now they know who he is… and he's going to jail." But her words were too slow, and bounced off the back of Brown when she left the conversation.

Meanwhile, the media excitement was too crazy to describe and Jim Daniels was now the national hero he desperately wanted to become. He was the man who caught the cop killer and by the second day had no problem recounting the actions he took to any media outlet with a camera. For six days after that "The Morning Hour," a popular morning program… featured the former cop in a tawdry segment where Daniels theatrically retold his dangerous encounter with the killer. He secured a book deal, landed a major personal security contract and his story was quickly becoming a tear jerking example of American resolve and perseverance.

Officer Daniels was riding high on the winds of celebrity fame, and suddenly, like a cool chill… something shook his life back to the day he killed Adam Anderson. It was a

haunting feeling… a haunting that woke him in the middle of the night and appeared like a shadow on the wall.
"What is that?" he said. He sat up quickly sensing something in his room. "Don't move," he shouted. The military trained Daniels used his split second quickness, rolled from his bed, and with one motion grabbed his gun from the table and raised his arm to fire, but the gun was gone, his hand was gone…and before his mind could process a scream, so was he. "Piece off the board. White to move," Marcus grunted.

4 CHAPTER
The Soul Of Black Folk

The darling of the nation, Jim C. Daniels didn't appear on the show the next day. He didn't respond to repeated texts or the numerous attempts to reach him by phone. Two days later America realized why.

"Breaking news just in. Apparently Jim Daniels is missing," said the reporter who looked confused. "Police investigators are concerned. After he didn't show up for several appointments his friends and colleagues called police. Officers went to his home and found signs of a struggle but no blood. They do suspect foul play. Anyone with information please contact law enforcement."

In the law enforcement world, the issue of the missing officers was a major concern. In the wide American experience it has been a problem, but it didn't change their lives. Outside of a traffic violation, few White Americans had encounters with the police. Knowing this, the pro-police organizations bombarded the mainstream media with slick ads to remind the public what was at stake. Many Black people saw the ads as propaganda designed to shame, intimidate and persuade members of the African American communities to assist law enforcement.

In an Op-ed article Malcom Ben Carter wrote:

The Problem with Still Beliefs.

No lie can stand forever, and yet you still believe you can just send out a few law enforcement converts and flash screen shots of Black people who portray the image of success you want us to believe… and we will buy it.

You still believe that Black people are so preoccupied with good sports, loud music, and fried chicken that we can't see the American police and values you want us to help preserve are the ones that still oppress us. I think you still believe Black people are stuck in a perpetual state of stupidity. Wake up America, the revolution is real.

The article was one of the most talked about things in African America, but not in mainstream media.

Tatyana was driving home from a pleasant visit with the pediatrician when a popular ad interrupted her mood. In a patriotic voice, the US president spoke over military music recorded for maximum effect on the radio. "With your help justice can prevail," he said. "Help us find our missing officers like Officer Daniels… and make America safe again." The heroic music slowly faded. There was no one in the car old enough to understand what she wanted to scream, so in the most spiteful tone she could muster, Tatyana softly said, "Maybe Officer Daniels got lost in that split second fog he was always talking about," and she chuckled. Tatyana had no love for the police. She saw them as evil, but her faith provided a balancing force of reason she could always find in the Orthodox scripture.

Tatyana was born in Moscow. By the age of twelve her talents in technology were nationally recognized. Her technical know-how was an invaluable contribution to the life she and Marcus chose.

In Russia, the government blocked a lot of the American music, movies and other things young people liked, so Russian youth learned to evade and overcome blackout protocols to access the things they wanted. Marcus knew little about the Dark Web but for most computer literate Russians, navigating the Dark Web was a common practice. They used it to download things and they cloaked their searches and destination IP addresses multiple times by using a censorship circumvention tool like the Tor network. It encrypted the data and sent it through a virtual circuit, comprising successive random-selection computer relays, making it extremely difficult for the government to track an individual's online movements. Most Russian techies had access to whatever they wanted, and Tatyana was well beyond that. She was adept at combing the web for hidden information and avoiding sophisticated government surveillance algorithms. The Russian government noticed that and developed her on a steady pace through university. After her university training, Tatyana plunged into the vibrant cyber culture of the intellectual youth rebellion. They were young Russians who wanted real answers to real issues about real people. That's when she first encountered the BRO. Over time she grew more than a curious concern for the plight of Black and Brown people around the world with a particular interest in the US. Fighting the fears of her family, Tatyana sought and received a fellowship to study Black life in America. Ironically, in her search for Black consciousness she also found Marcus. "Marcus was a lot of things," she once said, "but Black conscious wouldn't describe any of them." He was a fully gentrified pseudo- aristocratic Black man, a good looking male more interested in a short skirt, Judo and the scientific utterances of Steven Hawkins, than the current concerns of BDS and the Black Lives Matter movement. "I didn't want to get distracted, so I avoided romantic relationships all together," she recounted to a friend. Tatyana did not come to America to find a companion and she wouldn't have had the time for someone as culturally detached as Marcus G. Madison, but something happened. One day she thought, "God is funny. He reminded me that the best things come as they are, not as I imagine them."

Tatyana Gannibal was a direct descendent of Abram Petrovich Gannibal and his wife Christina Regina Siöberg. The Gannibals were a prominent Russian family with old roots in Russian culture. Her ancestral uncle was Alexander Pushkin, a nineteenth century Black man that Russian schools credited as the single founder of modern Russian literature. Her father was a prominent minister, her mother was a prominent artist and she was fed up with the whole idea of prominence. The independent Tatyana needed more than the boxed parameters of her comfortable life. She wanted to see the world, the real one. "Racism is all over Europe and definitely in Russia," she thought. "But there is something deep and real about racism in America. Like an addict in denial, White Americans pretend it doesn't exist. The overwhelming majority of Russians might be curious about Afro- Russians, but the Russian police don't pull us over and shoot our parents in the face because a Black driver appears more dangerous than a White one." To stay or not stay was always a question. After the discovery of the TOAMA documents the couple reexamined their previous decision to stay. Tatyana's parents were concerned for their safety. They couldn't understand why two intelligent people with the means and ability to live anyplace in the world would choose to live in America. It wasn't logical. "Why start a family and raise a Black child in a place hostile to his very existence?" her father reasoned. But he didn't know the growing relationship Tatyana had with Lisa Madison. Tatyana wanted to spend more time with her in-laws but life didn't allow that. She admired them greatly. Marcus often spoke of them. Both of his parents were kind to her the evening they met, but Lisa Madison struck a deeper cord with Tatyana. "She did say she could read my feelings for Marcus," Tatyana remembered fondly. "She said I was gushing. I didn't think I was gushing. She said, 'gushing is good. When a woman has someone to gush over it's a beautiful thing,' and we laughed like old friends. I still feel you Mrs. Madison," she whispered loudly.

Tatyana could feel the warmth growing a little bit everyday she spent in the family home. Slowly it was clear to Tatyana that Lisa Madison found a spiritual way to cross the sands of consciousness and stay connected to her son. It was that comforting feeling a person gets from a mother when she's not physically there, but she is actually present. In the mind one can smell her perfume… her hair, even hear her voice.

The way Marcus described his mother was deeper than that… the way her friends and family spoke about her… it was all present; there was no fear in the room. When Tatyana first experienced it she thought, "Why is this happening to me? Why is she coming to me and not Marcus?" And then it was clear, she was there to help. "She was here to help me protect her son," she whispered. As a Russian Orthodox woman, Tatyana strongly believed a holy spirit was involved, and welcomed the presence as a mentoring force in her life.

In the days they spent storing away his parents things, Marcus and Tatyana found more about his mother. Packing her office papers they discovered that Lisa Madison was a junky for justice. Marcus grew up hearing the stories about how his grandfather marched for justice and how the non-violent weapons of rhetoric and unity won the equalities and liberties we have today. His mother frequently spoke of it. "Wow, I remember these words," he told Tatyana. "At granddad's funeral, she eulogized her father drilling into her that judicial activism is the only reliable way to guarantee safety and equality in a free society. This looks like a draft of her eulogy," he said. Lisa Madison had a fundamental belief in the US legal system. She was raised to believe that the way to ensure fair laws and just treatment was to stay engaged. Having grown up around the justice system, his mother understood that bad things happened to good, even innocent people. She knew that every system had its share of bad actors, but it wasn't in her to consider the whole system was rotten; and she had no personal fear of it.

"Look at this Marcus. This award congratulates her for all of her work with the police." For some reason, Tatyana was not surprised. "Apparently," she added, "Your mother was a firm believer in the concept of community policing, and she served as the chair of her sorority committee to support local law enforcement."

"Yeah," he said. "I know about that one." He tried to fight it, but a proud smile took over his face. She was a kind, understanding soul who believed that fairness in fertile ground would always grow something beautiful. In memory of his slain parents, Marcus and Tatyana agreed to raise young Gerald in the USA until he reached ten years old… and together they would work to defend ordinary people against those who pledge their allegiance to the code of blue.

Mushin

After a grueling training session Marcus quietly sat on the cool tatami floor in the sparsely lit dojo. "Arigato Kondo," (Thank you Kondo) he said. "Our training sessions are better than any therapy I can imagine. When I am in the Flow I don't have to fight the recurring memories that are always threatening to take over my mind. How can I stop the images?"

"You cannot stop them. They come and go as they please. If you recognize this they will keep moving. But if you try to stop them, they stay in that place longer and longer. When images come, you should see them come and watch them go."

"What I try to do is concentrate on something else, but the images take over every time," Marcus responded.

"When you try to think about something else you are still thinking," Kondo said. "When you engage you quickly realize that the images are in control. Images are like pieces in fast moving river. What I say to you is do nothing, just watch them pass. No jumping, no thinking, 'no mind'. This is Mushin. You can do this can you?" Kondo asked.

"I can work on it a little every day."

"I will help with it, but it seems more is going on in you Marcus. What is it?"

"I'm trying to reconcile the myths I inherited with the realities I find."

"Why reconcile anything? Each thing is in its own place and happens in its own time. There is nothing to reconcile. It seems you still feel misled by your earlier schooling… and now that you are learning more, your former thoughts embarrass you. Is this so?"

"All that I learned about this place was a lie. Maybe embarrassed is not the right word. I feel cheated. Betrayed. Yes, betrayed is a better word."

"You say you feel this way. Examine your thoughts and tell me, who cheated you? If betrayed, who betrayed you? Who lied to you?" Kondo sat on the ground and waited for Marcus to respond.

He couldn't.

Kondo filled the silence, "Maybe your school? Your country? Maybe it was your parents? That kind of thinking always comes to the same place. Who? The reality is this, your parents taught you what they thought were the best things. They put you in what they thought was the best school. They lived in this country because they thought it was better. We are here training now, here in this place, because of the bad situation that happened to them."

"Yeah, but I would gladly trade everything to change that evening and have my parents back."

"You already know, we cannot change past Marcus; but we can learn from it… and we can live now."

"People who knew my parents, they want to know if I'm OK. What do they expect me to say Kondo? If I told them what was going on in my head they wouldn't sleep for a week. So, I lie. I do it so much I wish people would stop asking me so I can at least be honest in my silence. I will never be OK again Kondo. There are so many people, every day, everywhere, they mean well. But I can never give them the honesty they want. Police killed my parents and some days I want to kill them all. They splattered pieces of my mother all over my mind. I wake up in tears so often my tear ducts are dry; and my mind swings from day to day. Day one I want to pull the whole damn system down and day two I am plotting with others to improve it. I am falling apart Kondo. Tatyana has to glue me together every morning, it's not right… and it's not fair to her. Yes, it's true. My parents would find a place somewhere in their hearts to forgive these people. Tatyana is absolutely right when she reminds me of that, I know she's right ... but I am not like my parents. I don't trust this government." He stopped talking abruptly. He closed his eyes. Kondo spoke to him again.

"In your mind, see your anger. The feeling you have, the intensity, don't try to stop it. Let it happen. Imagine it has a shape. Don't try to contain it... watch it flow, like water in a river. You can't stop it, just observe. Can you see it?"

"Yes, I can see it."

"OK, describe it."

"It is fast. It is not clear water, it is brown, silty."

"Is it high? Is it overflowing the banks?" Kondo asked; his calm cadence nearly a whisper.

"I can't see the banks, but it is fast."

"Good Marcus. Let it flow. Understand that all things with a high will have a low. A fast moving body of water at some point will slow. It will level off, correct?"

"Yes, I know."

"So, now we will watch. And he folded his short legs like a pretzel until the soles of his feet lay over his thighs and faced the sky. He closed his eyes and slowly synchronized the rise and fall of their chests, and he softly continued. "Now we learn to expect nothing. Maybe the color will change. Maybe objects will be caught in the fast moving water and be pushed to the side or pulled down the middle. We will just watch it. Can you see moving?"

Marcus responded, "Yes. I can see the water. A boat floating. Now slowly drifting."

"Just watch the water," Kondo whispered. "Have no expectations. If the boat floats or sinks it doesn't matter. If other things come and go, it doesn't matter, water high or low. All you do is watch it. Can you feel it?"

"Yes, it's getting slower and the water level is changing."

"Go with the flow of your anger Marcus. Ride it like the wind, float on the surface like a boat on the water and your mornings will find the balance you are looking for; it is a principle of Mushin. Mushin is foundation of Flow."

"Yes, I see. It helps Kondo. Thanks again."

"You are welcome," he answered. They sat like still objects in an open space.

Between Tatyana and Kondo, Marcus was winning the struggle to find balance in his life. While he ironed out his private wrinkles, in the eyes of the public, two things prevailed above all.

One, there was an entity out there that tracked wrongfully acquitted officers and brought them to justice swiftly. And two, Black and Brown people have never been more united on an issue.

One cold evening after a few hours of careful research, Tatyana found something interesting. Speaking to Marcus she said, "Did you know there is no credible study comparing the number of police killed in the line of duty patrolling Black communities to the number of Black and Brown people killed by police patrolling those communities?"

"Ah, no. I didn't know that."

"Apparently, your government discourages this kind of comparison. I'm sure that's because the public will see who has more to fear from whom."

"That makes sense," said Marcus. His mind drifted, recounting every piece he took off the board. "As individuals they are not ready for much," he thought, referring to the officers the government considered 'missing.' They are trained to operate like pack animals. Like wolves, they want to intimidate with numbers, noise, and confusion; minimizing the risk of injury to themselves. "Kondo was right, the average officer is too weighed down with his own weaponry to fight a trained opponent," he remembered. Removing the targets from their place of comfort was not as difficult as he trained for it to be, but that was a good thing. "It's not that the officers were stupid," he thought. "They were arrogant. That's worse. I don't believe they spend much time preparing individuals for retaliation. At first I thought it would be hard to find them. Especially the ones in a protection program," he recalled. "With the hacking technology available these days, finding the daily movements of a rotten cop is a simple task for the BRO. Almost everything about them was on file in an easily hackable database. I guess the trackers didn't expect to be tracked." His eyes were open to the room, but his attention was still in a deep transcendent thought. A technique Kondo called analytical daydreams.

"Where is that beautiful mind of yours Marcus?" Tatyana asked, squinting her eyes in a failed attempt to see the inside of his head. He was too quiet, too withdrawn. She was concerned he was flashing back to a dark space. She was a woman determined to counter his random bouts of depression with reassuring words and a positive perspective. She assumed his memories were picking a fight with him again. She jumped in protectively. "Marcus," she gently reached for his hand, "From time to time God will send a reluctant, ordinary person to correct the wicked." She picked up a popular national newspaper.

He interrupted, "Tatyana, I love you, but please don't ask me to read another scripture. Please honey?"

She laughed. "It's the newspaper silly man…" and then she paused. Losing the laugh, she snapped out a serious question, "What's wrong with scripture?"

"Nothing!" he quickly replied.

"Yeah right," she huffed, and rested her weak hand on the right hip. This was an international Black woman signal that a profound message was about to drop on someone. Most Black males have been conditioned from birth to suspect it had something to do with us; so instinctively we look up to avoid the oncoming injuries of hard falling phrases. And that's exactly what happened to him.

"You need to know how God works Marcus." The sharp response was short, and it cut deep. Marcus reacted the only way a smart man could. He looked to the sky and said, "You're right."

"I know," she said. "Look at this." She pointed to the paper. "The people appreciate what you stand for. People are changing. They are losing the fear of government retaliation. The NAABP publicly published letter to you means they are willing to risk being isolated and branded a supporter of terror. Let me read it to you:

We don't know who you are, but many people from around the world follow what you are doing and support your cause. We just want you to know that Black people love you. It is now clear to oppressed people around the world that you are an anonymous avenger of evil. We see you as a mysterious figure fighting for righteousness against a corrupt establishment led by those sworn to protect and defend the public. You make us feel proud. You make us feel happy. You make us feel safe. Whatever you are, whoever you are, God bless you.

Donald Billings
Chairman, NAABP

National Association for the Advancement of Black People."

"Wow," he said. "I don't know what to say to that."

Tatyana moved into him and placed her head on his chest, his heavy arms held her close and wrapped around her shoulders.

"I was just thinking about a few good things," he said with a bit of emotion hinging in his voice, "but your love… makes the good things even better."

5 CHAPTER
There's Life In Every Moment

He was three years old and like most toddlers he was able to find the small important things responsible adults frequently overlooked. Children are naturally drawn to insects, and mothers are not. Her son was a handful of busy, inquisitive little boy whose mind was drawn to everything that crawled, crept, swam or could fly. Tatyana wasn't a squeamish woman. She was tough, intelligent, and a well-trained member of the Russian youth rangers. When she was nine years old her camping team was attacked by a rabid gray wolf. Her group was clustering in the cold and in a dangerous moment the wolf lunged, biting and snarling. Young Tatyana was the only one with the presence of mind to draw her utility knife and swing it with enough torque to nearly sever the head of the wolf. She has never been afraid of man nor beast, but she has always been afraid of bugs. Tatyana hated bugs - insects of any kind for that matter. Marcus on the other hand, had no problem with them. He was indifferent, which was a problem for her because their son always seemed to find the scariest bugs when Marcus wasn't there. On this day it was a green, wing-flapping, Cicada. It had huge eyes spaced far apart from the middle of its head. It was the size of a small bird and Gerald had the butt and back legs of the thing in his mouth.

"Look Mum," he mumbled with his mouth full of a living, moving something trying to flap its wings. She was trying to pray, but she couldn't move her fingers from covering her mouth. And then she heard it, a loud, distinctive, crunch.

He bit down. The front half of the severed insect fell to the ground; its little legs crawling, scratching forward in small circles and smearing pale-yellow bug pus across the light wood floor. As quickly as it happened, the lightning Gerald grabbed the moving half from the floor, shoved it in his cheeks and swallowed. That's when she lost it, and screamed like a white lady.

"Jeee-sus Gerald! No!" She grabbed him by the back of his jumper and forced an index finger into his mouth searching to retrieve the crawling thing her son just ate. Little Gerald was trying to yummy and laugh while his mother was searching past his tongue. She couldn't reach the bug, it was gone… and her finger was covered with a green gel she tried not to smell, but she did. Just when she was about to abandon her search, her finger touched it. She didn't expect it. She didn't even think about it. She was so preoccupied with the bug her boy had eaten, she was surprised when her roving finger pressed the throw-up button located in the middle back of every toddler's throat. She didn't mean to, but she pressed it…and he did it.

"Eww Gerald, it's a mess," she said when she grabbed his slimy hands because he was trying to eat it again. She wrenched the bug bits away from the boy and instructed Gerald to play with his blocks while she cleaned the pieces from the floor, but he didn't sit still, he didn't stop. She lost her voice screaming when she saw another two inch bug young Gerald retrieved from the shelf beneath her bedroom window.

"My God…" she looked to the sky and whispered, "This is why I prayed for a girl."

Discovered A Mole

All in all, this was a day of discovery, a day the BRO never wanted to see. Young Gerald discovered a bug in the room and it was gross but harmless. Hours later, Tatyana and Marcus received an important message from Leonard; it wasn't harmless. It read, "These are dangerous times. We discovered a mole in the BRO."

The following day Leonard had a meal with Marcus and Tatyana at the Black Diamond. The Diamond was one of the finest family restaurants in town. For more than two decades the Madison family created an environment where food and community came together. It had been years since Leonard sat at one of the tables.

"This place is still wonderful Marcus," he said. "I remember that photo there," and he pointed to a group photograph of familiar people standing in front of the Eifel Tower. Leonard was not one for small talk and he wasted no time getting to the point of discussion.

"Well," he said, "Here's what I know. The new protocols we put in place worked. As best we can tell anyway. Jamila Talame is a mole. She was a government insider for us for two years. Now she is working for us as a secretary to the mayor in Ballimore City. She doesn't know we discovered her. She's a new government agent searching for anything related to you."

"Did she find anything?" asked Marcus.

"There's nothing to find. You don't exist," Leonard replied.

"Ok great, how do we proceed?" Marcus asked.

"For now, we watch her, see where she takes us. So far she only discovered that we are an organization. She knows you have help but she doesn't know who. For some reason her superiors didn't tell her that they already know these things. The profilers have you as a Black male but they have very little forensic evidence to support it. They have a few fibers from the Daniels case, but our people in the labs tell us they belong to Daniels. The fibers that they found mean nothing without something specific to compare them to. This case is big though; they have over a hundred special agents devoted to it.

The fact that the missing officers have not been found is very unusual. It is devastating to the morale in every agency. The American law enforcement system has never had an experience like this. To them, it's like some Steven Spielberg alien, body snatching the police. When you are an arrogant agency, in an arrogant country, run by arrogant people, this kind of thing is scary."

"Is she the only mole?" Marcus asked.

"Yes. Thanks to the caliber of support we're now receiving, I can say that with certainty. Marcus, you have inspired a level of backing we could only dream about until now."

"Don't forget to tell him about the international criminal police organization," Tatyana lightly injected.

"Oh yeah, Interpol. Thanks, I almost forgot. Interpol has been consulted. You already know they share a database but here's something you may not know. The US borrowed two British Agents, One French agent and an Israeli Mosad person to work on this. Apparently your crusade may be the inspiration for something larger. At least that's the fear."

"Yes, my dear. They also think they can bribe the people to turn you in," Tatyana added.

Leonard laughed, "Yeah, the reward is beginning to look like the lotto," he said.

"OK, now we're talkin'! Does that mean I'll get the money if I turn myself in?" Marcus laughed and tapped Leonard, with an easy expectation that he would join in the chuckle.

"That's not funny," said a not smiling Tatyana. Leonard slowly looked away… he didn't chuckle. "And leave me with your son," she added… "Who eats bugs. Not funny Marcus." She paused for a moment, then she smiled and hugged his arm.

"Little Gerald eats bugs too?" asked Leonard, in the playful voice conspicuously absent a few seconds ago. "Marcus used to hunt bugs and he ate what he caught. He was about

Gerald's age. We use to call him the Hunter." Leonard smiled mischievously when he parted with those tidbits of trivia.

"Really," said the curious Tatyana. "Marcus you never said anything about that."

"I didn't know. I mean, honestly. I don't remember that."

"Do you remember the story about 'The Native Hunter'?" asked Leonard.

"Of course. My mother told me that story all the time." Tatyana followed each word between the two, her eyes bouncing back and forth like she was watching a tennis match.

"What's it about?" she asked curiously.

"On one level it's a story about perseverance and cunning," Marcus replied. "In the story a White colonial governor laid claim to the whole African forest and then he sentenced an African man to death for hunting in it. The hunter was smart enough to understand that he could not reason with the White man's law because all the laws were established by him to protect him. So the hunter decided to use time as a tool, a defense and later, maybe even an offensive weapon. He started by adopting a tactical delay. Because an opportunity to change his circumstance wouldn't matter if he died, the first thing he needed to do was stay alive. From there he reasoned: when life is present everything else is simply a matter of time. On another level the story was about finding the weakness of an opponent and waiting for the best time to exploit it. The governor was power hungry, so the hunter appealed to his ambition and won the governor's attention. The hunter was successful. The governor postponed the hunter's execution for one year in exchange for a secret technique the hunter would teach to him. Since the hunter had cheated death for one year, he appreciated each moment and lived every day in search of another one. He knew that living would bring a new opportunity to free himself. At the end he says, life is built on a series of moments, and I will learn to live in every one. You know, I don't remember her reading from a book. She always recited it to me, like one of Aesop's Fables. I didn't know she

wrote it, she never said."
"Marcus," Leonard injected. "You are the inspiration for the story. You used to get frustrated so quickly, but you liked stories. Your mother noticed that you retained information better when it came from a story. She said you had a tendency to see yourself in the characters. This was one of the things they used to help you. By the time you graduated high school, one of your most talked about traits was your determination."
"I didn't know she wrote the story. Why didn't she say it was her story?"
"Don't know, but she did write it. I remember when she did. You were like eight years old or so. I don't remember the full story though. It was a man hunting a deer right?"
"No, it's a gazelle," Marcus replied.
Anxious to know, Tatyana asked, "Can you tell me the story? I'd like to know it," she said in a funny, sarcastic kind of way.
"Maybe one day when he's able to sit still without munching bugs I can tell it to your son," and Leonard barked out a laugh that drew the attention of several people eating at other tables. Marcus couldn't help but laugh at the way Tatyana was looking at him. "Of course I will," he said lovingly. "I don't know why I didn't think about it before."
It starts like this:

In a forest not so near his village, a young hunter tracked the large gazelle he wounded, and found him lying lifeless against a fallen tree at the edge of a narrow brook. He removed the broken spear from the gazelle's chest and apologized to the animal for ending his life. Then he knelt, lowered his head and thanked the Creator for his own. After a few minutes rest he carefully bound the four long legs together and mounted the heavy beast around his shoulders for the one hour walk back to his village.

On his way home he was stopped by a band of passing soldiers. The soldiers arrested the hunter for stealing and killing the governor's beast, but the young hunter knew nothing of these men, or their strange laws. "What is a governor?" he asked.

The red coated soldiers confiscated the gazelle and dragged the young offender two hours away to a daily court, presided over by the governor himself. It is the habit of the governor's court to hear each case and render a judgment speedily before the people. Finally, the young hunter was standing before the great White governor. The governor asked, "What is your defense for stealing and killing my beast?" The hunter answered, "No person can own the creatures in the forest." "But the law is clear," said the governor. "The penalty for stealing and killing my animal is death."

Realizing the circular reasoning of the White man, the native young hunter paused in deep thought and calculated a lifesaving strategy. "Let me offer you a power you have never seen in exchange for my life," said the young hunter. "I come from a tribe who has mastered the mysteries of life and death. Soon, someone close to you will fall gravely ill and die. When this happens, I can restore that life and teach you the ancient secrets from my people. It takes two years to learn how to cheat death, but a man of your greatness, I can teach in one year."

The offer intrigued the governor. "I find what you say interesting young man. I do not know if it is true, but if you die today I will never know. Therefore, I will hold you captive for one year. If you can teach me to cheat death I will set you free. If you cannot you will be put to death. This is my judgment." And the hunter was spared and taken to a holding place for special prisoners.

One day an older prisoner said to the hunter, "I have lived in this land my whole life and I have never heard of a tribe who has the power to cheat death. Can you really cheat death?" And the hunter answered, "I have never tried it before, but when the time comes we will see." The man responded, "Then you have just wasted time. In only a year the governor will realize your deception and order your death, so why would you mislead him? It will only anger him."

And the hunter replied, "For me, time is a design in perpetual motion; it can never be wasted. At this moment I am alive, and anything can happen in a year. The governor may die, I could escape, my family may find me, or I can learn even more creative ways to cheat death. Life is built on a series of moments, and I will learn to live in every one." The End.

"Marcus," she said softly, "That is a beautiful story." Tatyana couldn't figure out why she was surprised, but it was pleasant.

She smiled and searched her mind for the best English words to express the level of admiration she was constantly accumulating for his mother. "Your mom," she added, "She's like the gift who keeps on giving. Where can I find this story?"

"I don't know… Me," he shrugged.

"Have you written it down?"

"No. I never thought I would need to, but Leonard said Mom kept it somewhere."

"No I didn't," Leonard quickly injected. "I said she had it, I don't know if she kept it."

"Oh, thanks for your unwavering support Godfather," Marcus smirked sarcastically. Trying to keep a straight face he added, "I just hope I can survive being crushed by the wheels of the bus you threw me under."

Without a moment's hesitation Leonard said, "Women stick together Marcus."

"What are you talking about Leonard?" Marcus shot back in a funny way. "You're not a woman anymore."

Leonard sat up tall in his seat, rolled his narrow shoulders back, pushed his chest forward, struggled to choke back his hearty laugh and said, "But I stay in touch with my feminine side." And they broke into a group laugh. It was a happy family moment.

The Price Of Freedom

Another Black man gunned down by a White South Georgia police officer on Wednesday.

Chelsie Police Officer Sam Michaels shot William Smith in the back as he ran away following a traffic stop in September, 2017, for driving his car with a broken taillight. A hidden witness took video of the killing. One hour after the incident the witness posted it online. It went viral.

Officer Michaels was charged with first-degree murder, but a judge declared a mistrial when a jury was unable to reach a unanimous verdict.

In a plea deal with the Department of Justice, the local prosecutors agreed not to refile new charges against Officer Michaels. The wording in his plea agreement described Michaels' actions as "objectively unreasonable given the circumstances."

Sobbing heavily, the victim's 70 year old mother said, "Even with a video of the murder, the dirty cop gets a plea deal. How is that right?"

Yet again, around the country community leaders marched and protested. The chants for justice were never louder. "We are tired of talking the same talk over the same thing," they chanted. "Stop the killing now." Everyone knew the words. The shirts and the signs were all the same. The journalists covered the ministers speaking and the political speakers offered the same solutions. Only the law enforcement agencies did something different. The federal government authorized full protection for the former police officer. Until the federal order was signed members of the Chelsie SWAT team volunteered to provide round-the-clock security for their colleague. It was a clear and present show of force to protect a fellow member. The National Association for the Advancement of Black People argued that the tax payers' money should not be used for the private security of the police, but their argument was ignored.

On the same day in another city, the federal investigators released the long awaited Jamal report. In the report the investigators found that the Boston police officer who fatally shot an unarmed motorcyclist last year had no legal reason to shoot. The officer was not in danger when he fired. This was the conclusion after an extensive six month internal investigation. It completely contradicted the officer's account.

The report, obtained by The Boston Insider, revealed that the officer and his partner violated many policies of the department. After a night of drinking, 28 year old Billy Jamal was driving at a high speed on Main Street. He ran several red lights. The cagey officers pursued him through the town, beat him to the intersection and cut him off with their squad car.

On the passenger side Officer David Larry flung open his door to stop the speeding motorcycle, but that didn't stop Billy Jamal. He collided with the door and slid by, continuing to speed down the street. Officer Larry decided to put an end to it once and for all, so he pulled out his gun and fired two times, striking his moving target once in the back and once in the neck.

In his report, Officer David Larry said the motorcycle pinned his leg between the door and the car and he only fired his gun because he feared for the safety of himself and his partner. But when the investigators re-created the incident and examined his injuries, they determined that Officer Larry's leg wounds were superficial and it was never pinned in the door. The internal police investigators also noted that Officer Larry's decision to shoot, "was not in defense of his life, nor was it in defense of the lives of others."

Because Officer Larry failed to turn on his body camera before the shooting, federal prosecutors who investigated the shooting determined there was not enough evidence to file criminal charges against him. It was a common assumption in America that police officers could be trusted to tell the truth, even when it conflicted with their best interest. To many Americans, an officer under oath was as credible as their religious leader. Across the country in the jurisdictions that saw fit to require officers to wear body cameras, it was common practice for them to trust the officer to turn the camera on and leave it on. Americans were surprised, sometimes appalled, when an officer did otherwise. In the case of Officer Larry he said, "I felt my life was in danger, and in the split second fog of the moment I didn't reach for my camera- I reached for my gun and I discharged it to protect myself, my partner and the community." The judicial trust most Americans have for the legal system and those who police it, has a name. Black people call it… White privilege.

On the evening the federal prosecutors determined there was not enough evidence to file criminal charges against Officer Larry, he and a few friends met at their regular bar to celebrate.

But someone was watching, quietly waiting with no regard for the one-sided way federal prosecutors made their determination. "In time, even the best soup grows cold," he thought.

His mind traveled back to an earlier conversation …

"How long are the people expected to put up with this? Why won't they fight back? Part of the reason your country treats the people so badly is that the people refuse to fight back. It is painful to watch Marcus."

He listened approvingly. Marcus was always a little amazed at how much Tatyana knew about US history. It was not a subject that stroked his interest in prep school. The only thing worse was when she assumed he remembered a basic Russian historical fact. When such a conversation arose he just smiled and repeated the same one word response, "Sputnik."

At which time she shook her head, smiled and moved onto the next subject.

"Marcus, it just seems like every oppressed people in the world who encounter the USA knows how to fight them except the African American." She spoke in a high pitched

irritated voice that carried a stroke of blame. "Why do you continue to put up with this kind of treatment?"
"Me? What did I do?" he pointed his thumb to his chest in sync with the question.
"Not just you Marcus. I'm talking about the collective. How does that poem go? 'You must make injustice expensive or the people will never be free.' It is so true. In my grade school World History class we studied the ongoing oppression of the American Black people. In Russia, the government wanted us to know what America was really about. We reason that the way to clearly understand the social ideology of a nation is to see how that nation interacts with disadvantaged people. The Russian revolution was a social rebellion driven by economic disparity. We consider our whole nation to be a large community. And though prejudice and racism exist in Russia as it does everywhere, it is not in the socio-economic best interest of a Russian communal society to exclude, mistreat or kill citizens because of their race.
The talents of all citizens strengthen our republic, like the ocean winds will move all boats. In our schools, World Humanity classes paid a lot of attention to the African and native descendants in America. Primarily because every opportunity American officials had to address the world community devolved into a human rights lecture led with a self-proclaiming of moral superiority. American leaders routinely portrayed the American lifestyle as the best in the world and presented our communist ideals as the epitome of oppression, so our teachers would frequently expose the contradictions in the American social logic.

Russian teachers loved to point out the high regard Americans claimed they had for freedom and equality, while racially segregating and socially targeting Black and Brown people. Still, this country distracts the world with proxy wars while they kill and incarcerate Black men at a rate they are embarrassed to admit, essentially culling the Black and Brown man from the American landscape. It is painful to watch.

It's like the American Black people are hoping that one day White people will hear your cry and stop beating you. And your march leaders are standing in front saying 'If we can just band together and cry a little louder we can shame them until they stop.' We used to discuss it in school. We talked about how White America terrified Black people for so long that the Black population was afraid to fight for their own lives. Most of us were around the same age Emmett Till was at the time he was killed. The way American school kids studied Adolf Hitler's Germany, we studied America's race problem.

But the Emmett Till situation was worse to us maybe because he was just a kid. He was only 14 years old. A White woman accused him of flirting with her and four days later he was kidnapped from his uncle's house and murdered. The old Jet magazine photo of Emmett's gruesomely mutilated body is an image I will never forget. When I first saw it I thought, wow, my grandfather was 14 years old at that time. If he were in America I may not be here today. And you know what sticks out most to me Marcus?" she asked rhetorically. "The men who were responsible for brutally killing Emmett were tried in the US court and acquitted; and they are still being acquitted all the time all over this country, and Black people still put up with it. Besides the actions of the White people something else bothers me. Two enraged White men came to the home of Emmett's great uncle. His uncle begged the two men to leave and not take his nephew. But here's the remarkable part, Emmett's uncle gave him up. He was so scared of losing his own life he wouldn't fight for the life of his nephew.

That is bothersome to me. Can you imagine what Emmett must have felt? I know we can't go back and re-live that situation, but Marcus, still today, we sometimes act like White people don't bleed too. I tell you if two people ever come to that door and threaten to take a family member from our home Marcus, I swear to you before the God I hold most high there will be a fight. Those men knew Emmett's uncle wouldn't fight for his life and they had no fear for their own safety. I find that crazy to think about; two strange White men drove up in a Black neighborhood, threw a Black boy in the back of a car and drove away, unscathed. In what other community can strangers show up and demand a 14 year old be given to them without a fight? We don't think about it this way, but it is happening today. Police will come into a community, brutalize someone and the people are too scared for their own safety to intervene. All White people aren't bad and all police aren't White, but the overwhelming majority of them are and from what I see, both of them behave as if they are superior to us because we treat them that way. When others in the world see that you are willing to fight and die for your freedom, they will help. And what do you have to lose? They're killing you already. For all of the protest rhetoric, America only really respects the rights of those who fight. Every year you celebrate the memory of colonial states who fought against the oppressive conditions imposed by the British. Americans praise the great rebel Patrick Henry but what did he say? 'Give me liberty or give me what?' Death. And, when your presidents comb the whole world looking for terrorists they... arghh! The hypocrisy drives me crazy!"

"Tatyana, you're not even an American. How do you know all of this stuff?"

"I told you, in Russia we get this in grade school. What I can't remember, I look it up online."

"Yes but why?"

"Because these people are trying to take some moral high ground, they are hypocrites. When the leaders in your government say, 'Make America safe again,' I think Emmett Till. It's wrong Marcus." Tatyana was angered to the point of distraction and she was justified..

6 CHAPTER
Prisoners Of Our Own Experience

Quietly he sat with his eyes closed because everything he needed to see was in his head. On his face he could feel what he needed to know: the wind… the temperature… the conditions and opportunities changed over time. Like a cat on a Ferris wheel he patiently waited. His body at rest remained at rest, but his mind would roam from a space to a place touching all the concepts in-between. Then he paused on a wandering notion, "For so many years I associated the word Apocalypse with the destruction of all things," he thought. "I understood it to be a negative word for complete and utter destruction. Now I discover it is actually a Greek word meaning the unveiling of hidden truth or knowledge. If I used a literal translation it would mean something more like, 'uncovering.' How did I get so far off track? That's not some little misunderstanding, I was just wrong. Actually it goes deeper than that. I never thought to question the meaning. I accepted it the way it was given to me. At the time I had no reason to question the fact and there was no one in my realm of discussion who articulated anything different. But I was wrong, and every thought I stacked on the face of my incorrect assumption took me farther and farther away from the truth. This small thing taught me a big lesson. Beware of the inherited assumption."

Before he could complete his thought, the figure he was waiting for appeared. It was a man. And he brought the stench of Old Spice and cheap beer. George Strait was singing in the background and the man was humming the song. He was still smiling from the joke that came with the last beer when he pushed passed the broken door and carefully stumbled to position himself mostly in front of the urinal. In the men's room the song was a muffled mix of voices with an under-towing tune. Above it all, was his moaning voice mumbling every word in a broken, drunken, toneless attempt to make music.

"I don't take my whiskey to extremes," he mumbled.
"Don't believe in chasin' crazy dreams
My feet are planted firmly on the ground
But darlin' when you come around
I get carried away by the look by the light in your eyes
Before I even realize the ride I'm on
Baby I'm long gone." He was loud and clearly tone deaf, but he continued, "I get carried away nothin' matters but bein' with you
Like a feather flyin' high up in the sky on a windy day
I get carried away."

He didn't really try to close his eyes, the alcohol did that. He stumbled as he stood to make the necessary adjustments, fumbled with his zipper, fingered his way passed the fold in his boxers and found the part he needed. Then he braced his other hand on the wall, released a few gasses and a glowing stream of urine relieved the pressure from his bladder. The song kept playing, his head kept nodding and he kept singing:
"I get carried away before I even realize the ride I'm on
Baby I'm long gone, baby I'm gone."

Someone was watching… and he spoke, "There's a lot of things the human mind can tolerate, but this ain't one of them." And suddenly the man stopped singing, the spray of urine hit the wall and then the floor but the stall was no longer occupied. "Shut up - George Strait is one of the finest artists this country has ever produced," Marcus thought, "and that demon was killing his song. Piece off the board. White to move."

As Time Goes By

Time passed and good friends always check on each other. Still laughing, two men went to see if their fully intoxicated friend was passed out on the men's room floor. He wasn't. Officer David Larry was not in the building anymore - he was gone and his friends never saw him again.

The international media ran with the story first. "The American justice system is being put to the test," the journalist wrote. "There is a fighter for judicial equality who lurks in the night and makes bad cops disappear. Until today the country was strictly divided. But it looks like things are changing. Another officer is missing, and more young White liberals are beginning to sympathize with Black and Brown America. Not since the Vietnam conflict have Americans been this distrustful of the government. The TOAMA documents triggered a massive influx of lawsuits and inquiries at every level. But the Democracy Today group was by far the most vocal, some would even say they were leading the charge.

Behind her back they called her the anti-Christ. Her hair was red to her waist and her eyes were the color of the sky on a clear day in Northern Ireland. She was barely five feet tall, her skin was porcelain white, and she ignored the government intimidation tactics like the subtle social cues to shave her legs.

Tiffany Doyle was a Berkley educated lawyer turned journalist who had long understood what the conflict was all about. She wrote an award winning book about justice in America. For a decade, she and a small team of graduate students tracked a consistent pattern of police misconduct and judicial bias. Her research found prejudice deeply imbedded in our whole system of jurisprudence. Her strong conclusions and radical remedy was considered by many to be too extreme. "Draft a new constitution and start all over again," she says. "We cannot gradually include oppressed people into a constitutional democracy that was deliberately designed to exclude them. That concept has not worked anywhere in the world and it is not working here. All people should see themselves as architects of the thing that governs them. The all White founders of the USA didn't work themselves into the British Magna Carta because they didn't want a second hand ideology. They wanted their own. So they drafted a constitution that begins with the words 'We The People.' It represented them because it was by them, for them. How can the Black and Brown people of this country trust the very thing that keeps them in bondage? I say it's time to call a new constitutional convention and rewrite the constitution. Bring representative leadership to the table and make a new one that reflects the will of all America, the true American people."

The conservative executives who headed the Foxhound Media Network hated Tiffany Doyle. They echoed the government assertion that she was a traitorous, treasonous, communist hell bent on using her rights as an American to destroy America. Doyle was unfazed by the right wing accolades. She was a forty three year old woman in a twenty three year old body. She knew who she was, she knew what she liked and she knew what she wanted… and she usually got it. Tiffany Doyle was a person the conservatives loved to hate and the progressive liberals hated to love, but the fire she brought to a discussion drove the viewership ratings of any talk show she appeared on through the clouds. She was articulate, eclectic and completely unpredictable. The Foxhound viewers hated almost everything she stood for but they couldn't stop watching her in a debate. In an on-air discussion with a right-wing host, Doyle once said, "I know your viewers don't like me. They want to see you take me down… put me in my place," she smiled. "That's why I charge you twice your normal guest fee to come on your show. It's like the Ali-Forman fight. You swing and miss, swing and miss, I rope a dope, you lose. I get paid and maybe we meet again for a rematch." It was that kind of quick witted taunting that drove people crazy. The liberals didn't want to like her because she was anti- establishment, anti- party and they believed her to be anti- white. The conservatives loved that the public mistook her for a progressive liberal, but they hated her command of the facts and her ability to argue both sides of an issue. Tiffany Doyle often said, "The problem with the party system in America is that both parties are committed to the preservation of the same constitution. One side says it's good, let's tweak it and make it better. The other side says, it's perfect the way that it is.

The US constitution is a breathing document that provides room for measured change over time to prevent anarchy." In her last interview she used an analogy, "Let me put it to you this way, America wanted a government to reflect the ideals of the inhabitants that mattered. So they took some land, they used slave labor and cheap materials to build a white house on a weak foundation. I say, the patterns of history are clear and this house will not stand for long. Eventually the land will be redeemed. The over-patched foundation will no longer support the weight of the house, it will rot, crumble and fall inward, I see it. Therefore, I believe we should negotiate a fair arrangement for the land, lift the house, add some color and build a proper foundation. Then the house may last… and we can live up to our potential."

Dismissively he said, "That's not a likelihood Ms. Doyle," and then he changed the subject. "I'm curious to know, what do you think of these killings?" he asked.
With a puzzled look, she responded, "What killings?"
"Oh, come on now Ms. Doyle. Don't pretend you don't know about these cop killings."
"I'm not pretending. I honestly don't know. Please enlighten me," she said with a very serious look on her face.
"OK. Let's start with the latest one. Officer David Larry last week. One minute he's drinking with his friends having a good time. He goes into the men's room and is never seen again. And then there is Officer Daniels before that, and so,

so many more. All over the country cops are dying. How do we protect the ones who protect us?"

She responded, "You asked me several questions at the same time. And your implication assumes that the premise of every one of them is true."

He sharply interrupted, "But you are a person who likes to talk about facts." His mid-western accent grew more excited, now the tone was raised and the pace was faster. "You mean to say you don't know someone is attacking our police?" he said sharply lifting the corner of his lips to produce half a smile. In his mind, he had her now; finally he pinned her down on an issue and he struggled to keep a professional voice. He thought, "She claims to know what's going on in the world but she is biased against her own people. Now the American people can see her squirm, they can see how she plays ignorant when it comes to the murders of our men and women in blue." "Please Ms. Doyle," he smirked, "Please look at that camera and tell the American people what you think about what is happening to the fine officers who risk their lives protecting us every day." Using the old theatrical lawyers trick, he pointed in the direction of the camera. But she out witted him again.

"Nice nails Mr. Quinn. Do you have someone come here to do them or do you go to a place?" She smiled when she said it but he didn't.

"This is a serious subject Ms. Doyle and you are making light of it." But it was too late. The technicians behind the camera couldn't stop laughing. Almost all of the support people were caught off guard by the comment. Most of them couldn't help but laugh, and though the American people didn't see the staff laughing, they could hear them in the background. The gotcha moment Quinn so carefully planned to have, didn't happen. "Let's cut to commercial. We'll be right back," he said grudgingly. When the cameras stopped rolling, Mr. Quinn slammed his ink pen on the table in a fit of rage, but it only amplified the laughter. Being the person she was, Tiffany

Doyle took advantage of the moment. She waited. After the short break the staff person signaled it was time to go back on the air. The room was quiet, anticipating the count down. The engineer started, "Here we go. 5, 4, 3…" A voice painted with humor said, "You know Quinn, lots of White men have small fingers. It doesn't mean anything. Just buy a bigger belt buckle or something. Anyway, it's good to keep clean hands Quinn," she said grinning like a school girl. "I mean it, good for you." The engineer couldn't finish the countdown. He was doubled over on his own lap trying to keep the sound of his laughter from the broadcast. It didn't work… and it didn't stop the cameras. The show returned from commercial with a rush of laughter that could have been mistaken for a comedy.

"We're back," he said using the most professional voice he could muster.

"Let us pick up where we left off Ms. Doyle. You didn't answer the question, so let me ask it another way." He looked down at the empty sheet of paper and pretended to read a profound question from it.

"Do you stand with," he paused and peered at the paper for a moment, and then he continued. "It looks like eighty percent of Americans, who see these murders as an act of terror?"

She answered with a serious inflection in her voice. "No, I do not."

"So, you don't believe this man is a murderer or you don't believe he is a terrorist? Which one is it Ms. Doyle?"

"I don't believe you know who it is, Mr. Quinn. You keep using the pronoun he. Are you so sure?" she asked rhetorically. "It could be a woman or more than one woman. I don't know and I strongly suspect you don't either. And who said anything about a murder? Do you have access to a secret FBI memo or something? A legal finding that someone is dead? To the best of my knowledge the officers have not been located. So, my short answer is no, because people need to be dead before we call it a murder Mr. Quinn. As to the second part of your poor question, do I think the persons or person is a terrorist? Hmm, that's more interesting because I don't feel terrorized at all. Maybe it's because I'm not a corrupt cop. It's the corrupt cops who are afraid. Cops who don't shoot children in the chest, motorcyclists in the back and unarmed citizens in the face, I think those cops have nothing to worry about."

He didn't like her philosophical response. She seemed to be blaming the missing cops for their own circumstance. To him, Doyle lacked the sound of concern he associated with feminine humanity, and she was eating up precious air time, so he interrupted her again.
"But this kind of terror is a threat to our democracy," he said in a rush. "We are a country of laws Ms. Doyle. I just said eighty percent of the American people agree with me on this." She heard what he said, but from the corner of her eye she saw the producer giving the signal to wind it up, so when he paused she stole a place to comment.
"But that's not the law," she interrupted. "That's a poll," and she quickly reached over and snatched the white paper from his hand, turned each side to the camera, snorted with a girlish grin and said, "But even those are fake."

The Carnival

The afternoon of the following day was the nineteenth of May and two old friends met at the annual fundraiser to support youth programing at the Marcus Garvey-Malcom X Caribbean Community Center. The carnival was supported by the finest West-Indian restaurants and entertainment in the region. The food and fun music attracted people from around the country. Every year Tiffany Doyle made it her business to attend and so did her good friend Leonard. She was standing in line thinking of the rice and peas and she reasoned, it must be the careful combination of coconut and spices that caused her addiction to Caribbean food.

"I can't really say that, it could be as simple as one ingredient in the dish," she thought. "But my mind can't quite separate an individual ingredient. Something is there, but I can't assign blame to the pepper… or the allspice and garlic. Being honest with myself, how can I accuse the salt, pepper, scotch bonnet, thyme, spring onion or the ginger when they are blended so evenly that one ingredient never overpowers the other? Do I fault them for bonding but not losing themselves in the potion, for working together to produce an experience beyond flavor? No, I cannot. Only a person skilled in the dark arts of culinary magic fully understands how to make that happen, and they must be aware of their propensity to create a dependence. They know exactly how and when to add the rice, peas and coconut milk… and how long to let it simmer. It's clear and convincing to me that this food is engineered to create an addiction, cuz they know just where to place the curried goat. Someday someone will catch on and ask the government to regulate the process. I just hope it's not in my life time. Let me die first." It was all a jovial thought, one of those pleasant daydreams that made her smile. Another voice said,

"I like it with crab and the king fish." It was Leonard. His friendly voice interrupted her daydream. "I can't take the goat anymore Tiffany." He had maneuvered his way from the back of the line, quietly asking others to help him surprise the

daydreaming Tiffany.
"What! Leonard!" The surprise worked. "How did you get up here?" she asked looking at the long line snaking behind her.
The fun-loving Leonard looked back, waved at the smiling line of mostly Jamaicans and said, "You know how it is Tiffany, 'I get by with a little help from my friends.'"
She hugged Leonard as old friends often do. "It is so good to see you my friend. I have heard so many things. This year has been a whirlwind Leonard. My God it's good to see you. Can we talk?"
"Of course."
"After I nab my beautiful plate of rice, peas and curry goat."
"And I have two people I want you to meet."
"Sure Leonard, but after I nab my beautiful plate of curry goat, rice and peas, right?" she laughed.
"Of course. But goat? Aren't you a vegetarian?" Leonard asked curiously.
"Yes Leonard," she laughed. "But it's curried goat."
"What?" he smiled. "How does that work for a vegetarian?" Leonard knew Tiffany for many years. He knew she had an answer and he knew it was going to be funny. So he waited.
"I am a vegetarian," she responded without breaking a smile. "You may not know this my dear Leonard, but Curry is a blend of crushed and finely sifted vegetables."

He laughed, "OK, but what about the goat?" By this time most of the hungry customers around them heard the clever banter between the two friends and found it to be a fun way to kill the time, so they listened for her to return something funny. It was brief, but she didn't disappoint them.
"Well," she said. "Goats are vegetarians Leonard. How could a man with your intellect miss that?" Her deadpan response broke the tension and Leonard's infectious laugh passed down the line of listeners like falling dominos.
Holding two full paper plates of everything they wanted, Leonard and Tiffany continued to chat as they walked across the lawn towards an old oak tree. The middle of May was not

like it used to be. Things that wouldn't blossom until June, found themselves in full bloom in the May of today. The green and colorful space where Leonard laid his blanket was already occupied and Tiffany was pleasantly surprised at the natural beauty her friend Leonard brought into her life. When they reached the warm space Leonard spoke. "Tiffany, let me introduce you to two of my favorite people. This is Tatyana and this is Marcus. Oh my God, how could I forget the little one? And running up the back end of the tree is their son Gerald." While Marcus abruptly left to chase after the tiny reflection of himself, Tatyana extended her hand with a smile. "It's a pleasure to meet you Ms. Doyle." She responded, "Please call me Tiffany. May I call you Tatyana?"
"Yes, please. It is a pleasure to see you in person Tiffany. I've seen you in the media and I admire your passion for fairness. Leonard shared a few things with us about your work together." "We definitely have a history," she said approvingly. "Your son is beautiful… and full of life." Marcus was rolling on the grass with Gerald, who was screaming in laughter at the top of his ability. Tiffany couldn't help smiling, watching, mimicking every move; shifting her body as if she were another kid on the ground with them.
"They are having a time… aren't they?" she said rhetorically.
"It's hard to be more accurate than that," Tatyana said.

"Yes, but it's great don't you think?" Tiffany was the youngest child and the only girl of seven children. She was a tomboy, through and through. She was athletic, never married, had no children and seeing them rumble made her want to tumble with them. When little Gerald popped up with a grass hopper in his hand she commented. "Chapulín. Oh my God, they are so good this time of year. When I am in Mexico you can get them with spice. They are toasted with garlic, a little salt, a drip of lime juice and if you touch it with a dab of chili, you rock and roll baby. Your son knows the good stuff Tatyana. Smart boy," she yelled, praising him for his find. Tiffany had no idea Tatyana hated bugs and the thought of eating an insect was not having the effect she intended. Tatyana thought, "Hmmm, of all the bad habits Black men pass to their sons, my mother failed to mention the bug eating one." But her smile covered her thoughts better than the first lady of the United States. Now that Tiffany congratulated Gerald on his find he felt compelled to run his prize over to her and she received it with warm regard.

"Thank you so much Gerald. This is the nicest thing anyone has given me all day. Thank you for thinking of me," and she hugged the boy tightly. He touched her dress. It was long to her ankles, with deep rooted bright colors in the style, worn like the French speaking women of Dakar in Senegal. He didn't know anything about Senegal, he just liked the colors. She was a very different looking woman. She was white, but she was colorful. Her hair was dread locked like his doctors hair, but it was red. She was holding his bug, but she was a woman… and she liked to eat them. She was pretty and she gave big hugs like his mother. And then, she gave him a kiss on the cheek. Little Gerald Madison was happy. Then she stood.

"Hello," she said. "You must be… Marcus."

He could feel it from where he stood. Leonard sensed something, so he spoke.

"Yes, this is Marcus. Marcus, Tiffany Doyle."

She lightly extended her hand and he took it.

"Pleased to meet you Ms. Doyle," he said.

Not for one second did her eyes break the track they were on. "Say something," she thought, but she was scared to speak. She felt like a girl in boarding school and the feeling wouldn't go away.

But the size of her smile betrayed her thoughts. He was easily the most beautiful human being she had personally encountered. "He has to be half your age Tiffany, get your head together." It was hard and she couldn't remember a time it was so difficult finding the words to conceal her feelings. She kept trying to show the right smile, anything to keep her thoughts from escaping. But he was exquisite and if the things going on in her mind were ever made public it would probably be illegal. It took her more than a few seconds to pull her thoughts together, but she did, and then she spoke.

"Well, first let me say… will you please call me Tiffany? And let me ask you this, may I call you Marcus?" Her cheeks were locked in the smile mode but the girlish giggle had dissipated.

"Yes," he responded. "Please call me Marcus." The very perceptive Marcus was clueless. Though he did notice that Leonard was uncharacteristically quiet, he attributed that to the overconsumption of rum, rice and King fish.

"I am happy to meet you Tiffany."

"The pleasure is all mine Marcus. This is great. I feel like there are some things I'm supposed to say or do but I can't think of them."

"No problem, it will come," Marcus smiled and said reassuringly. "That kind of thing happens to me all the time."

Receiving his warm comment she responded, "It's a strange feeling isn't it? I feel like I forgot to do something."

And Tatyana suggested, "Maybe you keep forgetting to let his hand go. Could that be it Ms. Doyle?"

"Oh my. I am so sorry. I apologize for kidnaping your hand Marcus. I wasn't paying attention." Tiffany was embarrassed but she didn't want to expose her thoughts by over apologizing so she quickly redirected the conversation to the food.

"You know Leonard, earlier you asked about these peas. They are not the garden peas you are used too. Actually they are beans, but the people of the Caribbean call them peas." Then she shook her head and whispered, "What was I thinking? I am so sorry."

Now with little Gerald perched firmly on her right hip, Tatyana just smiled.

Marcus and Leonard looked at each other, they continued to eat the wonderful spread of Caribbean food. Leonard drank more rum… and they said nothing.

First Impressions

First impressions can be deceiving because the rest of the afternoon was wonderful. Tiffany was a long time valuable member of the BRO. The professional quality of conversation she brought to the frank and open discussion was helpful to Marcus and Tatyana. She was a wealth of information and no stranger to struggle. She told Marcus and Tatyana how her parents left Belfast in the early seventies, at the time of the war the Irish call, "The Troubles." Her parents were both university educators who found a way to move seven children and themselves to Canada. Eventually they landed positions at the University of Berkley, California. When Tiffany was a teenager, her mother told her about the tender privilege they received when they came to America. "What has been happening to these Black people happened to us… and it will happen to you," her mother said. "Do not be fooled by these comforts. The people who run this country support the British, they killed my brothers and they killed your older brother Liam. Your pale Irish skin can hide your intentions here, but remember that the oligarchs who oppress and control these people are doing the same thing to you. So, their struggle is our struggle."

Tiffany shared her family's commitment to freedom. She said, "The fighting began in the late 1960s and didn't end until 1998. My family was part of the nationalists rebelling against British rule. They wanted an independent united Ireland. The British security forces undertook both a policing and a counter-insurgency role against the rebellion. There were many riots, mass protests and acts of civil disobedience. There were many places my family couldn't go because of who they were - a form of segregation the British called no-go areas. My uncles were a part of the rebel groups who retaliated by launching guerrilla campaigns all over Ireland and England, anywhere in Britain actually. The British police terrorized Northern Irish communities and frequently killed our young men. I have cousins who were killed, many people from the North do. The rebels retaliated by bombing the British political and commercial targets. Innocent people on both sides died. It's not a tactic my parents approved of, but it happened," she said. "Many people died resisting what they saw as British tyranny. Because many Doyles were part of the rebel leadership, the British hunted and killed members of my family. The BRO was an invaluable source of intelligence for the rebels and it played a major role in getting us out of Ireland, into Canada and the USA. I am here because of the BRO."

As the sun fell the conversation closed. Little Gerald had run and eaten himself to sleep. Tiffany, now full of curry goat, peas and rice, grunted a bit when she stood to leave. The rum had an effect on everyone except Marcus, who didn't take alcohol in any form. As Tiffany walked away Leonard leaned into Marcus and whispered, "So… that went well… you think?" Marcus paused. He smiled because he had a favorable impression of Tiffany Doyle. She understood our struggle, she was direct and she had a down to earth quality that he admired. He was just about to say that when Tatyana injected, "Well she has good taste in men, that's for sure. She also knows, it is better to be silent and thought to be lewd, than to open your mouth and confirm it. I admire the woman. She knows what she likes… and she fights. I like her."

7 CHAPTER
I Don't Know, We Will See

It was a rough night. There was no comfortable place for his mind to rest and his body had a harder time than that. Tatyana rode the wave of every nightmare and prayed for a moment of sleep but that prayer never came. Some nights are better than others but this was one of the worse. Now he was sitting, isolated at the far corner of the enormous bed. Sleep was never kind to Marcus and most nights he disrupted the hopes of any sleep for Tatyana.

"I woke you again. Sorry about that."

"Why do you apologize for something you cannot control?"

"I just… well I don't want my nightmares to keep you up. I try to move away so I don't wake you."

"I know… and I follow you every time you move away." He held a smile for a few moments, it faded and his head dropped.

"I saw the blood again."

"I know. I heard you," she whispered.

"You need to sleep. I'll just go in the other room," he said.

"And I'll just come in the other room with you."

"Ah ha… so, it's like that?"

"Yes. Just like that."

"Tatyana, tonight was strange. Most times I can let the images go by, but tonight for some reason I couldn't."

"Talk to me. Tell me what's happening in your head Marcus."

"It's not just me seeing me anymore. I'm seeing other things-as if they are happening now or have happened before."

"Are there voices?" she asked.

"Yes. Well no. I mean it's not random voices or anything like that. The best way to explain it is to say it's like a movie. Not all, but most of them are like watching a documentary. The spooky thing is, I can see myself in the audience; I can see everything but I cannot intervene.

They actually happened. A few nights ago I dreamt Gerald would eat a Cicada and you would freak out. Later that day, I was at the restaurant and you called… you were not happy. You were upset. Why? Because Gerald was crunching on a Cicada. That dream was true. The next night my dream was even stronger. In the dream I was walking home from my training session with Kondo. I stopped at the convenience store to buy an apple juice and the teller convinced me to buy a lottery ticket. In that dream, on that night, I won the lottery. The following day while walking home from my training session with Kondo, I stopped at that convenience store, bought the same apple juice, and I made it my business to talk with the same teller until he suggested I buy a lottery ticket, but we didn't win the lottery. That dream was not true.

Why were so many details accurate, but the outcome was not? It left me thinking. The dreams were like the river Kondo spoke of. I should see them for what they are, not what I wish them to be. Because the final outcome was not what I wanted, I declared the whole dream to be untrue. And because the dream I had the night before was consistent with what you later told me, I surmised it must be true. So I created a system of true or false based on my knowledge, or lack thereof. These dreams that shower me at night, they come to aid me. My challenge is to see them as they are, not as I want them to be. Tonight, there was so much blood, but it wasn't the blood from my parents. It was the blood of my people. I saw it before, but now I see it." She hugged his shoulders and laid her head on the middle muscles of his naked back."
"I didn't think about it like that," she whispered, "but a bad

dream can be a good teacher. They all serve a purpose."
"Yes," he said. "Wrestling with the simplicities Kondo brings to my attention helps me in ways I find hard to articulate."
"Well you articulated it pretty well just then," she said. "I hear it this way. There is something positive and negative in every dream. When I think about it, there may be something in a nightmare I need to know or remember. The vision may be horrific and useful at the same time and it doesn't have to originate with me. If you have the nightmare that shakes you from your sleep, it comes through you, but it wakes me too. The ideas that vision was sent to convey will stick with me because of the way it affected you. So I should accept the nightmare as an opportunity to learn something deeper than I - in my conscious state would not have considered. That's how I understand it. You are using your dreams as a teaching tool."
"Yes, that's it. Kondo talked me through it. It's a Taoist concept, a real game changer for me." "Amazing Marcus. The God we serve is awesome."
"All of this helps me Tatyana. I am getting much better at seeing a situation as it is. I don't need to try and predict the outcome. It's like the story, well let me ask… do you know the parable of the Chinese farmer?"

"No, but are you about to sit at the foot of this bed and tell me a story?" She loved the smell of his body…and the soft skin of her cheek pressed comfortably between the mountainous muscles of his back. She rubbed her hands over the gentle slopes of his hot brown flesh. Her eyes were closed but she could see everything… and her mind was wide open to the sensual, very sexual man she was stroking. She slightly lifted her head to speak, "Even if I knew the story, no woman could resist a story in bed Marcus." Turning to see her face he chuckled, "It's not that kind of story."
"When we are in bed and your son is asleep, and it's warm, and I'm close to your body, and you are naked… every story is that kind of story." Now he was close. His chest was in her

face and he didn't move. The low tones in his voice never raised above a whisper. She could feel the transfer of heat from his skin touching her lips.

"You still want it?"

"Yes," she said.

"OK, it begins like this. There was this poor Chinese farmer. He and his wife had one son and one horse. One day…" and before he found the next word, Tatyana touched him.

"I can't tell the story if you do that," he said. But there was a playfulness in her mood, a flirtatious flutter in her voice and the story was not the only thing she wanted.

"You want me to tell this story? Cuz you keep touching stuff."

"Yes I do. It's just hard to hear you when this keeps rubbing on my leg." The thin blanket that covered her shoulders slid down her back. She was trying to concentrate but he was too close for her to think about anything else. He tried to continue.

"The Chinese man and his wife were rice farmers. They had one son and one horse. One day their horse ran away…" Marcus wanted to finish, but she interrupted him with another touch.

He stopped the story. "Let me say this," he paused. His low tone seemed to stretch the meaning of each word into something more sensual, more sexual than his English was able to accommodate. His inflection changed, his body language changed. The muscles in his back and thighs seemed to thicken, the tone of his voice was more aggressive and his posture posed a threat that Tatyana wanted to ignite.

"Let me be clear," he said. "If you touch that again…"

"But Marcus," she interrupted, "You're talking about horses…and running. How can I not touch it?" She wasn't aware that her eager eyes slowly tracked down the length of his inner thigh and onto the upperparts of her own. "It's all in my personal space Marcus, how can I avoid it?"

It wasn't what she said, it was how she said it. When she reached this state, a heavy Russian accent took over her voice.

Her words were easy to hear but hard to discern. He was quickly losing the fight to manage the sexual energy that was swelling everything… including his state of mind. He re-focused. "You asked me to tell you about the Chinese farmer."

"Uh-huh… but that ain't Chinese."

"If you touch it again there will be no story on this night. I'm just sayin,' don't touch it again."

Tatyana could feel the heat emanating from his skin, the subtle pull from the playful threat in his voice. She could feel his pheromones moisten the tender hairs and sensitive place that line the inner folds of her labia, and it was throbbing. She knew his relentless spirit- he didn't bluff. Looking over she saw little Gerald was still asleep in the next room, but his door was open. "One more day," she thought. "I'll stop ovulating in one more day. God, please let me be practical. Help me resist myself. Tomorrow is better. Now is not the time to be playing around with Marcus, cuz he is not playing." But when she opened her eyes, all of it was still there…so she touched it. "The pheromones made me do it," she said.

Hours later, little Gerald rose with the morning light, but his parents did not. They woke when he bounced himself from the foot of their bed to the head of his father.

"You up Marcus?"

"I am now."

"Gerald bouncing around brought something to mind. I watched you training with Kondo yesterday. The moves were so quick it was hard for me to follow your change in motion. I can see the bits of Judo in there… but it's so, so different. After your warmup I can't tell what you are doing. I couldn't figure out exactly what style it was. It looks like, well I don't know what it looks like. Is it something Kondo created by patching a lot of styles together?"

Marcus smiled. "You know, I used a similar comparison once when I spoke to Kondo. For more than an hour he pounded me with examples, scenarios and philosophical reasons why there is nothing new about Flow. 'It is as old as mankind,' he said. 'Flow takes your natural abilities and develops you into the best you, you can become.' As for me, I describe it this way. Flow is art. For the sake of this discussion, let's say technique is material… and you are an artist. If I were to give seven good artists the same colors of paint, including you in the seven, you will create no less than seven different kinds of good art. Some will blend the paint and create different colors and hues, some will let the paint dry a bit and layer it like a cake to create different textures. You all will choose a suitable surface to display what you produce. Most of you will combine all these techniques in some personal way to express yourself. But your work will be different, it will all be good… and it will all be art; this is how Flow works. So, Flow is not as simple as a fighting form. It's everything you know, and movement, a way of feeling, thinking, doing. Ultimately it's a way of life. The way you fight, or more importantly don't fight, becomes an expression of you."

"I follow your premise and I have one question. How can you say the art will be good? A good artist is quite capable of producing bad art."

"Yes, and judging art is subjective," he replied. "But in Flow your life is your art and you are the artist and the judge. Every day you practice becoming the person you want to be and every moment of everyday you change something about yourself whether you know it or not; Flow says, get to know it.

Many people fall into the trap of trying to define all things according to their immediate base of knowledge. Over the history of human existence, people have done more things than any one person or entity is capable of knowing. So, because you haven't experienced it before, doesn't make it new. Let's just say, it is new to you."

"I like it. I want to do it Marcus. The physical training looks really tough, but I want to learn."

"Really? You never said anything before."

"When I was pregnant with Gerald it was all I could do to

manage my Tai Chi. Watching you and Kondo work out... it looks intense but I like it. You think I'm ready?"

"Of course you're ready. You move well, balanced, your fundamentals are excellent."

"When can I start?"

"You just did."

"Oh, one more thing. Will you tell me the story about the Chinese Farmer? It was hard for me to concentrate last night."

"You are funny," he said. "Ok the parable of the Chinese farmer goes like this.

There was a poor rice farmer. He and his wife had one son. They owned one horse and a small rice patch just big enough to support their small family. At the end of a day's work, villagers would socialize at the communal tea house at the base of the first slope in the heart of the village.

One day the farmer's only horse ran away. It was a significant loss because a horse was a source of transportation and field labor. When the farmer arrived at the tea house that evening, his friends and neighbors said, 'We are so sorry to hear what happened with your horse. What ever will you do? It's such an unfortunate thing.' The farmer replied, 'I don't know… we will see.' The next day the horse came back and a small herd of wild horses followed him. The farmer and his son quickly corralled the animals for good keeping. That evening when the farmer arrived at the tea house his friends and neighbors said, 'We are happy that your horse returned and brought so many others with him. You are a very fortunate family.' The farmer replied, 'I don't know… we will see.'

Less than a week went by and the farmer's son wanted to train one of the wild horses for riding. The son roped one of the horses and attempted to ride it, but the horse threw the son to the ground, stepped on his leg and crushed the bones. That evening when the farmer arrived at the tea house his friends and neighbors said, 'We are so sorry to hear what happened to your son. He may lose his leg. It is such an unfortunate thing for your family.' The farmer replied, 'Well, I don't know… we will see.' Two weeks passed and the military recruitment officers were roaming the country collecting able-bodied young men to fight in the new war. Every house with a draft age son was required to commit that son to the war effort. When the officers arrived at the little farmhouse they saw the condition of the son's leg and decided that he could be of no help to the war effort in his present state. That evening when the farmer arrived at the tea house his friends and neighbors said, 'We are elated that your son was not drafted. The other young men who left to fight in this war did not come back. You are a very, very fortunate family.' And the farmer replied, 'I don't know… we will see.'

Here the farmer is saying, if we pay attention we will see that life is always in balance.

When I apply this principle to me, I realize that my parents' death was not my fault. I could not have saved them, but I can work with the BRO to stop it from happening to others."

Tatyana's eyes filled with emotion. "Wow Marcus. To hear you say that is big for me. I listen to you and you have grown in every positive way I can think about."

In a failed attempt to conceal his emotions, he looked to the sky, hugged her closely and quietly responded, "We will see."

8 CHAPTER
Freedom Begins When We Lose Our Fear Of It

The abduction of Officer David Larry was too harmful to the morale of the enforcement community to accept diplomatically. The government credibility was taking a beating. Officers were forming private security teams to protect their own. Civil liberty groups and a few journalists were beginning to lose their fear of the law enforcement machine. Something drastic had to happen… and it did. Not since the Black Panther movement has the white power structure been more threatened. All over America, Black people were shedding their fear of the police.

At 8:15 am on the fourth day in April, children all over the country were leaving home for school, but in the city of Chicago, two young boys wouldn't make it to school that day… and what happened to them changed the lives of everyone who witnessed it. That morning, on the ninth floor of one of the last existing high-rise housing projects in the city, two undercover police officers attempted to arrest Cedric Noble, a low level drug dealer. The officers waited until Cedric exited his apartment and locked the door before they pounced from the adjacent unit and yelled, "Cedric Noble! Stop! Put your hands were we can see them, you are under arrest!" But Cedric didn't stop. He panicked and ran down the hall like a mouse in a maze. Still frightened he turned down another corridor in his attempt to reach an exit, unaware he was running into a trap. When Cedric reached the door to exit, several police were waiting. In a panicked state, he turned back towards his apartment, took a few running steps and both officers stood ready, with guns drawn and both barrels aimed at his chest. They shot him. They shot Cedric down in the hallway like a rat on the street. Both officers felt their lives were in danger. In the split second fog of the moment, they thought the man was going for a weapon. The hallway was lined with many doors. One of them was the home of Kathy Favors and her ten year old twins Devon and Deon. They walked out of their small apartment just as it happened and they saw Cedric drop to his knees with both hands in the air. They saw the young man plead with the two officers not to kill him. When the police shot the unarmed young man, Kathy, a registered nurse, instinctively hurled her body between Cedric and the officers.

"What is your name?" she asked, but there was a hole in his chest and the mortally wounded young man couldn't find enough air to make a word. The police threatened to shoot her if she didn't move. Hearing the police, the two boys quickly moved their small bodies to protect their mother. The twins stood facing the barrels of the police. Seeing the two boys were clearly no immediate threat, one officer lowered his weapon, but the other officer saw it differently. Children do what they know and these two were avid fans of the ninja turtle warriors. So Deon sharply mounted a pose mimicking his favorite character and jumped into position. "Yah!" In Deon's mind it was time to do battle with the deep dark demons of the underworld and he was ready. In the mind of the officer, he felt his life was in danger. And in the split second fog of the moment, he couldn't tell if the boy was going for a weapon. Then it happened - two head shots were fired - one for each officer. From a fair distance, someone with good training stopped both officers with a single shot to the head. Randomly the residents of the ninth floor apartments poured into the chaotic hallway. Many were angry, others were confused, but most of them were tired of the police coming into their community to kill unarmed Black people. To frustrate matters more, after the paramedics arrived and the investigators were finally allowed on the ninth floor to investigate the crime scene and interview witnesses, no one could identify the shooter. In every interview, witnesses said they saw nothing. One witness stated that in the split second fog of the moment he couldn't see anything that would be helpful to the police investigation. They didn't like that.

But the incident hit the news media hard. Kathy and the twins were seen as the heroes who faced down the police at gun point. All over Black media, people spoke with pride and a sense of empowerment. "In the face of certain death, we the people stood up to the occupying force of oppression," one man said on the radio. Thousands tweeted that they were inspired by the heroism of the small family. Social media was buzzing with comments about Kathy's compassion and brave assistance to the fatally wounded young man and most comments highlighted the brave actions of the two ten year old boys that stood up to the police.

Police investigators said among other things, most witnesses were obstructing justice and Kathy Favors will likely be charged with parental negligence and endangering the lives of two minors. When she was informed of the possible charges against her, Kathy said, 'Freedom begins when we lose our fear of the oppressor.'"

There were few media outlets that didn't carry the Chicago story. It seemed most people had something to say about it.

"They are threatening her with what? Criminal prosecution?" Tatyana said. "If she was White, she would be getting a medal for bravery under fire right now. And the stuff about her children is a scare tactic to punish Black America for having the audacity to praise this woman. It's clear. Everyone can see it. Like they care about her children…they don't give a warm piss for Black children Marcus. For some children in that city, just going to school is dangerous. They won't fix that, but this woman risked her life to try and save the life of another

human being and this city… this government is threatening her. Why? " Tatyana grabbed little Gerald and slowly stroked his hair. "This place… I worry for him Marcus."
"She is really upset," he thought. But before he could finish that thought she spoke again.
"Think about the little ninja turtle twins Marcus, they had no fear of the police. They had no fear of death when they acted to save their mother. They were too young to count the cost of shielding her from the police. Their minds were free, that's it." Gazing at their son she paused, "Like a bad dream," she said, "If we take a moment and think it through, we will see that these children and their mother teach us something big. That is, freedom truly begins when we lose our fear of it."
Looking at the picture in front of him, hearing her frustration, her concern, he reasoned, "Hmm, but my opinion can wait," and he hugged them both.

Tatyana's First Training Session

The subject of Kathy and the two ninja was a teaching point in Tatyana's first training session with Master Kondo and Marcus.

It was the first day and she was nervous. Training in the dojo was an experience she couldn't anticipate. There were five candles placed around the room. It was sparsely lit and except for them, the amount of heat a heavy breathing workout produced, was the only source of warmth in the room. The pace of constant movement left no time to even think about the cold. In fact, after the warm-up, she was wiping the sweat from falling in her eyes. A third of the way through the session she welcomed the coolness of the air, she just needed more of it. At some point, much earlier than normal, they sat. Tatyana suspected it had something to do with her lack of stamina. "But it's ok," she thought. "In a month I'll be able to keep up and you won't be pausing for me anymore." They sat still and silent for at least five minutes before he spoke.

"Before training start we talk about situation mother and two boys who behave like ninja." His words rarely rose above a hush. More than nine decades of life confirmed for him that speaking at a low volume brings the attention of the listener closer to the speaker, so he continued.

"We talk about how training of mother teach her to respond quickly. And we talk about how two boy, no training just instinct, they also move quickly. Marcus, why every time do we begin training with some story?"

"I think the stories are to give me something to relate to while I'm training, something to think about."

"If you are thinking about story while you are training then you are not training. You are thinking."

"Well, I walked right into that one," he thought.

"I understand," he said.

"Do you? Really. Tell me what you understand Marcus."

"I understand that thinking and doing are not the same thing.

I knew that when you asked the question but I was not paying attention to the way I phrased my response- it's a bad habit."

"Yes, I recognized it. But you must fix that. Because not pay attention in speaking and not pay attention in fighting is same. In both cases don't think… know. For example, sometimes you speak of the way you and your coach fixed bad habit from your Judo technique. It is good thing to have good technique for Judo, but Judo is sport. Sports have rules to get points. Your practice helps you to refine good technique. Is that so?"

"Yes, that is so."

"And good technique always stay inside rule. Because not stay in rule is cheating, or bad sport. Correct?"

"Yes that's correct."

"So, best technique always teaching good way to win point, but stay in rules, yes?"

"That's true."

"Every time in training you practice to act, react, act again, and react quickly. Your purpose is to respond within the rules without thinking. Make movement like instinct. Is this correct?"

"Well, yes."

"So, now you are successful. Your instincts work best inside rules. Do you see?

"Yes, I see."

"It was excellent beginning for your body for sport. But now, you train in Flow, already you understand. Human mind has no rules. Real instincts have no rules, Enemy has no rules. Flow has one rule, find balance. But balance, has no rules."

"Often people say it is bad habit to move this way or that way. No such thing as bad habit good habit. When fighting all habits are bad. A habit is a predictable pattern of behavior. If enemy know your habits, enemy will know you… and enemy will use your habits against you. So, as people we all have our way that is what makes us who we are, but in fighting you must have no habits, no forms; no style. You must be like particle, unpredictable. Like electron; be like that."

"Kondo, can you please use another example because now you are asking me to move like a subatomic particle." Marcus laid his back on the floor laughing and Kondo just smiled a bit. Unfamiliar with Kondo's direct and dry attempts at humor, Tatyana whispered… "Is he serious?"

Jovially, Marcus added, "Can I move like something a little less quantum mechanical please old great master?"

With a hint of a smile Kondo replied, "But you understand this concept?"

"Yes, got it. Particle."

At that point, Kondo turned to Tatyana, but the humor was gone.

"Have no habit Tatyana, but notice the habits of others," he said. "Notice the nature of others. Today was first day and good day. You move well, but you worry. About stamina you worry, about good enough, about cold, about light, so many things on your mind, I can tell. Here on this wall we say 'Mushin.' It means no mind. Also, stop checking for style. You will train every kind of style everyday but you will favor no one style. You will have no one system, but many… because enemy will not bring book of fighting style for you, only dangerous situation. Today is good day, tomorrow will be better day." He glanced at her with a look of approval. "But bring no mind…'Mushin.' He gave a gentle bow that signaled the end of training for the day.

"Whoa," she sighed. "All that time I thought he was talking to you Marcus, but that was for me?"

"Yeah, he does stuff like that."

Still whispering she said, "I am over here thinking… wow, I need to remember this because one day it will be me he's talking to."

Marcus chuckled, "You'll get used to it Tatyana."

"I hope so." She kissed his cheek and smiled.

"THERE'S A BUG!" he yelled quickly, but she didn't look.

"Grow up. There is no bug."

What's In A Name

"I don't know who shot the two officers, but it was a mistake."

"Jesus Christ Leonard, how can you say that? They were going to kill the two boys. How is shooting them a mistake?"

"Because it gives the blue shield an opportunity to go on the offensive. Now you have two cops killed in the line of duty to distract from their atrocities. They will use this to whip up public sympathy and open the door to a long awaited retaliatory strike on everyone who opposed them. The liberals cannot be seen as supporting the open violence against public servants less they invite it upon themselves, they will be silent, at best neutral."

Tatyana knew he was correct, but she still didn't like it. "So, what are we to expect from these bandits now?" She frowned.

"They will take this as an opportunity to mingle the actions of the shooter with the actions of 'Raguel,' Tiffany injected. Tiffany was silent until this point because the thought of things to come were so painful. But she knew Leonard was right- she had seen it all before. "The police know that the shooting of these two officers are in no way consistent with the way the vigilante moves, but they have to kill his image before they can kill him. These bandits, as you call them, are happy to use the death of their comrades to raise the level of aggression against the people. They will hit the Black communities so hard someone will give him up. That's how they operate," she said.

But Tatyana was confused, "Wait… who are you talking about?" she asked. "Are they talking about the shooter or the vigilante? She knew Tiffany had no idea Marcus was the vigilante the world was looking for. But Tiffany referred to him with a name… and she missed part of it. Tatyana needed to hear it again; and she asked, "Who are you talking about?"

Tiffany responded, "I'm talking about Raguel. The anonymous person the world is looking for." She smiled, but she was really puzzled by Tatyana's lacking knowledge of his name. "You know the people see this person as the great protector of justice. That is the biggest threat to law enforcement," Tiffany said. "In my opinion, it's bigger than the abductions they talk about. Now, with the shootings, they will certainly brand him the cop killer. That's all I mean."

"Do you know how they came to call the person that name?"

"That I cannot tell you my dearrr Tatyana." Her Irish accent often left her R's rolling at the end of a sentence. "I cannot know how that name came to be, but that is the name widely used. The one the police prefer of course is Cop Killer but the people in the Black and Brown communities call the anonymous person Raguel."

Tatyana fought the look of embarrassment. "How could I miss such a thing?" she thought.

They sat comfortably conversing in the lounge segment of the Madison family front office. Her mind raced until she had to excuse herself. "Excuse me," she said, and she politely stood and walked over to the office computer. She started to type. Her fingers were moving faster than anyone could tell, she nodded her head a few times and then… it just fell to her chest. When she gradually lifted her head, her face had a smile on it.

"Wow, they call him the anonymous avenger of evil police."

"Tatyana, if my ego wasn't so big I would think you didn't believe me."

Tatyana quickly responded in a reassuring way, "Tiffany, please don't take my surprise that way. I usually follow everything I can on this subject and I overlooked this. I was shaking my head because, here I am looking at the actions of the police and the activity of the people said everything." She stood with tears in her eyes and added, "This name means they will never give this person up. My next question is- why do they feel it's a man?"

"I don't know," Tiffany responded. "No one knows for sure. But people being who they are, typically assign this kind of action to a male, for better or for worse. It would be cool if the person turned out to be a woman though, wouldn't it?"

Tatyana grinned. "Yeah, how about that Marcus? What if the vigilante was a woman?"

"Sounds great to me," he said with a tone of indifference.

Sitting quietly and listening to the discussion, Leonard wore an uncomfortable smile for most of the conversation. Marcus was his Godson, the only child of his closest friend and sorority sister. Guarding the welfare of Marcus went well beyond the duties of a Godparent; he was Lisa's son, and it was hard for anyone who knew her to be around him and not feel her presence. Anytime Leonard looked at Marcus he saw a mirror image of his father. Most of his mannerisms and veracious appreciation for the feminine physique were also like his father. But Lisa's energy surrounded him, her patience and compassion protected him, and Leonard saw himself as an earthly set of eyes and ears helping to keep Marcus safe. Like Tatyana, Leonard didn't know the vigilante had a name and he couldn't ignore the chill of embarrassment he felt when Tiffany mentioned it. Despite his sometimes playful ways, Leonard was widely considered to be a cautious person and a tactical genius, but this surprised him… and he didn't like surprises. He spoke.

"I hadn't heard this stuff about the name. I missed it too."

"Well Leonard, you grew up in Hyde Park," Tiffany teased. "Not a whole lot of Black people out there to remind you. So, I guess this confirms you're not exactly a man of the common people." They both laughed and she pushed his head.

Laughing along with the conversation Marcus asked, "Why Raguel though? Do they believe the person is Latino?"

Tiffany answered, "I don't think that's it. They believe the name has a biblical reference to justice. That's what I understand anyway."

"They are right," Tatyana injected enthusiastically. She continued, "When I went on line to see for myself what Tiffany was talking about, I was pleasantly surprised. What the people are saying is consistent with scripture."

"Where Tatyana?" Tiffany anxiously asked. I looked and it

was hard for me to find, where are they looking?"

"Probably the Book of Enoch," she answered. "He is one of the angels who keep watch. Raguel is one of the seven archangels and among them, he is a big deal. God has given him the roll of handling justice. He judges everyone who rebels against the laws of God, even other angels." She glanced over at Marcus and spoke in a way that only he could decipher.

"Apparently many people see this person as a mysterious figure fighting for the restoration of God's justice against a corrupt establishment. That is nearly a biblical definition of The Angel of Justice, also called, Raguel." Her deep brown eyes worked themselves away from Marcus and back above the proud smile on her face… as if to say, I told you so. "Raguel is the Latin form of a Hebrew name that means Friend of God."

Tiffany didn't get the hidden meaning, but Marcus did… and so did Leonard.

"So," Leonard responded, "Please tell me what it all means." Leonard never read biblical scripture, or any other religious doctrine for that matter. Tiffany, who was raised in the Catholic tradition had a vague understanding of this archangel. She was trying to help Leonard, but only a few questions into the discussion, she was shrugging her shoulders and looking to Tatyana.

Tatyana spoke up. "He's important. When God sends Raguel, stuff has already hit the fan," she said. "He is incorruptible. This guy makes the other angels shake a little. He is also a part of the select team of angels who separates the souls of people who have been faithful from those who have not. Of all the secular super-hero names they could have chosen, they didn't. Instead they chose a biblical one… and an archangel at that. This is not a coincidence," she said. "It is a sign that God is guiding the people. This is foretold in the scriptures: 'The hand of God will nudge them… and the people will fashion a way out of no way. Collectively they will call on the Lord and He will send the spirit of Raguel, His angel of justice.' So you see that name is no accident," she added. "The name they chose represents a powerful archangel whose main responsibility is to create and maintain order in accordance with God's will. It sends a strong message that this person will punish evil. Especially that evil acting in the name of law enforcement."

Tiffany asked, "But do you think it's a real angel?" She chuckled in a disbelieving way.

"Yes," Tatyana answered.

Tiffany paused without a smile. She didn't expect an unequivocal response and never anything that strong in the affirmative. After that she was hesitant to ask another question.

The War Begins

At 4 am the following morning, a few hundred miles away in the windy city of Chicago, a fire started, and the O'Leary's cow had nothing to do with it. No one knew for sure how it started but the investigators said it began in the apartment of the Favors family. The flames quickly consumed the entire ninth floor. Police say all of the exit doors were jammed. There is some speculation that the tenants jammed the doors to protect themselves against police storming the high-rise-community in the middle of the night. The families of the victims saw the tragedy as retaliation. They noted that the police department and the fire department are siblings. Many people are skeptical and suspicious of the explanation the fire fighters gave for their historically slow response. Also the usually well-equipped teams were unprepared, wasting precious time as the flames grew stronger by the second. By the time the fighters successfully assembled, the flames were out of reach and out of control. The entire ninth floor, everything on it and everything above it was lost. The only tenants easily identified were the ones who leaped from the windows. It was one of the saddest days in Chicago history.

An international pool of reporters covered the story for weeks, but on that sad and frightful day the tears of the world fell for the victims. Of the tenants who lived on the ninth and tenth floors, those solemn sleeping citizens of the windy city of Chicago, not one of them survived. Among the identifiable bodies were Kathy Favors and both of her ninja warriors.

The next Sunday evening, in the little Swedish town of Lund, The International Consortium of Media Outlets, (INCOMO) invited a panel of esteemed Americans, one Swede and two Brits, to have a frank discussion about the growing racial discord in America. The world was curious, and the Chicago fire stoked the flames of misinformation all around the globe. The name of the program was the Euro-listic News Hour. The topic of conversation was, 'The Growing Racial Discord in the USA: How Can Friendly Countries Help Stop It?' Normally the well watched program ran sixty minutes, but the special interest associated with the subject more than justified the thirty minutes extended to the program, and some argued that the ninety minute special still wasn't enough time to properly cover the issues. In the middle of the discussion the notable Malcom Ben Carter said, "As we move on in our discussion I want to address a point made by the last speaker," he said calmly. "She mentioned the US Constitution being a living breathing document and all. She said she still gets a little choked up when she read the words.

Most of you are not American. Most of the people in Sweden will not trace their ancestry back to slavery. And a large number of you can at least in some part, identify with the intentions written in the documents that guide and govern your country because it was written by your ancestors for themselves, to benefit you." He turned slowly to each side of the seated body of mostly White men. He pointed his finger at one and said, "But that's not my story. My ancestors had nearly nothing to do with drafting the document that governs me. I am represented in it as an afterthought. The forethought that includes me talks about me as property. As the good lady said earlier, 'She remembers each word as a protection.' Yes I agree it protects her all the time. As for me, sometimes it might sometimes it might not. It depends on the person, depends on the police officer, depends on the judges.

It will depend on many things all the time but it will never fully depend on real justice for me. I am an afterthought." The panel of notables were glued to every one of his words. The woman who spoke before him injected a few well-polished words, but few heard them. Malcom Ben Carter was never trained as an orator. His words were bent and full of gesture, his heavy voice had a scratch in it and by public speaking standards, he was not a pretty speaker; but neither was Louie Armstrong. Like Louie, Europeans liked the sound of his voice, they loved what he had to say and they smiled when he said it. Ben Carter was captivating because he brought a level of profundity to a conversation that a concerned listener couldn't ignore. He was not conventional… he was effective… and he continued… "I don't know how familiar you are with American history." He paused momentarily, looked around the table and noticed almost everyone shaking their heads 'No.' He started to speak, but the same woman interrupted.

"Mr. Ben Carter is talking about ancient history," she said dismissively. "The Dred Scott case is an obscure situation that speaks to a period in our past when Black people were not seen as equal to the Whites."

"And it's different today," he sarcastically interrupted. But she continued.

"That case is so old," she puffed and waved her hand as if to say, it's not relevant. "There is no need to bore this group and the viewing audience with a long case like that." She spoke in that hurried way card tricksters do when they try to distract your attention. "We should stay in the present and work towards a better tomorrow," she sharply added. When she finished, no one spoke and everyone at the table cut their eyes back to Malcom Ben Carter. It was one of those silent moments that didn't need a single word. He continued by asking a question. "Are you familiar with the Dred Scott story?"

No one said yes, so he continued.

"I think it was in the 1840's. She calls that ancient history, but when the cab driver brought me here he showed me a few things. You have active barber shops older than that." The small group laughed. Many nodded yes at the same time. He waited a few seconds and then he spoke. "It is a famous legal case. It is a constant reminder to Black people in America that we are an afterthought. Today, some Americans who even know about the case will say, 'Yeah that was wrong but how long do we need to apologize for that kind of thing?' They miss the point completely. We are not asking you to

apologize. We are telling you to recognize… we hear your words but we know your actions…and they only changed shape, they didn't go away.
The Dred Scott story begins when the slave of an army surgeon from the state of Missouri moved to the state of Illinois with his owner. Slavery was legal in Missouri but it was not legal in Illinois. Dred Scott knew that but it is the nature of White Americans to assume Black people are less intelligent than we are. So the owner never considered that Scott would know anything about law. For four years Scott worked for his owner in the free state of Illinois. Being a resident in a free state erased his slave status. By law, he was a free man. Scott knew that, but he also knew that most White people respected the law only when it benefited themselves.

He waited until he found the right White people to help him. He did, and eventually he filed a law suit and won his legal case in the Missouri courts. He was free, but it didn't last. They appealed and he lost. His case made it to the US Supreme Court. This is the court that justifies justice. They tell the world who America really is. These justices are the final word on a legal issue. To remind myself of this I never leave home without my copy of the words the chief justice wrote. I keep it in my pocket every day. In an honest way he told the whole world what the American founders thought of my ancestors and me. Here's what he said.

Taney's Opinion
Mr. Chief Justice Taney delivered the opinion of the Court....
In the opinion of the Court the legislation and histories of the times, and the language used in the Declaration of Independence, show that neither the class of persons who had been imported as slaves nor their descendants, whether they had become free or not, were then acknowledged as a part of the people nor intended to be included in the general words used in that memorable instrument....
They had for more than a century before been regarded as beings of an inferior order and altogether unfit to associate with the white race, either

in social or political relations; and so far inferior that they had no rights which the white man was bound to respect; and that the Negro might justly and lawfully be reduced to slavery for his benefit. He was bought and sold and treated as an ordinary article of merchandise and traffic whenever a profit could be made by it. This opinion was at that time fixed and universal in the civilized portion of the white race....
No one, we presume, supposes that any change in public opinion or feeling, in relation to this unfortunate race, in the civilized nations of Europe or in this country should induce the Court to give to the words of the Constitution a more liberal construction in their favor than they were intended to bear when the instrument was framed and adopted....

And upon a full and careful consideration of the subject, the Court is of opinion that, upon the facts stated in the plea in abatement, Dred Scott was not a citizen of Missouri within the meaning of the Constitution of the United States and not entitled as such to sue in its courts....

We proceed...to inquire whether the facts relied on by the plaintiff entitle him to his freedom....

The act of Congress, upon which the plaintiff relies, declares that slavery and involuntary servitude, except as a punishment for crime, shall be forever prohibited in all that part of the territory ceded by France, under the name of Louisiana, which lies north of thirty-six degrees thirty minutes north latitude and not included within the limits of Missouri. And the difficulty which meets us...is whether Congress was authorized to pass this law under any of the powers granted to it by the Constitution....

As there is no express regulation in the Constitution defining the power which the general government may exercise over the person or property of a citizen in a territory thus acquired, the Court must necessarily look to the provisions and principles of the Constitution, and its distribution of powers, for the rules and principles by which its decisions must be governed.

Taking this rule to guide us, it may be safely assumed that citizens of the

United States who migrate to a territory...cannot be ruled as mere colonists, dependent upon the will of the general government, and to be governed by any laws it may think proper to impose....

For example, no one, we presume, will contend that Congress can make any law in a territory respecting the establishment of religion...or abridging the freedom of speech or of the press....

These powers, and others...are...denied to the general government; and the rights of private property have been guarded with equal care....

An act of Congress which deprives a citizen of the United States of his liberty or property, without due process of law, merely because he came himself or brought his property into a particular territory of the United States...could hardly be dignified with the name of due process of law.

The powers over person and property of which we speak are not only not granted to Congress but are in express terms denied and they are forbidden to exercise them.... And if Congress itself cannot do this...it could not authorize a territorial government to exercise them....

It seems, however, to be supposed that there is a difference between property in a slave and other property....

Now...the right of property in a slave is distinctly and expressly affirmed in the Constitution. The right to traffic in it, like an ordinary article of merchandise and property, was guaranteed to the citizens of the United States, in every state that might desire it, for twenty years. And the government in express terms is pledged to protect it in all future time if the slave escapes from his owner. This is done in plain words--too plain to be misunderstood. And no word can be found in the Constitution which gives Congress a greater power over slave property or which entitles property of that kind to less protection than property of any other description....

Upon these considerations it is the opinion of the Court that the act of Congress which prohibited a citizen from holding and owning property of this kind in the territory of the United States north of the line therein mentioned is not warranted by the Constitution and is therefore void; and that neither Dred Scott himself, nor any of his family, were made free by being carried into this territory; even if they had been carried there by the owner with the intention of becoming a permanent resident.

There was less than twenty minutes left in the broadcast and the table of articulate professionals were struck with an uncomfortable silence. The American woman who spoke so glowingly of her constitution was red with anger, even her red lipstick was redder than it was before. Despite her anger, she squeezed her thoughts together tighter than anyone could imagine and found a response and then she used it. She said,
"He fails to mention we changed that with the thirteenth Amendment. That amendment to the Constitution takes words from that Supreme Court opinion and used them to abolish slavery in this country forever. Maybe Mr. Ben Carter should carry that in his pocket too," she sniped.
He smiled when she said that. He thought, "One of the most irritating things a Black man can do to a White person is ignore them." So of course… he ignored her. "We are an afterthought in America," he said. "Most White people are afraid of us. They live in the perpetual fear of a Nat Turner style uprising. Now that they see it coming, people like the previous speaker travel the world trying to make our history sound reasonable. They word things so that you will adopt their phrasing, and over time, the meaning will change all together. For example, who chose the wording of today's topic?" No one spoke up. No one raised their hand or acknowledged credit at all.
"Hmmm, seem a little odd? When you say 'There is a growing racial discord in the USA, how can friendly countries help stop it?' You seem to imply that once upon a time, America was in harmony. In order for there to be a discord at some point there had to be an accord. I just want to know, when was that? At what place in US history did America have racial harmony?"

Again, no one spoke, no one responded. He encouraged the others not to take his experiences to be any more valuable than their own. But his life in America was perfect training for times like this.

The Europeans wanted to feel his authenticity, and if Malcom Ben Carter was nothing else, he was authentic. As the only American at the table with obvious African heritage he didn't want to leave viewers with a false image of expertise so he said, "Look…because I grew up in America as a Black man does not mean I am the expert on Black oppression in America. I am only talking about the things I have seen, the things I have experienced, the things I know. When the good lady here speaks, I believe she believes what she is saying. And when she talks so patriotically about the constitution, how it breathes and speaks for the people, I can feel her sincerity when she gets choked up about them. All I say is this, our experiences are different. The words she loves the most were never meant for me. The men who drafted the constitution never intended those big and lofty words of freedom to protect people like me. In fact, some of those words she gets choked up about, were used to choke my people; but we call it lynching. That is the truth. If we want to fix the race problem in America we have to be truthful about it. And if our government would stop misleading the public with fifty shades of gray facts about the police and the military, the vigilante wouldn't exist and whistle blowers like Edward Snowden and Chelsea Manning would have nothing to blow about. Our government is not trustworthy. You ask, how can friendly countries help?' Try to encourage the US government to allow a UN team of forensic investigators to do a proper investigation of the latest tragedy in Chicago. That would be a good beginning. A reliable source of transparent information about what happened there will help build a platform for trust. Let us search for the facts America and we may find the truth…and we will see that it has the inherent power to produce the desired effect.

Finally, one of you asked, 'Given all that has happened to

Black and Brown people in America, how can you ever feel safe and free in that country?' Well, safety is relative. Safer than what, I would ask. But for the most part we take the comforts of safety wherever we can get them. With few exceptions, to assume a general sense of safety in America is a luxury set aside for White people. About the issue of freedom … *'You can only be free when even the desire of seeking freedom becomes a harness to you, and when you cease to speak of freedom as a goal and a fulfilment.'*

I believe Kahlil Gibran was correct when he wrote that.

Sometimes when a free people have been oppressed for so long they forget what it feels like. Generations have come to accept the comforts of oppression and the human mind is an amazing thing; even in the most painful situation it will find a crumb of pleasure. In that space, survival is more important. But when we examine the evolution of life or the creation of all matter, nothing is designed in bondage. Living under the constant heat of oppression can produce the illusion of satisfaction for some… and generations of psychological trauma has conditioned the mind of many to conform or perish. These people will even resist their own freedom because bondage is safer. Some of our fellow sophisticates will not consider their fear of falling from affluence to be a form of bondage. To all of this I say…Freedom begins when we lose our fear of it."

As the program came to a close, the producers scrambled to invite Malcom Ben Carter back for another ninety minute show. He gradually developed a wet and hacking cough, until his fight to breathe forced him to sit. While the nervous staff dashed around the studio seeking water and waiting for medical assistance, a camera man from another studio was an emergency responder and he rushed to assist the struggling Ben Carter. He was gasping and his mind was focused on death; but his eyes were fixed on the American woman who stood only a few feet away. She was quiet…and she was smiling.

9 CHAPTER
Chaos Theory

Loosely put, the concept of the chaos theory provides that some things look predictable for a while and then they behave randomly. Any meaningful prediction of behavior cannot be made more than three times. From the perspective of anyone who met him, this was a perfect description of little Gerald. As young parents, Tatyana and Marcus had the energy to raise him.

His inquisitive nature often took them into obvious, average, ordinary things they thought they knew, only to realize on further investigation they did not. His mind was like a sponge that soaked up everything he saw and all the things he heard. After the Officer Friendly comment in the mall, they learned to speak carefully around his small ears. Tatyana and Marcus were the proudest people on the planet when Gerald learned to speak, they just didn't expect him to do it all the time. He was the greatest gift they could ever have.

"Before you say a word about the number of questions he asked, remember he's just trying to understand how the puppets work," Tatyana said.

"I wasn't going to say anything."

"But you were thinking it. I know you Marcus."

Laughing loudly he said, "They're not puppets remember. They are marionettes."

"Shhhhh Marcus. You'll wake him. And it was a good question by the way. Even the marionettist said so. All of his questions were good questions," she whispered.

"That's not the point," Marcus said teasingly. "The issue is how many questions. Tatyana the boy had a thousand questions. I mean, did he even see the show?" He laughed again, but this time he glanced back at Gerald fast asleep in his car seat.

"Of course he saw the show Marcus," she chuckled. "And stop laughing at my baby. He just wants to know stuff that's all."

"Seems like he wanted to know everything… except the story. He asked about the strings, and the wood, and how long did it take to learn how to move the hands, and the head, and the…oh my God. Yes it was my son but I could feel for the marionettist."

"Yes, he is your son," she replied. "And from what I have learned, you were just like that and more. Oh how soon we forget Marcus." Most parents love their children's growth stages. Marcus and Tatyana were thrilled to see their son evolve into someone who educated them at every stage.

"He is smart though," Marcus responded with the widest grin he could muster. "When he asked the guy about leverage and tension on the string, my jaw dropped. I mean, what? I couldn't use those words in a complete sentence myself until recently." He laugh proudly, then he added, "He's a handful, but he is magnificent Tatyana."

"Yes, he is," she answered in the most matter of fact way proud mothers often do. She was driving on a familiar road at a comfortable speed when she looked in the rear view mirror to see Gerald safely sleeping. She noticed a police car gliding one car behind them. Initially she said nothing to Marcus, but the car changed position. Now the cruiser was directly behind them matching their speed exactly.

"Marcus darling. There is a…"

"I see him," Marcus calmly answered, but he was different. His breathing had changed. There was a coldness in his face. Tatyana was nervously driving not to make a mistake. Her hands shook a little. The police car sped up; now it was less than a car length behind her. She glanced a worried look at

Gerald- he was still asleep and smiling.
"If they pull me over with my son in the back," she thought. She glanced at Marcus, and she glanced again. Something was happening to him. His eyes, they were not closed but not open…and the pupils were different. She had never seen him in that state. The police were so close to her bumper if she tapped the brake they would ram her. "These bandits," she said to herself. "They will die here today before I let them hurt my son." She gripped the wheel harder than ever before, preparing to weaponize the family vehicle. And then, a hand… it was unexpected, but Marcus gently placed his hand on her knee and said, "It's OK Tatyana, they'll pass." But the car continued to follow her. After a few seconds the lights were flashing and the sirens were blasting. The menacing car pulled around to the side of Tatyana, stayed for a moment, and then raced away.
Marcus leaned into her and said, "Breathe Tatyana, it's over." Her breathing was fine, but her face was a picture of a pissed off Black woman… and her Russian accent was heavier when she was angry. For a short while he could understand nothing she said. And then… he could.
"Marcus, if they think I was going to let them walk up and just…"
"Yeah, I know," he said.
"I hope they spoke to God before they would have come to this car because He is the only one that could've kept me from…"
"Yeah, I saw."
"Get out of my head Marcus."
"OK, if you insist." He started to make some light comment to break the tension, but he didn't. "When we are angry about a past situation sometimes a bit of humor dulls the pain," he thought. "Good timing is not everything, but it is very important." Just as he finished the thought she yelled.
"JESUS CHRIST MARCUS…that was so wrong." Her heart was beating double the pace of normal. She was too mad to be scared, but the rush of adrenalin that fear produces

lingered for many minutes after the threat was gone… and she was livid. The hands that tightly gripped the wheel were shaking and she couldn't conceal it. In the next block she pulled the car over, slammed the handle into park, turned off the ignition, took a deep breath and gave a long thankful look at her son Gerald; still safe, still asleep.
"No one should ever have to feel the way I just did Marcus."
"I agree," he said. Her eyes were still wet with anger and relief.
"Marcus, it is not normal for law abiding citizens to feel like their life is in danger when they see a police."
"Well, it is for Black people."
"Right. You're right about that," she said. And then she had another thought. She slightly changed the subject and spoke in a faster pace,

"What was that thing you did? The police were right there on the bumper, and you changed into something."
"What do you mean? I can't change into something."
"It looked like you stopped breathing. I touched your arm, it was cold. I looked at you and your body looked…well different. It's hard to explain. I never saw anything like it before. Your eyes rolled back and the lids didn't shut, it was…it was freaky. It looked like one of those movies when people get so angry they turn into something." He thought deeply about what she was saying. The close, almost symbiotic relationship he shared with Tatyana was built on a platform of honesty always. The personal covenant they created provided that honesty would prevail in all things at all times, so he couldn't evade the truth. He took a deep breath and he answered.
"No Tatyana that's Hollywood. I cannot turn into some strange thing. I'm just me, Marcus. But the Marcus you know does change under certain conditions… like that one. Let's just say he evolved a little."
"It seemed like you were waiting to suddenly spring an attack on them. Is that it?" There was an excitement brewing in her

voice. She pressed in with another question. "Were you going to strike those officers if they came to the car?"

"I don't know, maybe," he said. The thought of seeing her dear Marcus take down the officers drove a big smile across her face. She enthusiastically continued, "Marcus, it was like you had hackles on the back of your neck. It was, well, it was scary."

"Scary?" he repeated. "You didn't seem scared." He looked over to the loving face still recovering from a serious bout of mother protection fury. He could see the stage of relief and the early signs of a smile forming in the corners of her eyes.

"Yes scary," she said in a playful voice. "Now show me how to do it."

He replied, "But you didn't look scared to me."

"That's cuz' I was too mad to show it. I'm still mad," she said.

"Yeah, but now it's a sexy mad-angry Black Russian thing you got goin' on."

"You know what Marcus…"

"Yep, I know."

And a small voice interrupted their moment, "Is there food Mama?"

"Gerald… you're awake."

"Yes. I am awake, is there food?"

"There's food at home Gerald and we are almost there. I will give it to you then, OK Honey?"

"Yes, it is OK Mama."

Leaning into Marcus she whispered, "Later I still want you to show me that strike like a snake thing." He lovingly rested his hard hand on the soft flesh just above her knee.

The Will To Act

Nearly a week later in a meeting at the Madison home, Leonard brought disturbing news. "We know who the shooter was," he said. "She was one of us I'm afraid. We discovered that she was an ex-navy sniper. She was an emotionally disabled veteran living with her elderly mother and had been a member of the BRO for seven years. Her primary responsibility was collecting grass roots Intel from the rank and file in the navy. Based on our information from those in the position to know, she found herself in a situation where she had an opportunity to kill two bad guys and she took it. There was no planning or anything like that, just an opportunity and the will to act. She died in the fire."

"Do the police know she was the shooter?" Marcus asked.
"Yes, they know."
Tatyana had a concern, "Do they know she was with the BRO?"
"I can't be sure but as far as we can tell, no they do not."

"Then all of the night raids and deportations are a part of another tactic I suppose," Marcus said rhetorically.
"Yes, always," Leonard answered. "It's all a prelude to finding the vigilante."
"So bombarding the public with misinformation has been so successful for so long there's no need to stop doing it," Marcus stated in a slow methodical voice that lacked even the smallest bit of inflection.
"True, and there's something else," Leonard said. "The source of the fire was more sophisticated than the team of investigators predicted. There were actually three flash points, but someone with a great deal of know-how took the time to make it look like one. Though the multiple points of ignition were synchronized to look random they were not. Our investigator found an ash-bot that didn't ignite."
"A what? What's an ash-bot Leonard?"
"Oh, sorry Marcus, I'll explain. An ash-bot is a micro-bot

agencies like the CIA will deploy to infiltrate a targeted site and set itself on fire. Usually they are not detectable. This kind of micro robot is the size of an ordinary insect. It is programmed or remotely guided to snuggle up close to an electrical panel or conduit; sometimes a furnace, or a gas line - someplace that will accelerate the impact of ignition. The intense flame will incinerate the tiny robot and hide its own existence. One of the ash-bots malfunctioned and our person found the tiny intruder still leached onto the gas supply line under the stove."

"Wow, but shouldn't the private fire investigators have found that?"

"Usually no. It's an assassination tool. The civilian investigator wouldn't know what to look for. Even the more enlightened agencies would have no reason to suspect this level of sophistication.

Whoever did this knew what they were doing."

"Well this confirms it then… the mother or her children were not responsible."

"Yes."

"So Leonard, you think the CIA started this fire?" Tatyana asked.

"No, they had nothing to do with it. They did watch it develop and they know who did it. But they didn't participate. This is the jurisdiction of the FBI and a few other homeland organizations… and still, even they didn't launch the bots. Remember, the government enlisted two agents from abroad; both of them have extensive experience with this kind of action. These contractors specialize in destabilizing enemy organizations and governments in a way that gives their employer the plausible deniability it needs."

"You mean the British guy?" Tatyana asked.

"Yes, and the other was from the HaMossad of Israel."

Marcus asked, "I see that part of their goal is to intimidate the minority communities, but what is the prime directive? Who they are doesn't concern me nearly as much as their motivation. Let me ask you this, do you think these

intimidation tactics still support their endgame?"
"Yes, I do," Leonard responded emphatically. "If you inflict enough pain on any people, history shows they will crack. Brother will turn against brother, child will turn on parent, mother against child and they will surely turn on you. That is the endgame - increase the threat on the people until they turn."
"I don't agree with that this time Leonard," Tatyana said. "This is different. That may be their intention. And yes, people tend to turn on each other and rip themselves apart in times like this, I agree with that; but this feels different. It is true that the government will call on the vigilante to turn himself in. They will say, 'Innocent people are dying because of you. You are the reason for the unrest. If you care about the people turn yourself in and stop the killing.' I agree with your prediction about that. In one variation or another that will happen. It's what they typically do, double speak. I just believe the people will react differently this time. You know, some things look predictable for a while and then they behave randomly. Marcus is like that, he is not predictable; and because the people believe he will protect them, I feel they will not behave as the enemy expects."

"Tatyana you could be right. Either way, I feel we are in the beginning stages of a new paramilitary conflict."
She abruptly responded, "Sure… I can agree with that…but it's the war they wanted. Whenever oppressed people demand fairness the oppressor wants to fight. This government, like all the others in this situation, has might in its favor. It has the media, the press… and the diplomatic muscle to shut out the truth. With all of this and the threat of war, an oppressive government will intimidate a free people into giving up their God given rights and the oppressed people to accept and celebrate the status quo."
"Yep," Leonard added. "I also see how it will distract the world from looking at their present and prior bad acts. They need a war because they are losing the social fight. They can

no longer claim the moral high ground. A good war will allow them to reboot the agenda, claim self-defense, redefine the conflict, draw new lines of loyalty and make this an 'us against them' battle. They need to lure progressive thinking Americans into an ignorant cycle of circular reasoning. In other words, anyone who is not one of us is one of them and must be a terrorist. In addition to that, people are willing to look the other way on an untold amount of atrocities when they are linked to the word 'War.' So, tactically and historically a paramilitary conflict works for them, not us."

"But the vigilante keeps them in check," said Marcus. He was characteristically calm; and there was a noticeable change in the tone of his voice. Leonard mentioned it. "Wow Marcus, you sound like Barry White. What happened to your voice?"
"Don't know. Got up a few days ago and everything I said sounded different. It just happened. I was going to have the doctors take a look but I thought… what the hell just leave it. It doesn't hurt or anything … and Tatyana said she likes it." Sitting next to him, Tatyana confirmed his words with a raised eyebrow and a gentle smile. The pitch of his voice seemed to fall a full octave. It was smooth and resonate… but it wasn't simply the sound of his voice that was different. The inflection and intonation both changed enough to catch Leonard's attention. Gone was the quick paced conversation of a post graduate young man. His Godson was now sounding much older than his years. Marcus often paused at the edge of an unfinished sentence to hold the attention of the listener - a speech pattern vary familiar to Leonard and reminiscent of a time not so long ago. Hearing Marcus speak with such confidence and forethought, Leonard was more than impressed, he was proud. Marcus continued to speak.

"They know he has infiltrated the government, but they don't know how deep," he said slowly. "They don't know if he is actually a group. They don't even know if he is one of them or not. They are blind. Many in leadership agree that a rival government is involved in some way. And no war strategist from any professional discipline will strike a community under those conditions. In short, our friend Raguel has the whole government tied in one big knot." Marcus always spoke of the vigilante Raguel in the third person. It was a way to keep structure in his mind, in his life. Living with a dissociative identity, it was important to develop good boundaries and organizational skills. Raguel was flawless, Marcus was not, and speaking of Raguel in the third person diminished the chance of anyone accidentally disclosing that they occupied the same body.

It was a beautiful night and a comfortable evening conversation with the only family he had.

When Did He Die?

Marcus was an avid reader of obscure science articles. To him, it was a pastime like some people study baseball statistics. When she first met Marcus, it was one of the quirky things Tatyana loved about him. Now she found it to be an excellent distraction from the torturous images that threatened to cloud his mind. Sitting in front of the beautiful smoked glass window, in his father's chair, in what was his parent's office, he said, "Tatyana, this is amazing. I'm reading this article from the Smithsonian Institute. A few scientists from the University College of London took a 10,000 year old skull and used the DNA information to create a facial reconstruction of it. Apparently after running it through a battery of sophisticated tests, the scientists were shocked that the findings revealed conclusive evidence that the skull was in fact male, he had dark curly hair, blue eyes and very dark brown to black skin. "Tatyana, that's amazing! Did you know this?"

"About Cheddar Man? I heard something on the news about it a few days ago, but nothing in-depth."

"Really?" he asked surprisingly. "Where did you hear about it?"

"Oh, no place as prestigious as the Smithsonian, so it might not be accurate. Tell me about it darling."

"Well, they found the skeleton over a hundred years ago. Here it says 1903 in a cave. In an English village called…hold on…"

"I think it's the village of Cheddar dear."

"Yeah, you're right. It's interesting, don't you think?"

"Very."

"They populated all of Europe… OK, you had this in school already right?"

She laughed.

"Wow," he said, "Not here."

She paused for a moment. "Hmm, did you feel that?"

"Feel what?"

"Something is off."
"I don't feel anything," he said.
"I don't know, it feels well… maybe you're right. Anyway, I'm going across the street to the community center to pick up your son. If I time it right, it will be ending when I get there. When he goes into his Lego trance no one can snap him out of it. Marcus, that boy will start building one of those things and for the next three hours or so he will hear nothing. I call that a Lego trance."
"I used to do that."
"Used to? You still do that." He stood to hug her before she left and the enormous window shattered into crumbles of tempered glass. With the sudden explosion of glass and sound, instinctively Tatyana dropped to the floor and covered her head. Marcus fell to his knees and then, the floor. He didn't cover… he couldn't. When Tatyana lifted her head she called to him. He was there. His eyes were locked open. He wasn't moving and she was stunned with silence. Her body tried to produce a scream but her mind couldn't find the files that made the noise…and she held a great silent scream until the veins in her forehead were thick enough to break the skin. He still wasn't moving. Staying close to the ground she crawled to him. She was struggling to drag his body behind a table when the force of a heavy round slammed into his ribs with a thud strong enough to flip him over like a rag doll. "MARCUS!" she yelled. The handsome muscles of his chest were torn open and the tangled contents lay on his side and floor. The floor, the chair, the room, was red with blood. Searching for a response to the madness she lay over him. Working to gather a thought, the notion that she was also a target quickly passed through her mind, but it didn't return.

"My blouse," she thought. She ripped the garment from her body, tightly rolled it at the edges and jammed it into the open wound like a plug. She searched both sides of his body for the damage the second shot created, but she found nothing. "No, Marcus," she panted. Her mind, abruptly switched. “Oh my God, Gerald.” She took another prayerful look at Marcus spread haphazardly on the floor in front of his desk. “Hold on honey,” she said softly. “I’ll be back.” She didn’t stand, but slowly slid across the room in the blood of the only man she ever loved and then quickly crawled away to secure the safety of their son.

10 CHAPTER
The Warning At The Mourning

…He will try to divide your spirit. He will try to destroy your name,
He will try to discredit your message, for strategic political gain.
He'll possess your leaders with gifts and gold. His spies will look like you.
The leaders and friends he cannot corrupt will die in public view.
He will mimic the voice of reason, his words will please your ear,
He'll assemble with groups and committees to pacify your fear.
He'll window dress every demand and say that there must be change,
He'll strengthen the arms and forces, expand their scope and range.
He will reach the old established, to dim your youthful rage,
To organize your movement and patronize your age.
He'll screen your life by sky, by land and then by sea,
You must make injustice expensive, or the people can never be free.

His words rang in her head like a mantra from heaven. Tatyana couldn't tell if life at this point was a bad, bad dream. But there she knelt, shirtless, in the middle of a cluttered community center clutching her son. She noticed the puzzled look of concern on his face. She noticed the large spots of blood she transferred to his cheek and his shirt. She noticed that every eye… and ear… and word of nosey careless gossip was speculatively focused on her. But now that Gerald was safe and in her arms, it was Marcus on her mind. She could see the broken window of the family office from where she stood. The staff at the center, the people on the street, in the surrounding shops, even those comfortably eating patrons of the Black Diamond itself, began to gather at the base of the second story window. "What happened," they asked. It was the constant moving question they murmured amongst themselves. "What happened?" Ah, a face she knew; one she trusted. It was Beverly Oden, the director of the center and a family friend.

"Bev," she spoke hurriedly. "I'll explain later, I need your phone."

"Yes, of course."

"Please, take Gerald to your office until I…"

"Of course, I got him Tatyana." Tatyana made the only called that made sense.

"Leonard, it's me. They shot Marcus. I'm headed back to the office now… right now. Gerald is OK." She forced back the tears of anger and fear and she refused to give in to even the possibility that Marcus was dead. She spoke as if she knew he was only hurt. In her mind his present condition was simply a painful setback. The soothing force of denial was a relentless source of energy that overwhelmed all logic but Tatyana's personality wouldn't admit to being overwhelmed by anything. She spoke quickly, "Why would God allow this? This is evil at work Leonard. Marcus is a good man, the Lord I serve would never take him from us. They know something, they know who he is… and they… Leonard, they shot my beautiful Marcus." That was it. Those words touched something in her. It was like the light weight of the last card placed at the top of the tower. It often took years to construct an emotional tower of strength. Like paper cards, most people balance a life time of experiences on and against each other until their multi-layered edifice represents the idea of strength and success they hold in their minds. But every card has weight…. and every tower has a weight limit. Before she could say another word, the well-constructed tower of emotional stability Tatyana worked so hard to erect, crumbled. "HE FELL LEONARD. They shot my beautiful man… and he fell like a bird from the sky." She sobbed uncontrollably. Her quick pace to the office halted. She struggled to take a normal breath but she couldn't do it. Her legs, they wanted to stop but her mind kept moving her body back to the scene of her anguish and the site of her Marcus.

"Tatyana, are you there?" Leonard's voice called out to her, "TATYANA," he yelled again. "Can you hear me?"

"Yes," she responded in a way much calmer than before. Still overwhelmed with emotions, an emergency part of her mind seemed to default to an auto-function pre-set in a survival mode that somehow got her back to the office. "Yes, I'm here Leonard. Just trying to get back to him before the police or anyone else gets there."

"OK listen, someone is on the way. You will know how to identify them when they arrive. Let no one near him, I mean no one. Is that clear?"

"Crystal, but I had no intention of doing anything else."

"OK," he was worried. Trying to compose himself, Leonard's voice cracked with emotion on every question. "Umm, let me ask you this, it's important. Where was he hit?" Leonard was mindful of his questions. He wasn't sure how much experience Tatyana had with this kind of thing, but it didn't matter. The stress associated with witnessing a love one being shot down was typically enough to paralyze an experienced person with grief, silence or stress induced amnesia. He had to have the information, but he needed to approach each question with a great deal of caution and compassion. "Could you tell anything like that?" He only expected a nervous answer and Tatyana responded.

"He was shot in the back… and it looks like the bullet went straight through Leonard," she said clearly and without a waver in her voice. "The bullet entered his chest cavity from the back right shoulder region and it exited the opposing side at the upper right part of his chest," she continued. "It looked like he was sucking air through the hole, so I plugged it with my shirt and a piece of his torn skin. I thought that would stop the suction and equalize his chest pressure. It should have helped him draw air in through the airway and into the good lung. I was coming back to check after I saw to Gerald." The most immediate thing running through Leonard's mind he couldn't quickly express, but he had to say, "Tatyana, I don't think you will ever stop surprising me." She didn't respond. Tatyana was still on the move. He could hear the wind in the background and her quick steps racing over the street and pavement into the restaurant. She was a woman running on the fuel that fear produced and she was too scared to admit it, even to herself.

He asked another question, "Do you have an idea how much blood he lost?"

"No, but he lost a lot," she answered.

"OK, How far are you away from him now?"

"Headed up the stairs now, a few seconds maybe."

"While you were away did anyone have access to him?"

"I can't say for sure. There was the time it took me to deal with Gerald, but I could see the building even then. Someone would have to have been in the building already." In a crisis, Leonard's tactical experience often took control of his actions. He was widely praised throughout the BRO for his ability to cease his emotions when others could not. Fighting back the worry he had for his Godson, holding the heavy tears and hidden prayers for a safe and healthy Marcus, he said, "Tatyana, we don't know what we are dealing with so be careful how you enter the room. It's not likely but a sniper could be lurking around. Please be cautious. Let's pause a moment and look at what we have here. We don't know enough about the angle of the shooter to calculate distance or direction. We have no way of knowing who the intended target was, is it you and Marcus or just Marcus? We know nothing. Most snipers are gone within seconds after the target falls, but we have no idea if it was one shooter or two… or more. We know nothing. Please, listen to me. We can't calculate probabilities without information. How close are you now?"

"I'm approaching the office door," she said.

"Hold on, before you go in there let's discuss how. Or maybe even wait for help to arrive before you re-enter; we don't want Gerald to lose both of his parents." She was standing at the entrance and took a moment to gather her breath. Only a few of his words registered when he spoke and after a few seconds she composed herself enough to address them.

"Do your calculus Leonard, but I'm going back in that room for him. There is nothing to discuss," and she dropped the phone.

Blood was everywhere. She could see the tracks she made when she left. She panned her eyes around the open space. The noise from the street was gradually growing, including a siren in the distance. The police were coming, the ambulance was on the way, she was sure of that. Gathering onlookers had no idea what broke the window, that it was broken was the only thing needed to raise curiosity. People didn't know exactly what was going on, but it is the nature of the middle class public to call the police when they see a shirtless Black woman moving around the street. The fact that she was covered in someone's blood made police involvement a statistical certainty.

Tatyana had no idea what she would see when she entered the room. Instinctively, she found the floor and cautiously crawled into the room for the same reasons she crawled out of it. Staying as low as she could, Tatyana slid over the blood, the tangled mat of rug, the pea size pieces of tempered glass shattered throughout the room and scattered around the floor. She kept her head low and her eyes up, scanning and planning every sliding move forward. The poke and cutting sensation of glass raking across her nearly naked torso opened her skin, but there was no time to feel it. Her soft hands carried the weight of her body on wet blood and broken glass, but there was no space in her mind to know it. As a woman of devout principles, Tatyana had always accepted the works of God whether she understood them or not. The minutes were passing faster, the sirens were coming closer and for the first time she allowed herself to think about the worst thing possible. "To every beginning there is an end, which starts the beginning of the end again. It is the perpetual state of love and life gifted to us by God until he calls us home," she thought. Before she could trust her eyes to see anymore, she whispered a prayer she never dreamed necessary. "Whatever I am to face I will see it through you my Lord. When I lift my head, please grant me the strength to bear what I see." She was afraid. Even before she opened her eyes her intuition could detect no signs of life in the room. Tears forced their way from her tightly shut lids, until she opened her eyes to that place in every room were the wall meets the ceiling and reluctantly let them fall to the desk behind his body. When her eyes found the place where he fell, the source of her fear was real and her beloved Marcus was gone.

11 CHAPTER
Disbelief

"Tatyana, there is a purpose for all things, a reason for it to exist. To be mindful is to be completely aware. To hear everything, to see everything your eyes encounter, to feel and smell and sense everything around you. Let it go, or not. That is your dilemma."

"I do not understand."

"Your eyes are cameras, your ears are audio recorder, your skin is a big blanket sensor and your brain is computer that store every information. Even though you record and store information it does not mean you remember where to find it. You see everything your eye pass every day. Your brain records it, but you may not label it and place it in a particular space for your easy retrieval at a later time. Does that make sense?"

"Kind of, well sort of."

"For example, all the time you go into your home. You go up the stairs to your room yes?"

"Yes, I do that."

"Every day you go up and down the same stairs in your home. Is that so?"

"Of course, the stairs don't change."

"Oh, really? Never change do they?"

Tatyana was struggling with unpredictable waves of sadness and it was harder for her to be cordial in conversation.

"Hey, Kondo, I'm having a hard time following you right now. I don't see what my stairs have to do with anything. Please just make whatever point you are trying to make a little more riddle free. I mean, unless you magically have him hidden behind the stairway at our home, I'm not seeing the relevance."

"I understand," he said as if he hardly heard her…and then he continued. "So, every day you go upstair …and then you go down stair. Please tell me Tatyana, how many stair you have?" She thought about Marcus. She remembered the many times he shared his frustration with Kondo's style of teaching. Whenever he gave up on a problem and turned to Kondo for help, instead of an answer, Kondo would give a Koan style question that confused him even more. She remembered he didn't like it at first, and she remembered when it changed; the progressive way it helped Marcus see past the emotion, past the obvious, past the pain. "Kondo does stuff like that," Marcus said to her, "But the answer is always in the question. He believes that in life the answer to our problem is always in the question itself." With that memory she took a deep breath, threw herself down into the only office armchair and turned most of her attention back to Kondo.

"Kondo, I missed what you just asked me, I'm sorry."

"No problem," he said. "My question is how many stair to your room?"

"I have no idea," she said.

"Think, Tatyana. Every day you go up the stair and down but you have no idea how many. You only see, you do not observe." His eyes quickly cut to the direction of the sound rushing through the broken window opening. "Police coming now, we must go."

"But Leonard is sending someone. I should wait for them."

"They already come," he said. Tatyana had an uncharacteristically puzzled look on her face. "We must go now." He stood from his folded position on the floor, walked away from the main entrance towards the utility closet, opened the door, slid back the wall of shelves stacked with office supplies and descended a flight of stairs she never knew existed. The spring loaded wall tracked back into position as she passed down the stairway. It was an old servant's staircase that led to the rear corner of the wine cellar.

"Jesus," she whispered loudly.

"Not Jesus…I am only Kondo."

"Is he here Kondo?" She was trying to descend the dark winding cascade of stairs without stumbling, but her attention was not on the stairway. "Is he down here Kondo?" she repeated. Few questions mattered, and he kept moving. How did Kondo know about this place and she didn't. Was this a trap? Where does it lead? The only thing she wanted to know was the question she kept asking. The steps ended, the floor was uneven, and the space was dark except for one flickering light in a small room. It was cold and she could smell something, so she called out the question again. "KONDO, IS HE DOWN HERE?"

"Yes, I am here Tatyana." His voice was weak, she couldn't see much so she hurried in the direction of the voice. And there he was… sitting up, shirtless. His chest had a white patch over the wound, three people surrounded him… and one of them was Leonard.

Simply A Question Of Stairs

After all the moving of the day, now she couldn't move. "When you leave office and come to here, how many stair?" She heard the question, but her eyes were glued to the beautiful reality sitting up in front of her. Afraid of making a mistake, she slowly walked across the little room as if it were a mine field. "One wrong step," she thought "and my dream could be blown apart." The voice repeated, "How many stair Tatyana?" She was close enough to touch him by then. His head, his neck, the broad thick roundness of his shoulders….his scent, "This was no dream," she whispered. He reached and rested the weight of his unbandage arm around her. Marcus smiled in that perfect way she could never resist, and he kissed her skin. It was all so silent. She pressed her forehead to his, closed her eyes and the cold dark space was an empty heated paradise to them. No one, and nothing else existed. Cutting through the silence, one voice rang like a bell in her mind. "Tatyana, how many stair?" His relentless question broke into the imaginary door they closed behind them, so she answered.

"Thirty two," she whispered gladly, hoping to stop the piercing question from ringing in her ears. "There are thirty two stairs Mr. Kondo." Her lips moved, but she couldn't.

"Yes, and if we include the landing step it makes thirty three," Marcus added. Tatyana gently brushed his face. "My Marcus, all real," she thought, and together they laughed.

But before they could fully enjoy the mood, a professional voice interrupted. "So Tatyana, what was your dilemma?"

"What dilemma, what do you mean?" The question didn't have her full attention, but the questioner persisted.

"I mean, when you came back to the office and you saw Marcus was not there you nearly passed out. Kondo spoke to you for a bit and then he brought you here. There was so much blood in the room. Did you question that?" She slowly raised her eyes and pointed them in the direction of the question.

"What are you talking about Leonard? I had no interest in calculating how many God damn liters of blood there may or may not have been in the room, on the floor, or wherever else it was you think I should have noticed, in your infinite wisdom."

"I told you she would be mad," Marcus said to Leonard.

"Please Tatyana, if we think deeply we can see that there is purpose for all things."

"Oh, shut up Kondo. There is definitely a purpose for that." Marcus howled a laugh so big his ribs were hurting, and he couldn't stop looking at Leonard who was laughing at the incredulous look on Kondo's face, which gradually found a smile. Still she was hot, and she turned her attention to an unfamiliar face grinning in the room.

"So, who is she?" Tatyana asked. When no one answered fast

enough she asked directly.
"Who are you?" and her weight shifted with the question.
"Who me? I'm just here."
"I know where you are," she snapped back. "What I want to know is--- who you are."
"I am Catheryn."
"OK, now that you know your name Catheryn. Why are you here? Why are you all here? What is this?"
Leonard jumped in, "Tatyana, let me explain."
"Marcus is OK. Well, he was OK until he bumped his head and took a tumble down those stairs you just counted. That's how he nipped his shoulder and bruised his arm. In times of high alert the BRO will stage these drills and assess the response."
"WHAT! WHAT DRILL?" Tatyana was not happy. She glared at Leonard and then Marcus. Marcus tried to hug her and explain but she pushed him away forcefully.
It wasn't a scream that came next, but she spoke with an anger and disappointment too heavy for Marcus to measure.
"Marcus," she sadly said, "You lied to me?"
"No Tatyana, he didn't lie to you." Leonard was talking but she never acknowledged that. Her eyes were on Marcus.
"You lied to me?" She looked into his eyes, past the lens, into the open chamber and onto the retinal walls and optical webs where all Black women eventually go to find an entangled lie, or partial truth. She found nothing.
"Tatyana, I'm sorry. I didn't know about it until the last minute myself. It's a way the BRO tests its teams without having to pull people together. Because members are supposed to remain anonymous even to each other, telling them it's a drill before you pull them together will expose people unnecessarily. Think of it as a fire drill for people who never know who is who. They get the call to respond and the conductor, in this case it's Catheryn… the conductor keeps track of everything and everyone using her note pad; who responded, how long it took them to respond. How did they react to the situation? It's a very detailed operation Tatyana.

With makeup teams and all, like a movie production. Before you came down Catheryn and Leonard were explaining why it's so important to the BRO.
Malcom Ben Carter was poisoned last week. He is not a member of the BRO. But because we had members on the scene able to quickly muster the expertise of others in the area, the neurotoxin didn't kill him. If our family comes under attack Leonard wanted to be sure he had the right combination of people in place to support us. It was all set up before he ever brought it to me Tatyana. He said he knew I would tell you if he did it any other way."
"Yes," Leonard said, as he carefully entered the conversation. "The original idea was to surprise both of you but Kondo wanted to add a training scenario for Tatyana. He thought she was ready. Tatyana, I know it was hard to go through that, but you, Marcus and Gerald are the only family I have. I need to know that you are safe." The haze of anger surrounding Tatyana began to dissipate. She needed a little more than a moment to take it all in, and then she said,
"It was so real though. He was bleeding everywhere. How was that?"
Leonard answered. "That was the point I was trying to make earlier. He was bleeding everywhere. That was the first clue. There was too much blood. When you looked at the wound you correctly noted it was an open pneumothorax or as you said on the phone, 'a sucking chest wound.' You saw little blood inside the wound. In fact you stuck your shirt in the hole, which was brilliant by the way. I can think of few professionals with the presence of mind to do anything like that under that kind of stress. But you observed no arteries thumping blood into his chest cavity and you saw no veins oozing. Given there was so little blood coming from the victim one has to ask, where did all the blood come from?
Second thing - you saw him shot twice. The second time flipped him over. You did the right thing. You looked for the wound, but you found no wound. So where did it go?
Third thing - you went back into the room and found no

Marcus. You thought about that for some time. You even said, "Where did he go?" But it appears you never asked yourself, where did Kondo come from? On Catheryn's checklist there are sixty-five very important things to observe in your scenario; and you missed three. You did great Tatyana, and I really loved it when you told Kondo to shut up."

"That was funny," Marcus added. "Let me also say this, I told Leonard not to tell me when something was going to happen. That way, I wouldn't have to lie when you asked me about it later. My thinking was, if you want to really keep a secret, you must also hide it from yourself."

"What does that mean Marcus? You made it up?" She was still a bit miffed with Marcus. The fear of his possible death was not something she ever wanted to experience, even in a drill. The thought of losing him put her in a dreadful place but she was still so happy to see him there was no room to hold a lasting anger.

"Did I make it up? No I didn't make it up Tatyana, George Orwell did."

"Well it was stupid when he said it too," she sniped. Then she hugged him around the waist and gently placed her head on that particular crease in his chest.

"Never do that to me again Marcus. I was losing my mind."

"I will never do or take part in anything like that again Tatyana."

Still standing close enough to hear their conversation, Leonard responded, "It looked to me that your mind held up pretty well, considering." Tatyana didn't respond to Leonard's statement, she simply smiled and asked,

"Kondo did you say to be mindful is to be completely aware?"

"Yes, I did."

"To be mindful is to hear everything, to see, and feel everything around you. Is that true?"

"Yes it is true."

"Right now my dilemma is this. Marcus and I want to be

mindful but you are still here. Can all of you leave us now so that he and I can be mindful together?" The confused look on Kondo's face prompted a quick response from Leonard.
"Yes of course," he spoke hurriedly as he nudged Kondo and Catheryn from the room. "Let's go everyone. Laughing as he left he uttered, "I'll get Gerald and keep him with me until, well...I'll just..."
They responded, "Thank you."

The Life And Lines Between Truth And Fiction
More than eight days later, Tatyana sat in the cushioned green window seat nestled in the warm space of the east bay window that overlooked the lake behind their home. She enjoyed those precious evening hours. The time alone with her thoughts and a glass of wine soothed the mind and decompressed her day. Though she had a philosophical aversion to alcohol, and many of her family members wrestled with the debilitating effect of alcoholism, Tatyana's evening drink consisted of one glass of wine. It was a ritual that reminded her of home. For her, Sovetskoye Shampanskoye was the only wine worth drinking, the golden sparkle and balanced taste of fresh fruits were symbolic of her home and family in Russia. Many nights she reclined and contemplated the life they chose and their decision to raise a son in America. One evening while strolling the information highways on her tablet computer she noticed an article that made her leave the sanctity of her space, run to the next room and read it to Marcus.
"Marcus," she said, "On Feb. 8, 2017, Nina Renata Aron wrote a beautiful article in the Timeline News, titled
When The Black Justice Movement Got Too Powerful, The FBI Got Scared And Got Ugly.
She uses the acronym BPP to represent Black Panther Party. In my opinion, her article highlights more than a few tactical normalities the US government continues to use today. Despite the elaborate presidential window dressing the US predictable treatment of Black and Brown people has

followed that old southern cliché, 'If it ain't broke, don't fix it.' In part of her article she writes:
In a 1968 memorandum to 14 field offices, FBI director J. Edgar Hoover had instructed recipients to "submit imaginative and hard-hitting counter-intelligence measures aimed at crippling the BPP" within a context of "gang warfare" and "attendant threats of murder and reprisal." In the subsequent year, the agency sent forged letters, including insulting cartoons and death threats, to leaders of both movements, instigating the dispute that erupted on UCLA's campus.
The Black Panthers, founded in 1966, had grown to national prominence quickly. Their mission stood in stark distinction to the peaceful civil rights movement commandeered by Martin Luther King, Jr., and both their comportment and their tactics made for salacious press coverage: "Panthers emerged through the press in those days as a group of armed Blacks with militant attitudes and loaded guns—something only slightly more sophisticated than a street gang," wrote Tim Findley in Rolling Stone in 1972.

Of course, the group was far more varied and nuanced than the press was likely to report. But their diversity scarcely mattered anyway. J. Edgar Hoover had labeled BPP a "hate group" and by 1968 was convinced that they represented "without question…the greatest threat to internal security of the country." He launched a thorough, targeted campaign of surveillance, intimidation, exploitation, harassment, and in some cases violence, to destroy the organization.

Hoover and other rabid defenders of the status quo were right to be afraid of the Black Panther Party, which was in many ways uniquely positioned to improve the material reality of black Americans. At the core of the Black Panther ethos was a sophisticated critique not just of the American political machine but of capitalism—the engine that drove it, according to party doctrine. They opened community health clinics and introduced the Free Breakfast for Children program—initiatives that served to highlight the lack of adequate social services in Black neighborhoods. The group's socialist sympathies were a chief reason why they were deemed so threatening to national security, and programs targeting them were developed alongside those—like Operation Hoodwink—designed to gut the ranks of the Socialist Workers Party and the Communist Party of the United States.

The group posed a further threat because they were militant, armed, and sought to police the police by patrolling their own communities with guns, monitoring cops' activities. "We want an end to the robbery by the white man of our black community," read the organization's "Ten-Point Program." "We want land, bread, housing, education, clothing, justice, and peace."

Her article highlighted a stark reality. "The Black Panther Party was asking for most of the same things we are asking for now and that was over forty years ago. Now nearly all of the freedom fighters have been neutralized and justice continues to evade Black and Brown people." The tone of her voice carried the squeeze of frustration. "I asked this question in one of my classes and the professor simply smiled. But I am curious, why do Black people stay here? When pharaoh allowed the Hebrew slaves to leave Egypt, they left in mass. Black people in this country are some of the most spiritual people on the planet, surely they know the story. With all of the talent and know-how within the communities, why not just leave?"

Marcus nodded, acknowledging that she had his full attention, but he didn't speak. He knew where the conversation was going.

"If they won't leave physically at least leave ideologically. Why carry the social legacy of your captors into the next generation? If you keep the ideology of the master because it is more comfortable than building your own, you may look free but your mind belongs to him. We cannot raise Gerald to be a part of this hypocrisy. I will not raise him to idealize a capitalistic concept that craves money and material wealth over people. When the people were treated like this in Russia they fought back. We revolted, overthrew the oppressive government and gave the country back to the people. But here the oligarchs produce and promote a few people of color and the revolutionaries are lulled into silence. The oligarchs recruit a few Black or Brown people and promote their installation into politics or some other high profile position. Everyone knows that an honest politician is an oxymoron, so what is wrong with the Black middle class that they will not detach themselves from this myth? And why do they support school curriculum that under educates Black children while simultaneously celebrating the fairytale of a well-mixed melting pot?" He glanced past the piano room where Gerald had fallen asleep, and gazed into the comfortable cove where she lounged only minutes before, but still he didn't speak. She continued, "How can they rest so comfortably when it is so clear that the only thing that seems to melt are the rights and culture of Black and Brown people?" she said shaking her tablet at Marcus.

Marcus knew what raised her from her comfortable place. He knew what drove her anguish. He could see her worry, so he spoke to it directly.

"Gerald will be OK Tatyana. He is happy, he is safe. If at some point you feel these things have been compromised we can leave the country… and I will go wherever you want. Is that clear Tatyana?"

"Yes love. That is very clear."

"Now, I heard what you said and I completely understand why you see the African American predicament the way you do. But if you search closer, past the anger and above the fear, I really think you will observe something more than the frustrations of an oppressed people in a corrupt system. The revolution has begun, I am a revolutionary and so are you. The people see that other countries have caught up with the west technologically. The constant leak of top secret content has exposed the watchful eyes of the empire at home and around the world. Oppressed people are losing their fear of this government…and I believe in a very African American way, the people have risen. We are simply the front end of a revolution, but we will not be televised."

12 CHAPTER
Indiscriminant Acts

Formally convinced that their loyalty to the blue shield was an act of patriotism some police are changing. A sizable number of Black police officers have refused to support or defend brutality. "The status quo is wrong," barked the unnamed leader of the newly organized Band of Brothers and Sisters. The BBS was founded by conscientious officers of color who had members of their family abused by law enforcement. Many of them were victims of police abuse by officers unaware of their membership in the blue order. "We will not continue to condone the indiscriminate acts of brutality against our own people, and that's the reality of the situation," said an anonymous twenty year veteran of the force. "We know exactly what's going on and there is never a good reason to be silent and do nothing." The BBS campaign was one of a growing number of side groups in law enforcement who were breaking ranks with the traditional code of silence. Officers who bucked the code put themselves at risk of being ostracized or worse. The threat of an untimely death loomed above those officers. A staged death in the line of duty was the traditional payback for that kind of betrayal.

Tony Orlando Perez was thirty-two years old, the youngest of seven children in his family. His father worked as a janitor in his high school and his mother was a part time bank teller who couldn't resist telling anyone who would listen how proud she was that her youngest son was a policeman. On the night the famous Puerto Rican fighter Hélix Trinidad came out of his second retirement to fight the former champion Deroy Jones Jr., Tony was on his way to Madison Square Garden to watch his favorite fighter destroy Deroy. When he sat in the arena he found his dream. From the beginning, it was all Trinidad and he was thrilled. It was more than cultural pride that animated Tony. He closely resembled Helix Trinidad, in fact they were almost identical in physical appearance. He enjoyed it when people regularly mistook him for the famous fighter. During the bout he couldn't stay in his seat and for every punch Trinidad released, Tony threw another. Standing in the isle bobbing and jabbing he entertained the mostly Puerto Rican crowd with a mirror image of the action in the ring. Trinidad won the first two rounds but, in the end, Jones was too fast, scoring two knockdowns and finishing with a victory by unanimous decision. It was a bad night for Tony. At the end of the evening and outside the arena, another fight erupted in the parking lot. Tony arrived on the scene, identified himself and attempted to quell the conflict. Minutes later, two uniformed officers appeared on bicycles and without hesitation drew their weapons and shot the two men, both drunk, both unarmed, both killed. The officers reported that the two men did not stop when ordered to do so. In their written report they stated that the men continued to rush them in a menacing way and posed a threat to themselves and others.

They added that in the split-second fog of the moment they felt their lives were in danger and only discharged their weapons to stop the threat. But Tony Orlando Perez saw it differently. There was not a time in his life Tony didn't want to be a policeman and to him, the oath of an officer was the ultimate commitment to truth. Only a year before in a high profile case, Tony was held in praise for his loyalty. He and his partner were surveilling a man suspected of fencing stolen goods. They were informed of his actions by an undercover agent surveilling another case. At some point in the strategy of the prosecution, the government lawyers decided to use the report of Tony and his partner in addition to some inadmissible intelligence to boost their chance of success. A legal team of civil libertarians were able to show that the government was using secret evidence, evidence the defense had no access to because it was kept out of courtrooms and the public eye, a process known in the legal world as "parallel construction." Tony's testimony was so honest that the prosecution dropped the case to save what was left of its tattered credibility. But they will never forget the case and they never forgot Tony. On the deadly night of the big fight, the two shooting officers asked and expected their brother in blue to corroborate their story - he didn't.

"I arrived on the scene and the two men were obviously drunk," said Tony. "They were throwing punches at each other, but they were too drunk to hit anything. From my observation, they were doing more posturing and screaming than anything," he stated calmly. "I identified myself as a policeman and instructed them to leave the area. They did continue to scream but they were leaving. As the two men attempted to exit the circling crowd the other officers arrived. I observed the officers stepping away from their bicycles and shooting the two men multiple times. It was a horrible situation, like a bad movie. In only a few seconds the officers drew their weapons and shot two unarmed drunk people. When I made it known that I was a policeman the officers dropped their barrels away from me. In the aftermath of the evening they wanted to know what I saw. I felt that was a clear attempt to synchronize our stories, so I didn't engage much, I tried to stay busy with crowd control, then I went home and wrote down all that I saw, and blasted that email to my fellow members of the BBS for safe keeping." His girlfriend replayed that audio tape in a living room stuffed with journalists. "Tony knew something was going to happen to him, that's why he made this recording," she said stridently. "The police killed him. He tried to stand up for something good and decent in our profession and someone in our own ranks killed him for that. We will find out who did it and we will hold them accountable."

Not A Suspicious Death

The improbable circumstances surrounding the death of Tony Orlando Perez never sat with his family or his friends, but for his fellow members of the BBS, this was not a suspicious death at all, they knew what it was… and they knew why. What they were determined to do, was to find out who. After months of the traditional law enforcement investigation turned up nothing but the same story, a founding member of the BBS said, "I worked homicide for thirty years. I also knew Tony personally. He was a good young man, he was fair. What happened to him is not as it appears. Neither the setting nor the circumstances are consistent with the way he lived. Every murder has a pattern, like the pieces of a puzzle. Solving the problem means finding the right pieces and putting them in their proper place. Here we have pieces that don't belong, statements that don't fit and integrity problems with the investigators themselves. Trusting much of anything they find or produce is impossible and as a result the problem cannot be resolved. What we need is a new investigation with new and credible investigators. In an old Sherlock Holmes story he said, when you have eliminated the impossible, whatever remains, however improbable, must be the truth." As a Puerto Rican homicide detective he had served the people for more than thirty years. He was a trained reasoner and his finely adjusted temperament conditioned him to speak about the most horrific scenes and circumstances calmly with no hint of negative emotion, like eating fried egg for breakfast. He added, "So that we may conduct an independent study and investigation of what happened to our young brother, we ask on behalf of the family, that this government give us access to any and all information and evidence related to Tony's death."

Angry protests continued through the night on the streets of Puerto Rican communities in all five boroughs of New York City. In Brooklyn, the Bronx, and the Spanish Harlem and Loisaida neighborhoods of Manhattan, the rioting was so heavy that the governor deployed the National Guard. Protesters spilled out onto the interstate and blocked traffic in both directions. Breaking news footage showed angry protesters surrounding and attacking any kind of police car. In Washington, DC, the intensity grew when a multi-ethnic mass of protesters marching on the White House came to a tense standoff with a line of police in riot gear. After televising the unrest, the protest quickly spread to New Jersey, Philadelphia, Miami, Fort Lauderdale, Chicago and Hartford, Connecticut. A fire storm of social media spread around the globe enlisting the support of wealthy sympathizers. Within weeks, small groups of well-funded militia began to form throughout the country lead by former military officers and members of the BBS, starting in Tampa, Florida and Boston, Massachusetts. The BBS militia was comprised mostly of war veterans and ex-cops, all of whom were second amendment activists and libertarians. They shared a common belief in racial equality, individual liberties and civil responsibility, in addition to a disdain for the tyrannical leanings of the federal government. Most members were of African descent, with a slow growing number of Asian and White members trickling into the ranks.

Meanwhile, well-established White militia were preparing, Black and Brown militia were growing, the average White American was confused by the rhetoric, and the average Black or Brown American was not. The official government response to the growing national unrest was that it was all a part of a grand Russian plot to undermine American Democracy and to portray the racial divide in America as being worse than it actually was. The United States government ridiculously suggested that an international conspiracy might be behind the death of Officer Tony Orlando Perez. One FBI press release stated that, "The untimely death of Tony Orlando Perez may have been a counter intelligence tactic engineered and carried out by the Russian government in order to spark civil unrest and maybe even a revolution."

Donald Billings, Chairman of the NAABP publicly responded this way:

"The official response from the FBI to our cries for help and transparency rises to a level of federal disrespect that I have not seen in my lifetime. Instead of addressing the issues head on, the FBI is seeking to distract the nation with the childish maneuvers of a street side card trickster. I would like to remind the director of the FBI that before his office and his position was created, the Black and Brown citizens of the United States of America were being murdered by law enforcement, or killed with their tacit approval. Before the Russian government ever existed this kind of suspicious killing had been happening to us. The statements put out by your office insults the intelligence of millions. No foreign government can trick Black people about our racial division. We do not need the Russian government or anyone else to tell us what we have always known. When you float your conspiracy that a Russian grand plot to undermine American Democracy by portraying the racial divide in America as worse than it actually is, you imply that it is better.

Your statement suggests to the world that you know who we are, and you do not. The fact is, the American race problem has always been worse than those in your office have wanted the rest of the world to know. The Russian government has no idea how bad it actually is for the average Black and Brown person, but for you to try and manipulate us into accepting your representation of what has happened and what is happening to us… that is arrogant on a grand level. It's a childish mind trick, and we resent it." His internet posting circulated the Black media like the wind. The mainstream news picked it up and his words were soon an international household conversation piece used to open the next question that now stroked the curiosity of the public. "What happened to the officers?" It turns out the police protection program devised a strategy that was followed to the tee.

Whenever two or more officers were involved in a killing, to secure the safety of both officers, at no time should they be together. The theory behind the strategic policy was divide and you stand but together you may fall. Point being, it was harder to abduct both cops if they were never in the same place at the same time and, if one was attacked that would alert the other.

On the crystal cold evening of January 16th, that strategy failed. Both officers were struck at the same time. The morning hour was barely in place and the men were missing. Police reported that the protection officers on duty were found unconscious, apparently subdued by an unfamiliar airborne sedative. Traces of the weaponized tranquillizer have been collected and are being examined by the proper labs and agencies.

"We are taking a closer look at the evidence we have. This is a different type of attack," said the overworked spokeswoman. She looked tired, as if a good night's sleep was an uncommon occurrence in her life. But the press corps was relentless.

"If the police officers cannot be safe with your best efforts, what should the public do? Can we feel safe?" Before she responded another question pushed in, "Wait a minute… if you are saying the two men were abducted from two separate places at the same time that means there has to be more than one person involved." The room of scoop-seeking reporters was buzzing with suggestive questions swirling around that logical assumption. In between the moment of constant queries, a foreign accent yelled from the rear of the crowd. "Given the level of dissatisfaction with the investigation, do you now think the BBS has something to do with the abductions?"

"I…well, we don't know," she admitted, dropping her head in defeat. Her tired eyes said a lot but the strain in her voice said even more. The law enforcement agencies were baffled by these latest abductions. And the fear imposed by so many fellow law enforcement officers openly opposing the government's position was a major strike to morale and reminiscent of the bickering that took place before the Confederate artillery fired on the Union garrison at Fort Sumter and started the American civil war. That was one hundred and fifty-six years ago. For many American history enthusiasts, this felt like the residue of a fight long passed over an issue never resolved. Another question rang from the rear, "If this is a team or an organization do you believe they are home grown?"

She quickly responded, "I don't know."

"How did they know where to find these two officers? Earlier you said they were in secret locations in different parts of the country. How could one person or a small group be in two places at the same time? What you say, it just doesn't make sense. What happened here took precision. This was a coordinated attack with the help or direction of someone on the inside. Why not just say that? The American people deserve to know what we are dealing with. The members of the so-called BBS have all the capability to do this kind of thing. Are they under investigation?"

"Not at this time," she reluctantly answered.

"But this sounds like the work of an entity with the counter intelligence capabilities of a rival government," barked a pale beefy reporter standing in the front row. "Would it be fair to assume you're considering that?"

"We are considering all options at this time," she said.

"Wait a minute." The squeaky voice of the Right Wing Journal reentered the banter and he could barely contain his contempt. "It seems you people are always making excuses for them. If this were some White group of officers the whole world would be screaming right now, and you would be calling them what they are- a hate group. But in the era of political correctness you can't allow yourself to say that about an insurrection of government trained Blacks and Mexicans. When I just asked about the BBS being under investigation you said they were not."

"No I didn't. And, the Hispanic representation in the BBS aren't all from Mexico," she snapped. He stopped sharply, interrupting himself he cut his eyes down and quickly glanced at his pad of scribbles and uttered, "Now you're defending them." Then he read from the pad. "Your exact words were, 'Not at this time.' That is not consistent with your last answer." She was annoyed by the way he spoke to her, but she answered.

"My answer to your question is not just consistent," she tersely responded. "It is a fact. For your information, a consideration and an investigation are not the same thing. In the case of your question, we may be considering the launch of an investigation, but an investigation has not been launched."

He tried to ask a follow up question, but she didn't respond and abruptly concluded, "Thank you for your questions everyone," and she walked away from the microphone.

Don't Back Down, Stand Your Ground

The same day in another city a different voice took the mic. "White people of White America, you built this country. Some people want you to feel bad about that, don't bend to it. Stand proud of your forefathers and mothers. They died for this, so that you may have more than they did living under the crushing heels of the European monarchs. When Whites came to this land it was nothing and we made something out of it. We built it into the greatest something the world has ever seen. Our ancestors conquered this continent. When they came it was savage and baron, they made it bloom with industry, with art, with technology. These people who stand on the paved streets that we built, eat the food that we provide, drive the cars that we make; they live and raise their families within the secure borders we protect and defend. These people blame us for their shortcomings. They want to make us feel guilty about their condition. And they make fun of us because we love God. You know who they are, the ones pushing us to accept their perverted lifestyles and lazy ways.

They are the progressive liberal elite and their big bucks have control of the congressional leadership. Now they are using our federal government against us. Our founding fathers saw this day coming. The day when our government grew so powerful that it could ignore the basic wishes of the individual. They saw it. That's why the first five things they amended to the constitution were restrictions on government's power. The first amendment to the constitution prohibits Congress from making any law respecting an establishment of religion, hindering the free exercise of religion, abridging the freedom of speech, infringing on the freedom of the press, interfering with the right to peaceably assemble or prohibiting the petitioning for a governmental redress of grievances. And the second amendment to the constitution protects the right to keep and bear arms. They wanted to keep a president or a federal power from having authoritarian control over the people.

Local government, the people of the community, would be responsible for governing themselves and they would send a few of their own to state congress and to Washington, DC to represent their interests. That does not happen today. Today when we send a person to office, after a few months of wining and dining with big lobbies and big business, they change. Our representatives will represent the interests of their masters not us. The founders were smart, and they saw this day coming, so they vested the responsibility of each state to protect and defend its citizens. That's why they, the Washington elite, want to strip us of our guns. They want to deny us our God given right to defend ourselves. These people ignore the second amendment and want to disarm us while they take up arms against everything that made us great. I say to everyone in White America, it is time to fight back. Don't back down, stand your ground."

13 CHAPTER
A What?

"He was the smartest pup in the litter, well trained and very friendly. After a few years the agency retired him from bomb sniffing service and he worked a full year in Tanzania at Saint Matthew Hospital, using his talented nose to detect cancer and tuberculosis. His olfactory senses are so acute that he is astonishingly able to notice the most subtle changes in human chemistry. When he senses fear, he lays on his back and scratches his belly. For some time now the international body of research scientists have been able to show that the brain of every animal produces a distinct odor when it calculates something suspicious. My friend Sherlock is able to detect that distinct odor the human brain exudes when it calculates a deception.

When he smells a lie he puts his head down and paws at his nose; like a child with allergies. Whenever he detects danger, he backs into me wagging his tail and points his flaring nostrils in the direction of the threat. He's brilliant Tatyana, just what we need. Look at how Gerald takes to him. They are great together, and Sherlock is super clean, almost obsessed actually. The whole time I was in Tanzania I didn't once see him make a mess. Because he was about to retire, the organization paired us in the hopes that we would develop a bond and at the end of my training I would home him with my family. We developed more than a bond Tatyana, we are friends."

"It's... a rat."

"Well, technically he's not a rat. In the true sense he's categorized somewhere between a hamster and a rat. He even stores food in his cheek pouches like hamsters do, it's kind of cool when you see it." Marcus smiled approvingly, but she didn't react that way; she wasn't impressed.

Shaking her head she spoke in a low tone and kept her eyes pinned to the massive thing lying on the lap of her son, like a small dog.

"Marcus," she said slowly, "When you told me you were building a relationship with the company and studying the way their animals learn and work, I thought it was a great idea. I still think it is a great idea. That they are based in Africa and have a global impact is amazing. The work they do, the lives they save… how intelligent the animals are… the whole bit, I love it. I…I just didn't think--- you would bring one home with you. APOPO is a great organization Marcus, I'm with you on that. Can't we just go to apopo.org and send money like normal supporters do?"

APOPO is a Dutch acronym for Anti-Persoonsmijnen Ontmijnende Product Ontwikkeling. The English translation for that means, Anti-Personnel Landmines Removal Product Development. It is a Belgian non-governmental organization that trains Giant Gambian Pouched Rats to detect landmines and some medical conditions. APOPO had a noble mission to develop rat detection technology to provide solutions for global problems and inspire positive social change. But Tatyana had a problem with rats, no matter how noble.

"JESUS!" She didn't mean to shout but what she saw caught her in a crazy way that was hard to bring down, but she managed. "Marcus," she said quickly, cringing with every syllable. "Gerald just licked him." She tried to stay calm and for the most part she was successful but Gerald just licked the face of a rat, who was in every way larger than the neighbor's shorthaired Chihuahua and when the rat responded by doing the same, it was all any mother could bare.

"No licking!" she shouted. Everything about her wanted to grab Gerald and pull him away from what she saw as "the vermin" but she didn't. "No kissing Honey, remember what mommy said about animals. People don't kiss other animals Gerald… the animals don't like it." Even as she spoke, Sherlock contradicted her. He didn't seem to mind being kissed and happy little Gerald saw no signs of disapproval. While all of this was going on, Marcus was blathering on about something she was too preoccupied to hear, so she simply responded to the last thing she remembered.

"So, let me take what you just said and work it out in my mind. You are saying if a bomb were planted near us, some dangerous situation fell upon us, or God forbid one of us was stricken with a life threatening medical condition smart enough to evade modern screening and all of our high tech detection equipment, your good friend Sherlock will catch it."

"You sound like you don't believe me. He's not any old ghetto rat Tatyana. Sherlock is a private-trained Giant Gambian Pouch Rat. I don't understand why you are so pessimistic about him; he's even great for home protection. Once an intruder gets a look at Sherlock he'll run away wetting his pants," he said with a look of boyish pride on his face. But she responded cynically,

"Because he's a ten pound rat you mean?"

"He's got better credentials than any service dog in the country," Marcus quickly responded. "Come on Tatyana, let's be fair now. If I brought home a Russian service animal as well trained as Sherlock you wouldn't have a problem."

"But he's not a dog Marcus. He's a gigantic rat…and where I'm from we kill rats not pet them."

"I can't believe the woman I love just said that. You are exposing yourself as a rat bigot.

And look at them, look at how your son plays with the one your bigotry would deny."

"Oh shut up Marcus."

"OK, but seriously Tatyana, he's protective of our son, smart, clean and a great family companion; just what Gerald needed." She was skeptical. "Again you are saying it's what Gerald needs," she repeated. "That's what you said when you returned from Japan with that Rhinoceros Beetle. Gerald wants whatever you bring him Marcus. He's just like you." Marcus laughed at the flattering comparison.

"It's not funny Marcus. Obviously you have passed you're genetic abnormality onto my son. I am not in a good space with this right now." Marcus didn't respond. Folding his lips between his teeth, he fought off the nudging urge to comment about the bad-smell look she wore on her face. She continued, "You make me sound like a squeamish woman and I'm not squeamish. I just don't think it's necessary to raise a rat in our home. Can't someone else do it?"

"But he chose me," Marcus said softly. "And look at all the positive things he will bring to our lives Tatyana."

"Marcus, no matter what you say, at the end of the day, he's still a rat…with a great resume. Why can't we just have a normal pet, like a dog?"

"Tatyana you see what he is, but you do not see who he is."

She answered, "I see exactly who he is, my vision is very clear. You're the one who sees nobility, friendship and – and whatever the hell else it is you see. I see him for who and what he is… a big rat." Marcus knew she trusted his judgment but he delighted in the way Tatyana expressed her descent. She reminded him so much of his mother sometimes it was funny. Sherlock wasn't the only one in the room with strong instincts. Tatyana had a nose for negative vibes. If she felt Sherlock brought bad energy, she would have taken Gerald right away and Sherlock would go back to APOPO. What she felt was the opposite. Sherlock was a positive presence and she sensed it. What tickled Marcus was her struggle to admit it. Watching the anti-prejudice woman he knew struggle with her prejudice made him laugh. Even as she went on at Marcus, her brown eyes darted back to Gerald who was crawling on the floor imitating the stance and mannerisms of his new playmate.

"Oh God, now he's a rat," she said looking to the ceiling as if she was searching for heaven. Shaking her head she thought, "Why God? Should I expect bats too?" Without another thought she reached for her foot. Valenki slippers were a household comfort most Russian women would rarely relinquish. But instinctively, Tatyana took off one and threw it with precision between Gerald and Sherlock, who were nose to nose in a staring contest.

"Stop it," she huffed. "No nose touching either."

"Tatyana," Marcus responded, "Look at them. That is not a pet playing with his master. Sherlock is not a pet, he is a good friend. He will take good care of us and we will take good care of him. If you give him a chance, I think you'll see that he can be a trusted member of our family."

"Two things in life I will never trust Marcus: the first is a politician, the second is a rat," she said with a small grin.

Marcus responded, "Your bigotry is showing."

"OK, let me say this…if your friend ever licks my son on the face again I will kill you both."

Marcus cut his eyes to Gerald rolling around with Sherlock and the corners of his lips curled into a massive smile. "It's too late for that," he said.

Tatyana glanced over at the two new buddies, gave a very loud sigh and flashed an eternal look of disapproval.

Prosecute Them For What?

Two days from that one, on a very pleasant evening in the Madison home, a few trusted friends were having a frank discussion when the doorbell rang.

"Come in Tiffany, the others are in the back room." Walking through the pleasant atmosphere of the Madison home was as welcoming as any words could convey, and it was especially warming to Tiffany. "We know how you like Caribbean food. We have that and there are plenty of other things to choose from if you like. The plates are right there on the top and the utensils are all in this section."

"Wow, looking at this spread it's hard to forget you two own a restaurant. Sorry I'm late Marcus."

"No worries, it's not a business meeting; just a family discussion." By the time Tiffany entered the room the subject of a civil war was blooming in its infancy.

"It looks like the people are really fired up over the latest police killing," Tatyana said. "The boy was in his grandmother's yard for God's sake. They shot him in the back, he was running away, he had no gun and they still refuse to prosecute."

"Prosecute them for what?" Leonard responded. "Even if the prosecution were capable of being honest, it is almost impossible to show wrong doing because the law is so subjective. The law was written to be pro police, so the standard of proof is impossible to meet. The prosecution has to prove that an officer didn't feel his life was threatened. And except for the videos and community witnesses it has to rely on evidence collected by the police, investigated by the police, and hope that a good cop is willing to risk career, friends even his life to share the truth with a prosecutor who more than likely is already biased in favor of the police."

Tiffany barely sat down before she commented. "In my opinion, a good cop is like the Loch Ness Monster. Adults who believe in that are crazy. It's long past the time for us to stop letting the police police the police. The people who honestly believe the pseudo-facts that support those laws are severely misinformed. Remember the people who make the laws have no reason to change those laws. Law enforcement are on the front lines protecting the haves from the have nots. They are the fence that keeps you out. Whenever you threaten to breach it they are authorized to use deadly force. They just need to say the right thing that is 'In the split second fog of the moment I felt my life was in danger.' Say those magic words and you go home, relax, start a new life if you need to, all with the help of the tax paid relocation program."

"Not anymore," Leonard said. "There is someone listening, holding the police accountable."

"Yes," said Tiffany, "But no one knows who it is. I'd like to give him or her a hug. I completely understand why the vigilante needs to stay anonymous. But in times like this it would be beautiful if we saw a person. It would be an inspirational figure of hope." Kondo followed every word in the conversation, drank oodong tea from a cup that looked more like a small ceramic bowl, but he said nothing. Tiffany was the only one in the small group not privy to the secret identity of Marcus. It was better that way. The only people who knew the identity of the vigilante were the three people who played a role in his development. The best way to keep a secret is to keep it to yourself, they reasoned. In this case, it was decided that ignorance was a safe space Tiffany could go to if she were ever interrogated. Not knowing the vigilante was in her company she said, "There's a strong chance it might be more than one person." Her demeanor was more animated and her hopes were more stimulated than before. She didn't want to speak with food in her mouth, but the fear of losing the thought before she finished chewing forced her decision and she spit a slice of half eaten eggplant back onto her plate. The golden brown pieces of batter stuck to her teeth when she spoke, but that didn't slow her words. "The last two cops were taken at the same time from different places," she said. "I think the Black police groups finally took action. They did it, or they know who did it. It's a beautiful thought. It also puts the world on notice." Kondo looked at Tatyana who quickly glanced back, but they didn't say anything. Changing the subject Marcus said, "I understand that Malcom Ben Carter is out of the hospital and moving around now."

"I heard him on the radio just this morning," said Leonard. "He said the fear of death made him stronger. Now his lawyers are asking the UN investigators to step in."

"The US Department of Justice refuses to pay for a UN investigation. The government spokesman said Carter has access to the finest investigators in the world at US taxpayers' expense. And then he asked the radio host a rhetorical question: why would Mr. Carter want the American taxpayer to pay foreign investigators when America is offering him the best in the world for free?"

Marcus interrupted, "Oh my God… Malcom Ben Carter didn't let him get away with that did he?"

"No, he didn't. I'm pulling up the podcast now because his response was classic Ben Carter and I can't articulate it the way he did. Oh, here it is… listen." Leonard placed his phone on the large coffee table in front of them and close to Kondo who sat on the floor. The unedited recording of the live program started with all the polite greetings and respectful accolades of the normal progressive liberal talking format. Leonard forwarded the recording to the point of interest and the scene of the action. They sat, fidgeting, like four children in a short line waiting for ice cream. And then the voices came through. First a scaly, very measured male voice was speaking rapidly. When Leonard started the recording the man was in the middle of a sentence. "… and the person or persons responsible need to be caught and they should go to jail for attempted murder. As a government employee, I want this person to go to jail as much as Mr. Carter does. What I find incredibly difficult to comprehend is this: Why would Mr. Carter, obviously an intelligent man, want the American taxpayer to pay foreign investigators when America is offering him the best investigators in the world for free?" There was a short pause in the conversation. The show host responded.

"Well, he is sitting directly across from you. Why don't you ask Mr. Carter directly?"

"OK," said the spokesman, with all the strident vibrato of a trial lawyer. "Mr. Carter," he said, "Will you please speak into the mic and tell the American taxpayers why you want them to pay for a team of foreigners to investigate what happened to you? You are an American. You were poisoned in Sweden. The Swedish government launched an investigation. Why is it not appropriate for the USA to investigate what happened to one of its citizens?" There was another pause, a long silence. It was an uneasy mood that filled the room, but not one word exchanged. Dead space was never a good thing for radio, so the show host filled it with a question… "Mr. Ben Carter," he asked.

"Yes," he answered. "Would you care to respond to his questions?"

"No."

"I understand Mr. Ben Carter. Is there something you want to speak about?"

"Yes, may I?"

"Of course, the mic is open and the time is yours."

"Thank you," he said. "It was a chess move." Marcus recognized it instantly, and Kondo was uncharacteristically animated by the smooth way Malcom Ben Carter controlled the clock…and the discussion. Silence is a battle technique and this man just used it masterfully. He didn't bother to dignify the questions with a response, which defused the questions and belittled the questioner. In addition, it demonstrated that Ben Carter knew how broadcast programing like radio worked. For them time is money. People who tuned in and heard nothing, moved on to another station where they heard something. Broadcast executives hated that because a few seconds of advertisement may not be heard and that's what paid the bills. When a show was depending on dialogue or debate, the listener was expecting to hear people talking. Tactically, the person who controlled the microphone had more time to convey their ideas to the listener… and the host just gave the mic and the rest of his time to Malcom Ben Carter.

"Many months ago I was poisoned," he said with no strain or flare in his voice. "I was fortunate to have first responders available who knew what to do… and with the guidance of our God they used their talents to stop the spread of that poison and stabilize me. They then transferred my fading body to a well-trained team of physicians whose combined talents have me sitting here and speaking with you today.

Many of you have questions and in due time you will have answers. For now, let me assure you that we have interviewed and chosen a reliable team of investigators we can trust. I have every confidence that they will uncover what happened. It is only a matter of time.

What I want to do now is turn your attention to a more pressing matter. That is the injustice of this justice system. We must change it today, there is only one time to change it… and that time is now. Don't accept the view of those who ask for your patience, no people have ever been more patient than you. The waiting game, the stalling tactics that denies us liberty and provides a happy life for others, is over. Our fundamental right to life, liberty and the pursuit of happiness is not consistent with the way this government and her police agents kill and incarcerate us. In fact, the prison system is a money making mining operation that works in concert with law enforcement and the US congress to extract the poor and mostly Black and Brown people from the streets of America, and work them at a slave's wage. The private-public relationship is guaranteed a court ordered workforce and a hefty government payout. It is better than slavery ever was, because it shifts the moral dynamic to the side of the oppressor. No one wants to be seen as soft on criminals. The truth is, they are the most disadvantaged population in the country. The deal is this, those who make laws will pass laws specifically designed to trick and trap Black and Brown people. Let me give you an example: one of the most important jobs for a congressman is what I call net making. Nearly the whole first year of a freshmen's congressional study is devoted to net weaving. That is, learning how to weave a legal net wide enough to catch Black and Brown fish and let the others slip through." The interesting metaphor seemed to catch Tiffany off guard. She nodded and smiled. His voice thickened, his pace, quickened and his words grew even more profound. He went on.

"In those days every slave had a brand or a number; an identifiable recognizable mark. They were stamped and categorized as inventory, now how is that different today? It doesn't matter what your infraction is alleged to be, you still receive a brand and a number; a felon, an offender, a criminal, not a man. Gloat all we want about the strides we have made, but we are not so different today. As for the gentleman here who speaks for the government, he made a repetitive assertion that our government, the bastion of capitalism is offering me something for free. I am old enough to remember that in government and business if the product is free, the ultimate product is me." Malcom Ben Carter knew the impact of every syllable he uttered. Some people would hear his words as a call to arms. Others would hear them as motivation to dig deeper and create new and innovative ways to provoke change non-violently. But he spoke from the perspective of a Black man who survived more than seventy years in America. His near death experience showed him that the current approach to changing America's behavior was designed to fail. It would only provide enough hope to quell the hopeful and disrupt the potential rise of violent unrest.

That was the pattern; slow, arduous steps in the direction of change. Picking up one very small piece of achievement at a time, and by the time any real change of that small piece could be seen, the people who deserved it were dead, scattered, paid off or lost track of the issue. He had time to reflect and re-run the many years he spent in this country.

He realized that people often bragged about how Americans can do anything. "If that is true," he thought, "Then this kind of change is not supposed to succeed. It is the carrot that hangs just out of the horse's reach; but I am the horse," he concluded, "And my struggle for peaceful change is a fool's errand." It was a deep reasoning that hadn't occurred to him before. At that moment he got it…and his eyes were opened. He resolved that the people who run America will lose America if it changes in a way that would satisfy Black and Brown people. More than a country, America is a big company and the president is the CEO. The president, will not ask… and the congress will not agree to push an agenda that would put itself out of business. Therefore he reasoned, "Petitioning the American government to change is a road of hope and dreams that lead to nowhere." The thoughts rushed by in an instant. He took a sip from the bottled water one of the assistant producers handed him, then he asked, "How am I doing on time?"

"Six seconds sir."

"Well, in six seconds, let me say, I know that it is much easier to fool the public, than to convince the public it has been fooled. I used to believe that working within the system was the best way to change it. Today I am telling you, I was wrong. Thanks for having me on your show… and thank you out there for tuning in and taking the time to hear what I had to say."

Closing the show, the host only had enough time to quickly thank both men for coming. Then he praised the companies who sponsored his show, without whom he said, the podcast would not be possible. It was over, and the cozy room at the Madison home was silent. For a moment they looked at each other wondering what to say. The glow of the scented candles no longer matched the mood in the room.

"He is right," Tiffany said.

"Yes, I think all he said is correct," Kondo added.

Leonard was about to enter a comment when he was struck in a way that left him speechless. He clinched his chest, his arm was numb and he couldn't move. Being closest to her old friend, Tiffany asked, "Leonard, what is it…what's wrong?" But he couldn't speak. His right hand still clinching his chest, he pointed to the table of food in the adjacent room. Leonard was her closest friend and she knew his family had a history of heart disease, but he seemed to be choking. His behavior was alarming to everyone and all eyes flashed over to the buffet table stocked with an assortment of very hot food. Tiffany panicked when she saw the tail… and then the strong natured Tiffany Doyle, the naturalist who didn't mind piddling with bugs, linked arms with Leonard and the two of them leaped onto the couch screaming like damsels in distress. The sudden screaming shocked Kondo to his feet, but he didn't know why until he saw Sherlock. His eyes scrolled to a wide open setting and stayed there for a long moment. It was his only reaction before he guided himself back to the comfortable place in his mind, and his seat on the floor. And then Marcus spoke.

"It's OK everyone. This is my friend Sherlock," he explained. "Sherlock is a Giant Gambian Pouch Rat I met in Tanzania, he's our friend," he said. With a bit of admonishment in his voice he shouted, "Sherlock, away from the table. Tatyana doesn't like you near the food. Come." And he did come, better than the most obedient dog. Marcus barely tapped twice on his thigh and the giant rodent rushed across the room, jumped over the ornately carved coffee table and landed most of his massive body softly in the lap of Marcus. His tail however, brushed the full plate of rice and baiganee Tatyana was eating. Needless to say, she was not happy. But she did maintain her composure when she stood, lifted her beautiful plate of food, walked the few steps to the waist bin and dumped all of it, including the plate and silver. When she returned to her seat she noticed her space beside Marcus was occupied with most of Sherlock's playfully moving tail. Gracefully, Tatyana didn't use a word. She looked at Marcus attentively petting his new friend, but Marcus didn't sense the look, then she slid her eyes over to Sherlock. Sherlock noticed everything she did. He stopped moving and followed her eyes. She stared at him for only a second, and then she moved her attention to the coffee table and the steak knife on Leonard's plate. When she looked back to her seat the tail was gone, and so was Sherlock. To herself she whispered, "Smart rat."

"Where did it go Marcus?" Leonard asked, he was still afraid, he was still on the couch, still tangled up with Tiffany.

"I think he heard something in the other room," Marcus innocently assumed. "It was probably Gerald moving in his sleep. It could be anything, but he hears everything."

"That is the biggest rat I have ever seen in my life," Tiffany said. "What in your world convinced you to get a rat for a pet? Who trained it like that? Does he patrol the property like a German shepherd?" She spoke with a nervous laughter that loosened her fears and she stepped one foot from the couch to the floor.

"Actually, he does patrol the property," Marcus replied. "But we didn't train him to do it, he does that on his own, and he's not a pet, he's just Sherlock. He's a part of our family now. Speaking of family, Leonard, why are you jumping up on the furniture? Can you please come down?" Leonard had a visceral fear of rodents. His knees shook, his whole body constricted into a crouch that contradicted his stoic personality.

"What do you mean why am I jumping on the furniture? It's what normal people do when they see a big ass rat in the room Marcus." Craning his neck to see around the room he cautiously stepped down, "Is it coming back?" he asked.

"Probably not. Sherlock is pretty nocturnal. He tends to move in the garden at night, patrolling the house and grounds you might say. He'll come if we call him of course."

"Well there's no need for that," Tiffany said. But another vantage point existed in the room. From his coveted place on the floor, Kondo found the words of Malcom Ben Carter and the talents of Sherlock to be foretelling.

"This African Rat, with pouch in cheeks, is very intelligent animal," he said in his typical tone that rarely exceeded a whisper. "Him have very strong nose and instincts. I think it is very good idea. Also every enemy who may come, maybe no one expect rat as your detection, or rat for your protection." When he spoke he caressed the bottom of his bowl shaped cup in his left hand and slowly swirled his right index finger around the smooth surface of the rim. He didn't hesitate with his words. Every broken English phrase came from his mouth as a complete and polished idea, as if he said it many times before. "I think maybe any person suddenly see giant rat first time will be scared, they run away, they make a noise, or they make mistake; all are good things for you."

"Kondo you say this," Tiffany said. "But you didn't look afraid of Sherlock."

"I like rats," he said, "But when I first saw him, I saw something suddenly moving, something not there before. I was surprised and I was scared. So suddenly he come. I think many people who do not know him and see him for the first time will be scared. As for me, I am Japanese.

In Japan, name of rat is Nezumi, usually we just call him, 'Ne.'

We have totally different relationship with rats than you do. You tend to see everything about him as bad, except when he is white. White rat you see differently. But this country is very strange about things like that. In Japan, the rat is good animal to us. Not in the west, but in Africa and Asia many people hope to have the character of rat. He is polite, smart, reliable, determined, with strong body and ability to do anything. Rat is strong thinker, he thinks before he acts and is honest with his actions. For me, when I see Sherlock I think it is good for Gerald... and very good luck for the family."

14 CHAPTER
Beyond Good And Evil

"Our core is solid, and our new few are strong. Building as we have, the BBS will have a well-armed militia in twenty-three states very soon. Believe it or not the strongest resistance we are getting is from the left wing liberals and the so-called Black leadership. Personally, I have no confidence in the antiquated approach they continue to promote. They say we are wrong to arm ourselves. They say we are violent but we have harmed no one. The other side keeps killing us and these false prophets continue to speak as if their non-violent approach is making progress. They are weak hypocrites and ideologues who hope that the world will feel our pain and stop America from killing us. These progressive liberals who believe they have a monopoly on morality are the most arrogant people on the planet. Life is only right if they say so and speech is only free if they approve it. They have anointed themselves the "thought police". Now, they are asking our young people to take hits without hitting and fight a war without killing. These people are the worse kind of sheep, and the moment a major hardship befalls them, they will scatter and we will be on our own." He was tall, bald and not yet middle aged. His skin was deep dark like the Dinka of South Sudan and his carefully trimmed beard had spatterings of white, making him look older than his thirty eight years. The semi-automatic weapon that usually hung on his shoulder was always loaded and he was always ready to use it. "I fought for this country," he said. "I fought to preserve the constitution of this country. We have a second amendment right to be armed and stay armed. And I will fight those foreign and domestic who try to step on my pursuit of life, liberty, or happiness."

His was the face the rebellion needed to have. Tall, tough and talkative.

He was a recruiting machine. Black militia membership jumped four-fold the first week his social media campaign went live. The government slapped a warning on each site, but it was too late. The word was out. His slogan was simple: Black and Brown lives matter, all lives do, you don't f**k with us and we won't f**k with you.

On the day America commemorated Martin Luther King, a park in Washington DC filled with fed up millennials heard a powerful voice broadcast media refused to air. He had no official place on the platform. He was not scheduled to appear or speak but more than a thousand hands had cell phones and nearly all of them recorded him that day.

"Since the beginning of time, all of humanity and animal nature has been divided into two broad types of living things," he said. "Animals that are naturally herd animals and animals that are loners. Some animals are predators and some animals are prey. We all know this but the thought police want to suppress our saying it. Some people are naturally fearful, they need the security of others to feel safe or comfortable. They are herd people. And some people are born daredevils; they go it alone and avoid large groups. They are loners. You know them. They are the ones we see on the survival shows. They take off from civilization and move to Alaska and live off the land." He smiled and the overstuffed Meridian Hill Park of people laughed and nodded their heads.

He continued, "The philosopher Nietzsche refers to us as sheep personalities and wolf personalities. Or crudely put, slave type and master type. Whether you are a sheep, mouse or turtledove it doesn't matter because you can't change it. You can't make yourself a wolf, hawk or lioness. That is not your nature. Yes, you can act that way, you can fake it, but you won't make it, because it is not who you are. The master types admire risk-taking, strength, boldness; they are independent, resourceful and need a constant challenge. They make poor servants and slaves because their nature is not to follow, but to rebel against the confines of social pressure and conformity. They explore life, instead of fearing death. For example, Nat Turner was a wolf, but he was hiding in a sheep skin." The park full of people irrupted in applause. The park police harassed the event organizer to seize the microphone and remove him from the stage, but that didn't happen. The ears of the crowd swallowed every word he uttered.

He continued to speak. "The slave types love conformity, the systematic approach, fundamental fairness and judicial decrees. They feel safer with close neighbors surrounding them and crave the attention of others like themselves. It is natural for them to stick together, they are herd animals.

This does not mean the wolf is better than the sheep or the master is smarter than the slave.

This I believe, is where we get tripped up. The system today tries to make us act the same and we are not. Failure to acknowledge that fact divides us. It is at the root of our conflict. We can change that. Respect the sheep as a sheep. Respect the wolf as a wolf. If you are a person who likes to be chained up and spanked, go for it, but don't try and do it to me- I don't like it. It's not my thing." Again, the crowd laughed and applauded; virtually every face carried a smile.

Rhetorically he asked, "Now, how do we relate this reality to who we are socially and morally?

If you have a sheep personality, a crucial part of your morality is fundamentally different than the wolf or hawk personality. You will most likely enjoy a safe and peaceful place to graze close to others like you. That would work. What you will not like are wolves or anything you perceive as predatory near your neighborhood; in fact, aggressive people and behavior will make you uncomfortable. You don't like to fight physically, you think it's barbaric. You prefer peaceful protest, economic sanctions, and social isolation to resolve conflict because you believe they are the most effective ways to sustain harmony. In your mind, guns make more problems than they solve. A civilized nation should ban them or at least heavily regulate them so that the average citizen wouldn't have easy access to them. You believe that a strong liberal arts education is the best way to lift people from poverty and kill their desire to do bad things. You are sure that hiring good security, well trained cops is the best way to secure the safety of a free people. To you, individuals relying on self-defense is chaotic because the public has no assurance that the individual will do the right thing. In your mind, a well-meaning citizen may make a mistake and kill an innocent, hurt themselves or in many ways, make the matter worse.

You think we should leave our security to the professionals. Therefore, it is best to hire well trained guards and police and they will protect the public from those dangerous, predatory wolves. It may not be perfect, but it is better than every man for himself. These are valuable positions that dominate our social conscience today. Holding such beliefs is not a bad thing, it's just a real thing. If the personality I just described fits you, raise your hand." He spoke to the crowd as if they only came to hear him, and it seemed that way. There were other acts who had performed on stage before he commandeered the microphone, most of them stayed and stood around the covered stage listening intently. Some of them raised their hands. In the park, half of the people had a hand up but he wasn't satisfied with that. He spoke again,

"Come on now, you know who you are, be proud of it." More hands went up, first one by one and then two and so on… until the number of palms in the air completely dominated the crowd. "See, see how many you are?" he urged them on. "There is strength in numbers. Now, here's the hard one. Are you ready, you wolves and hawks?" His voice dropped a notch. "Show us who you are. I know you're cautious." He pointed to the crowd and his down home approach commanded the attention of everyone out there.

He seemed to speak to each person directly. "Let us understand their dilemma. In today's society wolves are shunned, so they usually cloak themselves in sheep skin. Once they are exposed most sheep will be uncomfortable and the wolves will be isolated, ostracized. So let's see how many hands will go up. By the way," he chuckled, "I have no doubt some of you lied and said you were sheep." The crowd applauded. They looked around pointing fingers at each other in fun and fellowship. It was a joyous evening and the tightly packed gathering of twenty through thirty year olds were thoroughly enjoying the honest interaction. He paused to let the sound of laughter and conversation die down. Then he said, "If you are a wolf… raise your paw." Simultaneously he reached his long arms to the sky, adding a grin of white teeth that lit up the night over the park.

"Do you find yourself surrounded by weak people making policies designed to outlaw your hopes and devalue your strengths?" They were fewer than the previous crowd, but they were much, much louder. They didn't politely raise their hands. These people brashly pumped their fists and cheered like the crowd at a football game. "You don't want a neighbor so close they can smell your meal when you make it," he shouted. "You don't want your neighbor or government snooping, not that you are doing anything wrong, you just won't tolerate an encroachment on your freedoms. You don't trust the government, but you will fight for your government to protect your rights, and, you will fight against your government to protect your rights." When he said that there was a thunderous roar that shook the air around them, and it only got louder. "You don't run from aggression, you are not scared of the police. Yes, you can be aggressive if you have to be and you refuse to apologize for that. Death doesn't frighten you, BECAUSE-YOU- ARE –NOT –A –SLAVE!" The thundering grew, people started pushing and moving in an uneasy way. The wolves were less than a third of the people in the park, but the majority group shifted and grouped themselves into a mass. He added to their discomfort by saying, "As for my gun…I call him The Game Changer." And he reached to his waistband, pulled his revolver from his trousers and pumped it towards the sky. The wolves were loudly cheering but the sheep were silent with concern. His wasn't any old hand gun, it was the Russian made RSH-12, a huge fifty caliber revolver with a five shot cylinder and twenty rounds in reserve. This was a hand gun so powerful it rendered US military issued body armor useless. It was at a time when many gun control activists were rallying against those who carried assault style rifles in favor of hand guns and shot guns. He wanted to make a point. He didn't bother to carry his rifle, but his revolver used the same caliber round as an assault rifle. It was the kind of gun those in the gun industry called a handcannon with one hit kill capacity. It was a 12.7x55mm revolver developed by the Russians for their special forces to destroy anything it hit with one shot. He was waving one of the most powerful production handguns in the world. The massive weapon fit in his hand like a cell phone and he bought it from a company on the internet; a fact he spoke about with pride. The park police didn't like what he was saying. They didn't like the way he galvanized the crowd. But one officer sensed a change in the mood of many onlookers. He could feel a growing discontent with the semi-violent way he expressed himself.

Those who saw themselves as sheepish were demonstrating signs of discomfort. The patient park police officer waited for a lull in the audience. He found it and his strident voice called from the left side of the crowd. "Why would you need a gun that pierces police body armor?" People turned to see who asked the question. The question was clear. Those on the left side heard it best. Others in the back and far right didn't hear it at all; but they knew something was said. On the stage holding the microphone, he heard it. To him it was little more than a heckle. He didn't mock the question and he didn't berate the uniformed questioner. He carefully placed his revolver back in his waist belt, placed that hand high in the air and carefully pointed the head of the microphone in the direction of the officer. Please use this so that the people in the back can hear your question." Maintaining that posture he moved in the direction of the officer now near the stage. "Here you are sir, ask your question." Seizing the moment, the young officer confidently looked at the mic and spoke into it. "My question is: why would you need a gun that pierces police body armor?" The exchange took no longer than a few seconds, but it seemed like the crowd was quiet forever. He looked into the grey eyes of the officer and brought the mic back to his own mouth, and without hesitation he answered, "In case my enemy is wearing one." Dropping his smile and the hand he held in the sky he asked the young park policeman, "Are you my enemy?" The officer responded, "No, I am not your enemy." He replied, "Then we have no problem you and me."

It was at that point the park reached a level of unity no one would have expected. Sheep and wolves alike cheered his cool demeanor. He walked back to the center of the stage and took a deep breath. "Let me finish by leaving you with these thoughts," he said. "My gun is not for aggression… it is for protection. Our struggle against oppression needs both sheep and wolves from every gender and culture. We are not evil people, but we are different from our parents. We are peaceful and practical, but we are not non-violent. You will not beat me without a fight and you will not take my life without the fear of losing your own. This is all we are saying. BLACK AND BROWN LIVES MATTER, ALL LIVES DO, IF YOU DON'T F**K WITH US, WE WON'T F**K WITH YOU. My name is Thurman Hawk and thank you for hearing me."

15 CHAPTER
Burdensome Stone

Spring fell faster that year. The summer heat hit an all-time high every day for two weeks, and the first morning in June brought a welcomed rain that opened a smile on the face of every flower and vegetable in the Madison family garden. Before noon the sky was clear, the ground was dry and the small boy ran throughout the garden pathways, carefully pausing from time to time, not to venture long steps ahead of his best friend. His parents were inside. He could see them, both of them, holding a cup of tea, watching his movements and talking about something that made them smile. A tall wooden privacy fence surrounded the rear end of the Madison home. On the side of the house, protecting the only exterior way to access the garden, were a pair of French intricately carved 17th century wrought iron gates. The gates were an expensive piece of trivia his father purchased in New Orleans and installed one year before Marcus was born.

Those iron gates locked the path that fed the walkway around the garden. But on that day, two strange White men appeared at the gates. They saw the boy playing in the garden and they shook the locks and called out to him, "Little boy! Hello! Little Boy, is mommy or daddy home?" His parents couldn't see or hear the men from where they sat. But Marcus saw Gerald abruptly turn and run towards the gate. He was fast. Before Tatyana and Marcus made it off the porch he was touching the gate. One of the men had already crouched down so that Gerald's face was barely above his own.

He extended a hand through the gate in a friendly gesture and suddenly, without warning, there came a loud thrash against the ornate iron patterns in the gate. There was a screeching hiss and claws that sank into the flesh of the man like talons from a bird of prey. He screamed out in pain as the weighted grip of the ten pound rat, ripping and tearing, continued to pry meat from his bones. The yellowish pigment of the rat's heavy teeth was red with blood, his long tail was reaching for the other man, but the other man wasn't there anymore. The sight of so much blood and his partner's arm nearly severed by a giant rat disoriented him. He panicked, dropped the wad of documents he held and ran back to his car. Arriving to the site and huffing with anxiety, Marcus yelled his name. "SHERLOCK!" It was as if Marcus flipped an off switch. Immediately the rat leaped from the bone he was digging into and positioned himself between Gerald and the bloody gate. Gerald was confused and he was scared. "I'm sorry mother."

"It's ok my darling. You did nothing wrong." Tatyana was busy consoling her sobbing son, but her eyes never left the bleeding intruder. Sherlock sat at the feet of Tatyana and Gerald. He peered into the face of the still screaming man and his long smooth tail wrapped loosely around himself like a lasso on the ground. Having assessed the situation Marcus started to open the gate in an attempt to look at the man's wound and to ascertain his purpose for being there. But when the gate lock was removed all the bleeding man could imagine was the gigantic rodent rushing through the open gate. Before Marcus could open the gate completely, the man snatched back his tattered arm, ran to his car and they sped away up the road.

Marcus turned back to his family. He walked towards Tatyana who was clutching Gerald in her breast. "He is so young and this was obviously a traumatizing situation," Marcus thought. In his mind he tried to piece together how it happened. Every time he did he couldn't find fault with Sherlock, he was protecting Gerald. He knew Tatyana didn't like the big rat, she barely tolerated him. "What if she wants to throw him

out because of this?" he thought.
Standing in front of them, Marcus put his hand on her face. Gerald was quiet, he had sobbed himself to sleep. He reached his arms around them both and kissed her forehead, and then her nose, landing softly on her lips.
"You OK?" he asked.
"Yeah, I'm OK."
"I don't know what to say Tatyana. I mean Sherlock was just defending. I had no idea he would react that way but at the same time, I can't say he was wrong either. When he first came I asked you to give him a chance. You have done that. I hope you can extend that chance to this situation." She held onto Gerald, gently laid her head on the chest of Marcus and returned the kiss.
Marcus added, "Looking at the paperwork they left behind, the two men may have been harmless. I'm not sure but I think they were with the Jehovah people. I'll ask around tomorrow, find out who they were and see what we can do to help with his arm at least."
"They looked like police to me," she said. "Jehovah people aren't in the habit of sticking their limbs through an iron fence. Also, they won't visit a home and not have a bible in their hand."
"Good point," he answered.
"And Sherlock sensed something more than two annoying Christians," she added. "I remember you said whenever he detected danger he backed into you, wagging his tail and pointing his nose to the air. After you called him off the man, he did exactly that. While you were opening the gate, he backed into me, tapped my leg with his tail and sniffed the air until they were long gone."
"Really?" he asked instinctively, "I didn't see that."
"Yes," she responded. "Let's find out who they were, but our Sherlock is pretty sure they weren't Jehovah People." That was a change. Something had drastically shifted. This was not some incidental slip of the tongue. She meant what she said and it was at that moment he knew Tatyana accepted

Sherlock into their family fold as an important part of their lives.
Tatyana was happy in her life with Marcus and sometimes she couldn't help staring at him. She didn't mean to do it, it just happened… and this was one of those times.
He saw her looking, "What?" he asked curiously.
"Just you Marcus. Leonard is right, you are a lot like your mother."
"I'm glad you think so," he answered. Then his attention turned to the ball of fur on the ground by his feet. "Sherlock, what are you doing? Come on now, dude I almost tripped over you. Besides, we had enough excitement for today."
Sherlock hadn't moved. He sat panning the area with his nose, sniffing for anything or anyone new. When Marcus called his name, Sherlock stood on his back legs and stretched his big front paws to the sky. Then he rubbed the hairs of his head against his loose blue denim pants, in that cuddle me way that cats often do. Instinctively, Marcus reached down and stroked Sherlock's hairy head until his eyes rolled back in pleasure and his bald tail rhythmically tapped the ground.
"I thought you would hold all of this against him."
"He's fine Marcus. He got to the gate before we did."
"Yeah, he did."
"Did you know he could move that fast?"
"I had no idea he could move like that," he answered.
"When I see him walk he looks clumsy" she said, "but he moved differently just then. Is it normal for rats to leap like that? I've seen him jump around with Gerald, but what he just did was amazing, he sort of – pounced, like a leopard."
"I don't know how he did what he did Tatyana but he covered a lot of ground in a hurry." She looked down at the rat she never wanted to like and she didn't mind smiling.
"You know Marcus, I thought he would be like a burdensome stone hanging around our family's neck. I was wrong about him. Sherlock showed me something we spoke about when you were in the hospital a few years ago. Love is

not something you say to those you feel good about. Love is what you do to protect them."

The Judge

Days later Leonard brought news from the BRO.

The two people who came to your gate were intelligence officers. We don't know exactly what they wanted but we think they were interested in Tatyana. They're moving around the country interviewing Russian nationals who live in America. They are supposed to follow established legal protocols to obtain an interview. Complaints are flooding the ACLU and other government watchdogs because several government agencies have not been following the protocols of law. Harassments have been happening all over the country. We feel certain that's what it was. As for the agent who accidently scratched his arm on your gate, after a full ten hours of surgery he will maintain about eighty percent of the function in that arm. When he returns to service I doubt he will be using the other arm to lure little boys from their gardens, but you never know for sure, he's a federal agent. There is an emerging matter of importance you both need to be aware of.

The judge in the Tony Orlando Perez case is a good man under a lot of pressure. Today at 11:26 am, the jury finished deliberating. Last week, in open court without the jury present the judge called the prosecution incompetent and accused them of trying to throw the case. He has made it clear to the public that he plans to launch an inquiry into the government's actions in this case. Many legal experts critical of the government applauded the veracity of this judge. The people on the inside say this man has a background and a demeanor very similar to Tony Perez. How he ended up with this case is mind blowing to those judicial watchers who keep track of this kind of thing. It is especially odd because the chief justice is the one who assigns cases and she is a well-known supporter of the blue shield. She would never give a case like this to him.

"So what happened? Some kind of mix up miss-assignment at the clerk's office or something?"

"No one seems to know Tatyana. We do know that now he's getting very credible death threats. We know it is not the first time the judge has been harassed or threatened, but it's getting worse. Two days ago he was jogging through the park with his wife and dog. A sniper's bullet cut through the branches and killed the brown lab with a perfect shot to the forehead, no doubt intending to send a strong message. That was on a Sunday. The next day the judge was on the bench as if it never happened. He is stubborn, smart and brutally honest, definitely not a team player. He was never a part of that judicial group devoted to the support and defense of the blue shield."

"This is good to know Leonard, how does it affect us?"

"We need your help. We know the blue shield is going to kill him, but we don't know when and we don't know how to stop them."

"No thanks," Marcus quickly answered. "We don't do personal protection Leonard. You know that."

Tatyana added, "Doesn't the BRO have a group of professionals devoted to protecting those who protect the rights of others?"

"Yes, and no. We will track everything we can but we can't protect them all. Sometimes we lose people. It is the most frustrating thing anyone can imagine. The BRO will extend our intel, but we are reluctant to expose our people to protect this judge. You see, some years ago one of our people was exposed as a whistle blower. The government charged him with treason and this was the presiding judge. We tried everything we knew to expose the government tricks and maneuvers in that case. We couldn't risk exposing ourselves, so we tried every personal channel available to get honest information to him. We had boxes of information the government was withholding, but he avoided all of it. If it didn't follow the legal bureaucratic process he didn't hear it.

A good person was about to go to jail for life and he was

more concerned about the damn process. Ultimately, he didn't hear us and the government got its way. Many of us in the BRO find it hard to forgive that. We were not offering him a bribe or anything. We only asked him to review a small file, but he wouldn't even look at it. We were asking him to bend a little, show a human heart but he didn't have one. The only thing beating in his chest were the rules of law. He believed in the law, not the people. To him if the legal system was broken we should keep tweaking it until we get it right. He absolutely believes that the law is the only thing keeping humanity from killing itself."

"He sounds like one of those sheep Thurman Hawk talks about," Tatyana said.

"Oh yeah. He's the ultimate sheep."

"So why do we want to get involved here?" Marcus asked. "Why not just let nature run its course?"

"I can't just let him be killed without trying to do something Marcus… and the BRO is clear, it will not commit any more resources to his security." Leonard's concern was obvious to Tatyana and Marcus, next came the question.

"Leonard you seem a bit overly invested in this situation. Why is his security so important to you?" As he asked the question Marcus tried to remember the man Lena was married to before her gender change to Leonard. He vaguely recalled a beard, but he couldn't place it on a face of any consequence. Marcus was about to ask another question but Tatyana beat him to it.

"Is this someone close to you Leonard?"

"Yes," he said.

"Someone close to your heart?" Tatyana used a different smile this time. This was the…yes, of course you have my full support smile. Leonard answered.

"Yes Tatyana, very close to my heart. Always."

Marcus injected, "Why didn't you just say that at the beginning. Of course I'm in. I didn't know your ex-husband was a judge. I was trying to remember his face and I couldn't. I guess I was too young… and he wasn't around me as much as you were." Leonard adjusted the crumples in his shirt and sat roughly on an overstuffed chair. He squinted a little when he spoke,

"My ex-husband was rarely around you Marcus. You were too rambunctious for his over disciplined mind set. In addition to that your mother didn't like him, neither did your father. My ex-husband was a lot of things, but he was never a judge. It's my ex-brother I'm concerned about."

Marcus coughed a giggle of surprise and a look to match. "You have a brother! Why didn't I know that Leonard? I'm your Godson. You never told me you had a brother." Tatyana chuckled at the display.

Marcus repeated, "I'm your Godson." Turning the perspective lightheartedly, Leonard replied.

"Yes Marcus, I'm your Godfather and you never cared enough to inquire, not one time." Cold with disbelief Marcus stood staring at Leonard.

"Judas Priest Leonard!"

"No, it's not that bad is it?" Leonard said with a smile. "Now would you feel a bit more informed and less betrayed if I told you he was my twin?"

"What!"

"Yep. And I'm two minutes older than he is, so that means, he's my baby brother." Marcus plopped his large body in the stuffed chair with Leonard, squishing his Godfather over into the soft leather of the armchair until the smaller man could barely breathe.

"So, I guess we'll work it out between us three ha Tatyana?"

"Yes my Marcus. Including Kondo we are four."

"There we have it," Marcus said teasingly, "The partially miss-informed league of Just-Us." Tatyana couldn't help laughing at the playful way Marcus and Leonard interacted. Nearly smothering the man Marcus asked, "Any other siblings we should know about Godfather?"

"No, just us," he wheezed.

Predation

It was more than a week from that day and again he didn't move. After calculating the possibilities around him the probabilities were clear. To be mindful is to be clear, aware. Not only to see, but to observe. "If we rely too much on the eye we can lose sight of a thing," he thought. He could see down the barrel of his high powered instrument, the target was clear. The wind was light, elevation was perfect, the shot was good and it was time to take it. The target was stationary, unaware and apparently without concern for his safety. The target had fallen asleep in his patio chair reclining by the pool at his home; not a worry in the world. "After more than a hundred thousand practice rounds and over a hundred targets, I'm here clipping old fat men in their sleep," he thought. "This was no challenge shot. I had more fun shooting Palestinian goat herders running along the border fence in Gaza. At least they were moving."

He had taken well over a hundred targets before and he would take this one. It was an easy shot, and it was time to take it. He sat on the stable arm of a big oak tree a little more than two hundred meters away and settled into a relaxed state. His finger gently caressed the arc of the trigger, then he inhaled one final thought… and it was over. The brutal impact rocked his body and he fell from the tree like a piece of rotten fruit. His rifle slammed against a sharp protruding root, dislodging the scope, contorting the stock and bending the barrel, but it was still hot, still smoking. His vision was fuzzy from the fall, he tried to stand but the new crack in his leg wouldn't allow that to happen so quickly. He was still a bit dazed, but he was alive. Gathering his thoughts, he rolled on his back and scanned the trees to find the source of his predicament. Camouflage is the art of not being seen, and Marcus was almost impossible to detect in falling light. After the first strike that severed the sniper from his weapon and slammed his broken body to the ground, Marcus remained motionless like the mamba, observing the hired gunman. Abruptly, it was a bird, a squirrel or a person, he wasn't sure but something moved. In one fluid motion the man drew a pistol from his waist belt and fired five times in two seconds. With the unpredictable gunfire Marcus flinched, and the sharp eyes of the sniper tracked that motion. Without a blink, he locked a deadly aim on Marcus but he couldn't see the outline of a man. He couldn't identify the object. "I don't know who or what the hell you are," he whispered. "Let's find out right now. But before his finger moved she fell from the tree above him, landed her knee to his throat and cut off his hand with a high temperature cautery weapon. She was completely silent and faster than anything he could have expected. "He won't be killing anyone with that hand anymore," she whispered. "Like the man said, be unpredictable like electron. No rules, no style, no habits, now no hand." Piece off the board.

16 CHAPTER
A Source Of Philosophical Inspiration

The judge didn't die that day, but every new day brought a fresh opportunity for that to change. The Tony Perez case was over. Despite the government foot dragging the officers were convicted of two counts of murder and the judge was not at all lenient with his sentencing. In addition to that, the judge kept his promise to pursue an inquiry into prosecutorial misconduct, evidence tampering and federal government interference in a criminal trial. The FBI extended many offers to secure his safety, but he declined them all. It was almost easier to watch Gerald than to keep Leonard's brother safe. Adding to the task, his security had to take place without his knowledge. If he knew who they were he would report them to law enforcement. Even if they only broke the law to save his life he would turn them in to the authorities. Leonard's baby brother was an ideologue committed to the dream of US legalism, which in his mind could only be attained through strict adherence to the rule of law. He was a fat man who went to sleep with his mouth open, smoked tobacco from a pipe and had the most disgusting eating habits.

The weeks that passed landed them at another Friday evening meal in the Madison home. Tiffany was there, Kondo was there, and any important conversation was halted because Leonard was instigating an amusing discussion between Gerald and Marcus.

"But they are so delicious uncle. Did you make all of them by yourself?"

"No Gerald, I didn't make them at all. I just went to the

Friskie Fries shop and bought them. The people at the shop cooked them. Then they put them in the white boxes and I brought them here for us to share."

"Who made the first french fries?"

"I don't know the answer to that Gerald."

"Did you have these when you were a boy?"

"This store didn't exist when I was your age Gerald, so I didn't have these, I had other fries." Everyone smiled at the way Leonard answered that question because Leonard was never a boy. He skillfully deflected the attention to Marcus. "But I did bring fries to your father when he was a boy."

"Really father?"

"Yup," Marcus answered, crunching with a pattern of two fries at a time.

"Does everyone eat french fries on Friday Mother?"

"No Gerald, it wasn't my tradition Honey. I had them, but not so many times as now."

"You didn't eat them so much?"

"No, I didn't."

"It's not healthy?"

"No, Gerald they are not a healthy food choice, but it is OK to have them sometimes."

"Yes, like French Friday," he said enthusiastically. As long as we don't have too many right?" "That's right Gerald," she answered.

His cheeks were puffed with the crispy fried potatoes, but it didn't stop the questions.

"So we are French people every Friday?"

"Absolutely not," she sternly responded, and all indications of humor fell from her face.

"Well, Andre eats fries," he said curiously. "His mother is French. Andre said so many good things started with French people." Sensing the moment to tease Marcus, Leonard said,

"Didn't you spend a lot of time in France Marcus?"

Marcus started to speak but an overarching smile had his lips. He couldn't find anything age appropriate to say about the memorable time he spent in France as an exchange student.

He could feel the gaze of Tatyana burning the skin of his ear and from the back of his mind the words came.

"Well, Gerald," he struggled. Little Gerald sat holding a fry meant for his mouth. His attention wouldn't consent to chewing until he heard the next words.

"There are good things about all people Gerald and there are very good things about the French people also." Tatyana smiled and only raised an eyebrow.

"So, did God make the french fries father?" Gerald's questions were all over the place. Tiffany thought it was the cutest thing she had ever heard and Kondo was so inspired he actually commented.

"This boy has very strong mind," he uttered.

Grabbing his son by the waist Marcus lifted the laughing boy to the sky and gently landed him back on his lap.

"Did- God -make the french fries- father," his small voice repeated, quivering with chuckles.

"Yes Gerald, God makes everything," he said.

"Even french fries?"

"Yes, even french fries."

It wasn't long before the evening hour and fried potatoes sapped the energy from Gerald and he was asleep. That's when a deeper conversation took place.

"So, tell me," Tatyana asked. "What is an ex-brother Leonard?"

But Marcus injected, "Sounds to me like a brother who wouldn't accept you for who you are and decided to disassociate himself from his only sibling."

"That's about right," Leonard answered.

"I love my brother in a way that's hard to explain. Even if he's angry, and wrong, and sometimes stupid, and usually unyielding, I can't stop loving him. We are connected by genome. It's like not loving a part of yourself. I feel him, you know? I hope that make sense. It's hard to articulate."

"You just articulated it pretty well," Tatyana replied.

"Sometimes twins have this funny kind of dual existence thing going on," Leonard added.

"My brother believes that the system is not broken; it's the people who are broken. The system should be preserved at all cost. In the BRO we call that kind of person a System Saver," Leonard said.

"But it's the people who make the legal system," Tatyana commented. "How can a process created by and for the people be more important than the people themselves? What is the point?"

And Tiffany answered, "He belongs to a school of US philosophy called American legalism. People like him believe that humans are fundamentally selfish, and therefore bad. They feel that the average person wouldn't sacrifice their best interest for another unless they were forced to.

The principles of legalism say, if it is in one's best interest to kill another person, when the best opportunity appears, that person will be killed. They believe it is the nature of people to behave that way. To prevent our natural instinct towards chaos the enlightened minority will create a system of laws to guide people's selfish nature toward the best interest of the state."

Tatyana thought a moment and said, "It just assumes all people by nature are immoral."

"Almost like that," Tiffany responded, "But morals have nothing to do with it. I'll explain it this way, the mind of the legalist is not concerned with the predilections of any citizen, unless or until they interfere with the will of the state. If a person likes to kill small children, the legalist finds the killing of state children punishable, but that action might be useful against an adversary. It's different from a moral because behavior follows the law not vice versa. As applied, a person with a predilection to kill children would be useful in a special military unit, to terrorize the enemy or even discourage rebellion. The person is happy with their fetish, and the state benefits by having a dedicated soldier, it's a win-win situation. So on one hand, killing a child intentionally or accidentally is considered murder or manslaughter. On the other hand, killing a child intentionally or accidentally is justifiable or collateral damage. By contrast, some of us would expect a moral definition to say killing any child is wrong, but that's not our world." Tatyana squinted in disgust before she commented,

"So except for themselves, people are innately selfish and ignorant and the best way to control that is with written law. Is that it?"

"Yes," said Tiffany. "And strong penalties will deter people from breaking them," she added. "What kind of person finds this kind of value to be valuable?" Tatyana asked.

Marcus couldn't miss the intense look Tatyana was wearing. He put his hands on her waist, pulled her into his body and squeezed until her beautiful teeth lit up her face. Rubbing her nose with his own he whispered, "You OK Tatyana? You look like you just ate some bad Borsch." It was a reference to her favorite beet and meat soup topped with sour cream - a Russian food she rarely found in America, and the few times she did find it, the taste was a horrible example of the real thing. It was a Marcus attempt to make her smile, he was thoughtful that way. She smiled, licked her thumbs and brush them over his eyebrows. Tiffany was there. She was watching. She was close, and could feel the under-anguish stirring in Tatyana. But more than that, she could feel the draw she felt for Marcus pulling at her in ways that she was finding harder and harder to restrain. She felt wrong about the things she thought, the way she felt, but she couldn't help feeling it. Typically, she stayed away from him and cut visits to the Madison home and business to a rarity. But his was the kind of soul that boiled the blood and Tiffany was secretly addicted to any space he occupied. The affection between Tatyana and Marcus pushed something possessive in Tiffany, so the principles of legalism were a helpful distraction. Tiffany spoke slowly.

"Also," she said. "Leonard's brother is the last symbol of hope to many people in the Black community." Nodding her head to signal she understood, Tatyana uttered, "Sometimes God works through the strangest people."

From his seat on the floor those words drew a deep comment from Kondo.

"But some strange people are not wrong," he said. "Maybe the road is different, sometimes even direction is different, but looking for the same thing they are."

"What thing is that?" Leonard asked. He was encouraged by Kondo's perspective. Leonard spoke with a faster pace than before.

"What do you think Kondo?"

"I think you talk. You go to him, you talk."

"I can't do that Kondo. If I speak to him about anything substantive I will be risking the lives of other people. He is very insightful."

"Hmm, see right through you I suppose? But, as you say twins can feel each other more than most. Maybe now he needs the other part of himself that you have. Maybe now he's looking, asking, you are hearing but not listening. Seeing his actions, but not observing his feelings in a way only a twin can do. I think maybe this can be so. How do you think?"

The proud, logical mind of Leonard broke into little bits of liquid emotion and ran down his face.

"I don't know where to begin," Leonard said softly. "The last time we spoke he utterly rejected me. I just don't know where to pick up from there Kondo." He didn't trouble himself to look at Leonard. His gaze stayed with the steam from the tea in his cup but when he spoke, his words cut through the haze of confusion Leonard harbored for too many years.

"Leonard, what happened then is finished. You should remember that now is now and it will always be so."

Leonard held out his hands to gesture his confusion. "I don't understand Kondo."

"I mean nothing is ever the same," Kondo explained. "The tea I drink today will taste different tomorrow. In life everything keeps moving, changing. When we come to accept that, we can appreciate today for what it is. We can love tomorrow for the opportunities we may see, but we will know that yesterday is finished. Your brother may be angry with you still, maybe not. Either way you cannot say, you cannot control. You must say to yourself, am I angry? If so, why so? All anger will stop if you let it."

Leonard thought a moment, and then he repeated, "All anger will stop if I let it, hmmm. Interesting."

"Still yourself for a moment Leonard, close your eyes. Trust yourself, don't fight your emotions. Allow yourself to just roam around in the space between your thoughts." Leonard sat quietly, his ears were like baskets catching every word. Kondo continued, "Now breathe… slow… deep… when your lungs are full, let the weight of the air fall away from your nose." Kondo was speaking to Leonard but everyone was listening and following. "Move away from the center of your thoughts. The most dominate thing on your mind may not be the most important thing for that space, for that time, let it go. Now tell me, when you remove the anger and the fear, what do you see?"

Stripped of the barriers he created to protect his fragile feelings, Leonard emotionally responded.

"I want a relationship with my brother Kondo. I just don't know how to begin, or where to start."

"I can see that," Kondo replied. "Maybe he feel the same."

"You think so?"

"Yes, good chance I think."

"My fear is so strong. He hurt me deeply."

"I see that, but no pain will last forever. Fear can remind us of the pain. Pain can remind us of the fear and the perception of both can keep us going around and around forever if we let it."

The moment seemed so personal, the room so familial. Leonard had opened an uncharted part of himself and Tatyana weighed in with a constructive comment.

"I think you should talk to him Leonard," she said. "I'm sure we can find a creative way to reach out to him and not expose ourselves. If we are careful, what do we have to lose?"

Marcus added, "Like Muddy Waters. You can't spend what you ain't got, you can't lose what you ain't never had."

Leonard was confused, he didn't know who Muddy Waters was. "What muddy water? What are you talking about Marcus?" His Godson could always make him smile and this was another one of those times. Marcus repeated a little louder and slower. In a lighthearted voice he said, "Muddy Waters, the great blues theologian! Leonard, you are not going to tell me that my parents trusted you to be my Godfather and you don't know who Muddy Waters is."

Leonard was smiling now. He knew Marcus was conjuring up something funny to say but he just didn't know what.

"I know you grew up in posh America Leonard, but I am astounded that you don't know who Muddy Waters is. Don't worry, I'm here for you. I am a good and loyal Godson. I will help you plug that gaping cultural hole in your upbringing."

Coming to the aid of Leonard, Tatyana happily interrupted, "Marcus darling," she said with a major smile on her face, "Are we going to pretend that you grew up in 'Da Hood?" Her dig stopped Marcus midsentence, and the incredulous look on his face filled the room with laughter. The mood in the room was a lot thinner than before and after a few minutes Leonard turned to Kondo again with a question.

"Kondo, what you said makes sense to me. Where do you suggest I start?"

"You start at the beginning," he answered.

"OK, where is that?"

"It is now. The beginning is always now."

"So I start at the beginning of now?"

"Exactly," he answered.

The Gorilla's War

Hate groups and revenge organizations were popping up like bubbles in a glass of champagne.

Tuesday, the sheriff of Sans County Virginia said the public's negative attitudes towards law enforcement officers had created an atmosphere where Gorillas can roam the country killing police officers at will. "It's what any reasonable thinking person should expect when people demonize the very law enforcement officers that protect them," he said. "Without warning, one of these so called Gorillas walked up to the window of a family restaurant and killed three on-duty deputies who were sitting quietly and having a meal. Then the gunman calmly sat on the sidewalk and shot himself in the head. It was a brazen attack on our democracy, our peaceful way of life," he added. "The only thing these officers were guilty of was working to protect us. They just wanted to have a quiet meal and go back to work."

Later in the evening the Governor of Virginia released an official statement. "The killer was a wicked man and he was a coward. Any person who hurts a law enforcement officer is truly evil," he wrote. "We will not tolerate violence in our state, especially against the police." Other than that he said nothing about the killer. Few media outlets spoke about the man, except to reiterate their declaration that he was a monster. But why? Because government officials believed that an open, even discussion about the man or his group was a recruiting tool for that group. They were growing, and he was one of them. The group was actually a movement called the Kamikaze Gorilla Network, usually referred to as the Kamikaze Gorillas or Gorillas. The Gorillas were a growing phenomenon in America. Unlike the suicide attacks commonly seen in Europe and the Middle East, this group modeled their methods after the Japanese Special Attack Units who initiated suicide attacks against superior forces in World War II. Their tradition of death instead of capture, death instead of shame, death instead of defeat was traced from Japan back through China and India, to its origin in Africa. They did not fear death, rather they welcomed it as a means to an end of the long life in servitude and suffering for Black people. They asserted that the police are the enforcement arm of a totalitarian order. The message found at every attack was this: We members of the Kamikaze Gorillas Network will gladly sacrifice our lives to strike the oppressive hands of the blue shield until they let our people go. A Dark Web message from a person representing themselves to be authorized to speak for the Kamikaze Gorilla Network wrote this: Suicide Is Painless. We find that the US Government hypocrisy has no boundaries. One of the most racist sheriffs in the grand old commonwealth of Virginia had the audacity to say that his officers had simply sat down to eat and the killer just walked to the front of the restaurant and shot them without provocation or warning.

Now, if a Martian were passing through Virginia on his way back to Mars and he had no prior knowledge of that sheriff's department or Virginia's history with Black and Brown people, that Martian might mistake his three deputies to be three saints. Around the country, law enforcement officers choke Black people in the street, shoot Brown men in the back, raid our homes, kill our children all without warning. And because they have not taken any of our members alive to parade an image through their farcical justice system, they call us cowards. The most powerful government in modern history is reduced to name calling. We will not submit to your brand of justice. You have determined the course of life and death for too many Black people for too long. We agree with Malcom Ben Carter: 'When I am free to choose the time of my death, my life has more meaning.' We agree with Patrick Henry: 'Give me liberty or give me death!' So to you in law enforcement, our message is simple, this is what it feels like to be profiled, targeted and killed. Whenever we see a blue shield we will kill the one wearing it.

Truly yours.

17 CHAPTER
At The End Of All Things There Is Always A Reason.

Business was booming at the Black Diamond and the beautiful old building that housed the Madison family restaurant received a glowing report of inspection from the city council inspection committee of historic landmarks. Thanks to the restorations and upgrades paid for by the R.O.B film company who more than a year before, staged an elaborate action scene that blew out the front window and shut down the block with nearly a hundred official looking actors, extras and stunt people. The R.O.B was a front company owned and operated by the BRO. The primary purpose of the company was to produce real looking readiness drills sophisticated enough to fool even the most experienced members. To the rest of the world it was just another independent film maker, but to the BRO it was an indispensable readiness tool for testing and refining the response of the members. Their last covert production at the Black Diamond staged a shooting death of Marcus that Tatyana will never forget.

America Was Changing.

The BRO was stronger than ever and America was changing in ways few people could predict. New bodies of young rebellious Americans determined to rid the country of racism and judicial terrorism were rising all over the country. Some, like the Kamikaze Gorilla Network, were committed to a long and violent fight to annihilate the blue shield. Others like the People Patrolling The Police, were committed to a non-violent approach dedicated to exposing police wrongdoing by posting, tracking and tabulating it for the world to see. The motto of one was 'We are watching you.' The motto of the other was 'We see a blue shield, we kill the person wearing it.' Both were anonymous, both were effective, the choices were expanding and the people were choosing. The country was bright with individuals and organizations competing for a growing space in the minds of the American public; some seeking to oppose the rise of rebellion, others plotting to enhance it. One side said right is right and wrong is wrong. The other side said wrong is right and right is wrong, but the question remains 'Who is right and who is wrong?' In the past, this was the kind of thing that gave birth to civil war… polarity.

The Impact Of Marcus

The tragedy of Gerald and Lisa Madison was a common occurrence in the United States, but the ensuing actions taken by their son sparked a revolution that changed the course of America forever. The fact that the oppressed American had been suppressed for so long was a testament to the physical brutality, psychological abuse and the tactical acuity of a society who dangled the American dream metaphor like a twenty-four carat reality. But the growing winds of discontent proved the old cliché to be true; no lie can live forever. The impact that one young college student had on a country will always strike the faithful as prophetic. To them, his anonymity made him a mystical figure. His rise to action made him a hero, but it was his will to act against the power of the growing police state on the people's behalf that made him the majestic, angelic image in the mind of so many Black and Brown people in America and around the world. The undeniable truth of those who loved him and those who did not, was that the acts of Marcus Gerald Madison inspired a nation to dig deep into its history, open the hard issues of today and face itself in a serious fight for real justice, for real change. The prophecies of Isaiah promised a man like Marcus at a time like this; a guided man rising like the arm of God to strike down the great power. But it was Wonuku Mila, the African economist who wrote the Tendencies Of Timing. He stated that there was one thing the politician, the general, the musician, the historian and the theologian can unanimously agree on. That was this; 'Sometimes timing is everything.' One can never really know why all the right things come together at the right time to produce the promised effect, but the eponymous "Vigilante Effect" swept the country with change. There was always time to wait, but the time to act for change is now.

The Vigilante Effect, The Media, The Truth And The Internet Phenomenon

Finding the facts and discerning the truth was easier than before. New news and media outlets emerged to surpass and in many places replaced the traditional mainstream media outlets; many of whom had grown so comfortable with the status quo they couldn't credibly criticize it.

A record number of people were learning about the world of things they never knew existed on the internet. A credible body of international researchers agreed that only 4% of the internet was visible to the general public and 96% was made up of the Deep Web. Since governments had a hard time tracking everything on the Deep Web they tended to demonize it. There was a rich variety of credible information most people may find useful if they knew how to access it. The Vigilante Effect inspired a rebellious group of journalists, nonviolent educators and activists who launched a project called Free Your Mind. Their mission was to teach people of the world how to access and use the Deep Web and Dark Web for legal and peaceful purposes - to find government censored news reports, freely explore the arts, ways and research sites of other culturally diverse information and people.

"When governments track or control the communications of free people, we are not free," they wrote. "We don't trust people who are watching and tracking our legal actions in the name of national security and law enforcement." On their very user friendly website they taught the basics. Even a first time visitor would find easy-to-understand instructions on how to access the Deep Web. With short study, one would quickly learn the difference between the Clear Web they typically used with a basic search engine like Google and the other 96% of the Deep Web that Google couldn't search. The majority of the Deep Web did not have anything illegal on it. And then there's the sub-set of the Deep Web called the Dark Web that contained all sorts of websites, both legal and illegal. Free Your Mind was in direct opposition to the growth of American legalism. It was a change movement created by mostly millennials with a fundamental belief that when given an opportunity to do good, most people would. As a movement they said legalism was an affront to humanity. Tiffany Doyle was one of the founding members of the organization, she was also the oldest member. She was a lawyer, a journalist, a longtime member of the BRO and a trusted friend of the Madison family. Her award-winning book about the injustice in the US legal system won international acclaim and her fiery command of the facts made her a popular person to listen for in the media. "Some things behave like cancer in a free society," she once said. But when she made that statement she didn't know how personal those words would become.

Understanding Why

"When the genes of any animal change in a way so drastic it can no longer regulate the normal growth of cells, the cells can grow out of control," Tiffany Doyle explained in her last interview.

"And when those abnormal cells reproduce they form a mass, and doctors call that a tumor. A tumor can be harmless, or it can be an uncontrollable growth of dangerous cells clinicians refer to as cancer." Unfortunately for Tiffany she was diagnosed with late stages of the latter. The professionals called it breast cancer because the dangerous tumors were confined to the breast, but it didn't always stay that way. Over time, dangerous cells could spread from the breast tissue, make their way into the blood stream and invade the small organs and other parts of the body. Imagine a normal smooth surface invaded by an unstoppable bunch of growing grapes impeding the function of each infected organ and reproducing its self almost exponentially. That was the lasting image Tiffany had in her mind because it was the example the oncologist used to explain the aggressive way her cancer was behaving. Breast cancer was always caused by a genetic abnormality, but the specific cause of an abnormality in any individual was harder to know. Tiffany understood the science behind her ailment. What she never understood, was the "why."

Brothers

In the midst of a nation in transition Leonard and his brother Leon rekindled a relationship that never should have ended. They were two very different people produced by the same pregnancy; biological twins and ideological opposites. The years they mutually avoided contact stripped them of an opportunity to gauge just how different their lives had become. Physically they didn't look alike, but intellectually they were identical. Both very logical, both very methodical with an exceptional intellectual processing speed always associated with genius. In life, two very different people can work very hard to solve the same problem and be happy with a different result. Life was funny that way. These brothers rediscovered the things they had in common and resolved that their biological bond was stronger than their ideological differences. The brothers found that they could laugh at their differences, enjoy their similarities and love the life that God intended them to have. Not only did Leonard renew a relationship with his brother, he also developed a kinship with Kondo. Since the first day of his training, Leonard hadn't missed a session. He found the concepts of Flow to be helpful in his daily life. A principle of Flow was a primary component of reasoning when he first cleared a space in his mind for his brother. One day after a session, he sat for tea and a quiet conversation with his Godson. There he remembered a sentence, "All anger will stop if you let it." He never forgot how easy it was for Kondo to conjure those words. When he first heard the sentence he was embarrassed. "It was so easy to see, so simple to understand I felt stupid," he said. "I actually laughed at myself, why didn't I think of that? My brother and I share the same life circle. We are like one big magnet producing an equal force in the opposite direction.

We are different, we are free, we are alive… and I love him for that. This is the concept of Flow."

Friends Always Talk

"Leonard, Tiffany wanted to keep her medical condition private. And for the last few days it seems that every discussion begins with the same three-word question, "How's Tiffany doing?"

Today I was in the community arts center and it seemed like every other person asked me that question."

"Yeah I know. For such a private person, a lot of people seem to know she is sick. Just this morning I ran into a mutual friend who was very concerned about Tiffany. She was somewhat confused about the idea of survival rates." Marcus shook his head. He cringed at the possibility of someone approaching him that way. In a raised tone of voice he asked,

"What do you mean?"

"She was under the impression Tiffany had five years to live," Leonard said. "No that's not what it means. Survival rates are created to give you an indication of how long people with the same type and stage of cancer tend to live. I told her that when Tiffany speaks about a five-year survival rate she is not saying she only has five years to live. A five-year survival rate is the percentage of people who live at least five years after they were diagnosed with cancer. Now Tiffany is talking about stage four. That's not good I said, but it's not the end either. Only about twenty two out of a hundred people live at least five years after they were diagnosed with that stage of cancer, compared to a person with stage one, where ninety nine out of a hundred people are still alive five years after they were diagnosed. But you know Tiffany," I said. "She wants no one to feel sorry for her. Already she researched a ton of options and when I spoke to her that morning she was gearing up to push through a new treatment schedule, so I don't think we need to worry about her. I think our old friend felt a lot better about Tiffany after I told her that."

"Yeah, me too," Marcus said. Then he abruptly changed the subject to something more maternal.

"Leonard, Tatyana has something to say to you and Kondo while we are all here." Leonard looked curiously at her belly and then back to her face. He hoped she didn't notice that he noticed anything. But she stared right back at him, squinted her eyes to show, "I saw you Leonard." And he thought, "Damn. She noticed everything." Smiling in admiration he said, "In the eighteenth century, the Europeans would have burned you for those supernatural powers you have Tatyana." She smiled for a moment, and then that changed.

"You don't have to go back that far Leonard," she said. "There are some places in this country where you can still burn Black people and bewitchery is not a requirement. For any reason they deem legal, the people in charge of the military, and the police, and the courts can kill my son, or my husband, or me. The Black man and boy they found two days ago is evidence of that. Some depraved person mutilated that man and his child Leonard, and then they burned them. They were sending a message. It was a public execution, a lynching. It is the beginning of the Rosewood massacre all over again." Tears streamed down her face, and her lips tremored when she spoke. "I saw the images of the charred bodies and I felt the words of the Billy Holiday song my father used to play when I was a girl. I knew few English words, but those words came with an image still stuck in my head. She was singing about the strange fruit, hanging from a Poplar Tree. The words painted an image of dead Black people, hanging from trees. Their bodies were beaten, and burned, and left there for days to stink and rot like some kind of strange fruit. Leonard, it's a horrible picture to have in my mind."

"Tatyana, I am so sorry. Sometimes I kid too much. I didn't think about that horrible crime when I made the witch comment. I didn't mean…" The look on his face was one of great regret. She noticed his concern and addressed it.

"No Leonard, it's not anything you did. This has been

bothering me for years now. But this latest incident, maybe it touched a nerve." Her brown eyes, still hazy from holding the weight of her tears glance passed any place a persuasive word could comfort. Kondo slowly stood from his coveted place on the floor and gradually made his way to an empty space beside Tatyana. In a normal way he sat, and gently sank into the over plush leather of the overstuffed sofa, but he said nothing. She hesitated a bit before the words came. She knew what she wanted to say, but she didn't know how to phrase it. Then she sat up straight, shook the negative thoughts from her head and said to herself, "This is family." Marcus softly placed a comforting hand on her back. She lifted her eyes, took a deep breath and said, "I'm leaving."

18 CHAPTER
The Last Discussion

"The state of this world is so uncertain." Those were the first words from his mouth, but he didn't know why. He was stunned, and so was Kondo.

"OK, when you say you are leaving… leaving who?" Leonard looked at Marcus; he wanted to feel something from his Godson, but he couldn't. Marcus was quiet, and his attention was on Tatyana. It was a difficult time for her, she was protective, her hormones were raging, her body was changing and her Marcus could only watch. She instinctively stroked the space above her naval and Leonard's analytical eyes didn't miss a stroke. He had questions.

"I'm not clear Tatyana. What do you mean you are leaving? Leaving who?"

"We are leaving America Leonard."

"OK, now you say we," he said with a confused expression. "Leaving America!" he loudly repeated. "To go where? To live where? What about Gerald?" he ranted. "I totally disagree with that. Where would you go?" His fair brown skin was flushed with the hot blood his fast beating heart was pumping. "We need to think this through," he said. "Study the options, consider some alternatives." His eyes darted back and forth between Tatyana and Marcus like he was watching a tennis match. He lifted his index finger to emphasize an important thought he was going to state. He glanced at Marcus, looked one good time at Tatyana then he dropped his finger and stopped talking. "Her mind was made up," he thought.

"Leonard, Gerald is five years old. I worry about him in this country. We planned to stay until he was ten, but I can't…"

"But there are problems everywhere Tatyana," he said softly. His emotions were beginning to settle. He thought about Sherlock.

"Tatyana," he snapped his eyes open like a man with a revelation. "So have you thought about what to do with Sherlock? Did you think about that?" he asked.

"He comes with us Leonard. He's a member of our family. What did you think we were going to do, leave him here?" She was being extra careful not to snap at Leonard. His questions were straddling the lines of being offensive, but he was hurting. Marcus predicted it would be this way. Leonard was indeed struggling with the thought of his Godson and his family leaving the US and never coming back.

"Where will you go?" he asked.

"Home, Leonard."

"This is your home," he said without hesitation.

"Yes, it's one of them. Now we are going to the other one for a while," she replied calmly.

"Can't we talk about this Tatyana? Marcus, come on now. This is a big step."

"But we are talking," she answered.

"So, you're going to Russia?" Now his words came faster, and his patience was thinner than before. "What do you know about Russia?" he asked quickly.

"I am Russian Leonard, I grew up there. Did your fine mind forget that?"

"I was talking to Marcus Tatyana."

"Yes, well I'm talking to you Leonard!" she shouted. "You mistake yourself. You talk like we need your permission to leave the country."

"Well apparently that's not so," he snapped sarcastically. Tatyana was losing the ability to hold her anger and Leonard didn't seem to care. He changed the question.

"I asked about Gerald. What about his schooling? You want to experiment with raising him in a cold strange place? You may know it Tatyana but Marcus and Gerald know nothing. What will they do?" Again he was talking to Tatyana but he was looking at Marcus, who shifted his body to avoid eye contact. Marcus touched Tatyana gently on the thigh. She responded, "He'll be fine Leonard. The schools in my home land are quite good," she said proudly.

"He'll be different. The other kids will pick on him," he snapped.

"He's different here Leonard, kids do that everywhere."

"He doesn't speak the Russian," he said. But his words didn't have the same snap. It was like a beaten fighter flailing at the opponent before an obvious defeat. The breakdown was apparent now. Even his speech started to slow.

"He'll learn Leonard," she said in a lower, softer tone. His analytical mind deconstructed her words and the nuances in her earlier phrases. He latched on to every sentence, drew a circle around it in his mind. He was searching for a deeper meaning, maybe a hidden understanding, but there was nothing else. When his shoulders fell Tatyana could see the sadness surfacing, his brow, bending around the corner of his eyes.

Kondo saw it. But Marcus saw more without looking. He could feel the loving plea of unspoken words spilling from the soul of his Godfather. He couldn't look at him, not without breaking down in tears himself.

Kondo spoke to Leonard. "Leonard, when we see so many problems in a thing and we see no solutions, usually it is because we do not want to find real answer. There is so much happiness in this room now, but we feel sad, why is that?" he asked rhetorically. And then he added, "I remember one time you and me we speak about the three important things to good strong life and happiness. First is Simplicity; second is Patience; third thing is Compassion. We agree maybe Lao Tzu is correct with this thinking, do you remember?"

"Yes, I remember. You called it homework."

"Yes, it is what you take home from our session and work every day to make it a part of your life; it is home work.

To be simple in actions and thoughts because most things have a very simple beginning, solution is also simple. But often we want to bend wrong solution into correct one. It takes more time, more work, maybe never it fit. To be patient with friends and patient with enemies, you learn to see things as they are, because over time the truth will always show, if we wait and watch for it. Compassion, when you are compassionate and forgiving toward yourself you learn to respect that privilege of others.

Today, Marcus and Tatyana; they show love, compassion to me and to you. They understand your feelings, your pain about their leaving. Sometimes the questions you make, were maybe even disrespectful. But Marcus, he say nothing. Tatyana almost the same. Her conduct, I watching her, she work very hard to be patient, and Marcus, he still saying nothing. I think he understand. I think he recognize that the truth is simple. Every question you ask, every problem you raise, but you bring no solution. You are with BRO. If you want you can find answers to every question, even solution to each problem. But you created imaginary problems, because you do not want them to go. Now the next question is why? It is not because you want to see them unhappy here in America. That is not true because I know you love them. Do you fear something dangerous happening in Russia? That cannot be so because you know Tatyana has a big and well established family there, it is her home. For them, opportunities to live free and happy life are much better in Russia than here.

You even say education for Gerald may not be good, but do you believe that? No, you do not. You already know most important component to a child's good education is the parents. And you also know Russia has one of the most sophisticated education systems in the whole world.

All the time you say learning opportunities in this country are very limited when you compare them to the best in the world." Leonard's eyes dropped, his shoulders had already fallen. Kondo sat up taller in the leather cushions. His small frame extended until they were face to face, and the pale brown light from his eyes cut through the cloud of Leonard's. It was like an invisible truth serum that Leonard couldn't resist. The heated gaze of Kondo pushed passed the ports of his pupils and sat by the door in the back of his head, like a parent, waiting for the truth to come home. And then came the question. "What is your fear Leonard?"

It Was All My Fault

"It was not supposed to happen this way Kondo. Now I'm losing him too. Every time I attach myself to someone they leave me. I was so much happier with my loneliness. I had nothing to lose, now here I am again." The fear of loss was deeper than his initial words could express, but he couldn't stop talking. Kondo was in his head opening doors and he found a room of thoughts Leonard locked many years ago. A magnetic energy was pulling memories from Leonard's head and the truth kept falling from his lips.

"Gerald was not supposed to love her," he blurted. "He was not supposed to love anybody. He was the most ultra-entitled self-centered Black man anyone I knew had ever met. His parents were wealthy, he looked good, he dressed well and he was smart. But he treated women like toys on the playground. When he finished playing with one he just moved onto the next one. When he met Lisa every sorority sister in the country warned her about him. She knew who he was and what he was, him and his fine suits, his custom-made shoes and custom made cars." Leonard paused to wipe tears from his face with the back of his hand. Then he reached for a paper table napkin and swiped the corner of his nose. "He wasn't even her type. She thought he was a shallow upper-middle class Black man. And then they were good friends. Gerald would talk to her about his dates and she would do the same about hers, it was like that. She was dating some community activist. He was dating every skirt he saw. He was a very good friend to hang out with, to laugh and talk with, but he couldn't love anyone, he would tell you that up front. He always said that. They were never supposed to be a couple. When she told me she was going to try dating Gerald I was shocked. But I was the first one in our little group to wish her well, because I knew it wouldn't work," he said sharply. Leonard never lifted his head when he spoke but his words were clear…and the room was silent. "I supported the friendship," he added. "I supported the dating. What else could I do? She was my best friend." He was relaxed, and he

spoke at that peaceful pace some Catholics do in confession. Shaking his head he continued to speak, "After a year or so, she was talking about marriage. TO GERALD," he shouted. "What! Dating was one thing, but marriage? Gerald was not capable of loving anyone but Gerald. We spoke about it. I said to her, I couldn't believe he would want such a thing. We fought, we talked, we agreed, her life her choice. What could I say Kondo, she was the only person I ever truly loved and she was my best friend. It was a different time then. I couldn't tell her how deeply I loved her. Not at that time, it would seem like I…well. I supported her. I had never seen two people more happy than they were Kondo.
Of all the people in the world he could have loved he fell in love with her. Why her? He could have a thousand different women but he had to have the only woman in the universe that I wanted, Kondo. They did everything together. At some point I felt like a third wheel. They tried to match me with people, so I wouldn't feel so awkward in mixed company. But all I wanted was to be with her. She was the only one I ever wanted and he was the only one she ever wanted. And he, he adored her, to the exclusion of everything and everyone. He absolutely loved her. I was no match for that. At some point I knew she would not love anyone but him and she would never be with another woman. So I just settled for being close as a friend. I got married, I tried to fit in, I tried to disguise it. But it didn't work, it wasn't fair to my husband. I should have told him that I couldn't love him and I just needed to stay close to her. And then came Marcus. When she learned that she was pregnant with you, they asked me to come over. We sat in this room, I sat in this chair. They told me I was family to them, and the only person they trusted to care for you in the event they could not. A few weeks later I saw your first sonogram. I was there when you were delivered, when you opened your eyes to this world. When you took your first step, your first swim, your first breath, I was there Marcus. You may not be my blood son, but I love you like you are. And you are all I have left of your parents,

of your mother." He paused and wiped his eye. It was a gentle moment and Marcus was compelled to speak.

"Leonard, I love you as I have always loved you. I remember when I thought I couldn't make it across the pool. I was in the middle, it was deep water and I was really scared. You were on the deck, I called out to you, do you see me? You said, 'Yes Marcus I see you, just keep swimming.' I wanted you to get back in the water because I could grab you if I couldn't make it, like I always did. But this time you stayed on the deck. 'I see you Marcus, just keep swimming.' It was the first time I swam the length of the whole pool. A few times my legs were so tired I didn't think I could finish but the voice kept ringing, 'I see you Marcus, just keep swimming.' I made it to the end. When I got out you were there, my parents were there, and everyone was happy. I asked, did you watch me the whole time? And you…" excitedly Leonard interrupted.

"Yes, I remember that day," he said.

"You remember what you said to me?"

"Yes, of course I remember, you're my Godson." Excited to know what was said, Tatyana turned to Marcus, and then Leonard, they both were smiling. She asked,

"What happened?" Leonard responded.

"He was ready. At least a week before he was able to swim the length of that pool. I stayed close to him the first few times, well within his reach. He needed to know that he could grab on to me, and he did that the first time. The second time I stayed just out of his reach, but I stayed in the water, right in front of him, so that he could see me watching. When I was there, he knew he could do it. It went on like that every day that week. At the beginning of the next week I wanted him to know that he was ready. I wanted him to know that he could do it without me. So I got out of the water and I watched and encouraged him from the deck.

I said Marcus, God has given me one green eye and one brown eye, as long as I am able to open at least one of them, it will always be watching you."

"Yep, that's what he said," Marcus shouted. "That's exactly what he said! From that time to now, I know that love is not something you say to those you feel good about Leonard, love is what you do to protect them… and I never forgot that. You have helped me so much. We are not ending anything. We are beginning a new extension in a different place. When you walked back into my life you told me that you came to all of my high school and college wrestling matches, sat in the stands and told no one. The person who did that will come to Russia." Leonard smiled at his rationale. He could see the influence, the bits of himself imprinted in the thinking of his Godson. Marcus continued, "I have no doubt you will come to Russia to visit. My parents knew what they were doing when they chose you Leonard. They chose well. At the beginning and the end of all things there is a reason. Often, we are confounded by that truth. When I think about my parents, my family and my life in this country, I realize that my struggle was not only with the police in America. My biggest struggle was with my unrealistic expectations of American justice. You and the BRO helped me see that. In this country we have a proud history of revolutionary war against oppression. In every country on this planet there were oppressed people who at some point in their history had to rise against their oppressor and physically fight for their freedom. We celebrate that, because a revolution gave birth to America. But we don't celebrate Black rebellion. Descendants of the slave rising in revolution against the long legacy of oppression is a terrifying thought to most Americans. As children we learn to celebrate our rebellion and canonize our civil war as a fight for the right of all people to be free. But when Black people advocate an armed revolution, even other Black people oppose them, mostly in fear of losing the little freedoms they have. The Black American will protest injustice and march for freedom, but few are willing to die for it. As a people we have chosen to work within the system to change it. I was one of those people. But after all this time what I found was a unique definition of justice that slides around like the pointer on a Ouija board. I was trained to think that it is the greatest system in the world. I was taught to repeat phrases like. 'Our justice system may not be perfect, but it is the best in the world by far.' But when I had an opportunity to step back and examine the claim, I asked a deeper question. What self-respecting country wouldn't claim that their systems of governance are the best? When I was able to experience other countries, other governments, other people, I had something to compare. Before then, all of my information came directly from, or filtered through, the same western or American based sources. When I look back at myself, it is strange to see how much I thought I knew that I really didn't. I thought I had free choices and when I discovered that I was only choosing from the things placed before me I was dumfounded. I was in denial at first. To think I was free to choose only what others wanted me to know was a revelation. For a time, I beat myself up with questions. Why didn't I seek other ideas? Why didn't I independently explore other ideologies? I couldn't know why at the time but when a person doesn't know a thing even exists that thing is not a choice… and I couldn't hear other perspectives because I didn't speak the other languages. For me, America was the best, American culture was the best, American food, technology, entertainment, sports, arts, military, ideology, American everything was better than anyone else's anything. Given the horrible history of slavery and Jim Crow treatment I knew about, I still felt that way. It was all I knew, there is always a bit of security in ignorance. My parents trained me to be safe and secure in a country where many Black people are neither. When they died, they left me with you to finish my training. You and the BRO showed me that there is more to life than the world I knew. I am still learning Leonard. Russia is a new extension of life and learning in a different place. I remember how Kondo says when we discover our ignorance and leave the terror of losing, we are free, and we can truly live."

"Yes, it is so," Kondo uttered from the back of the conversation. "And, my thinking is this," he added. "You have reason to stay, you have reason to go. After you consider all the things most important to you, where ever you are is OK."

"Yes," Tatyana said with an easy voice. Picking up on Marcus' statement about his American upbringing, she introduced a different perspective. "When I came to this country I noticed the Americans have a tendency to be good at everything, except Black and Brown people," she said sarcastically. "But one day, very soon, those people will lose their fear of law enforcement, and the game will change." Everyone nodded. Leonard knew she was right but his mind was somewhere else. His large head was full of unfinished thoughts and his fighting nature needed to persuade them to stay without seeming selfish. Besides his brother they were the only family in his life and Russia was a long ways away. He hesitated before he stood, and in a soft voice he spoke few words. "Please," he said. "We still have work to do." That was it. It was an honest reach for something he felt he was losing and needed to hold onto. But he knew the facts, he worked with the team that tabulated most of them. The relationship the BRO forged with his Godson produced the most effective wave of change that has ever swept across the American continent. As long as there was injustice in America there would always be work to do. But Marcus Madison was the invisible force the people produced to oppose it; he would always return. He was a proud product of an environment that could honestly be stamped, Made in America.

The End
Book One

"Why carry the social legacy of your captors into the next generation? If you keep the ideology of the master because it is more comfortable than building your own, you may look free but your mind belongs to him."

Tatyana Gannibal

BE YE NOT AFRAID

From The Book Of Short Stories
By Venson Jordan

One day in the middle years of his life a Black man said, I am blessed to have an older brother. When I was a boy my parents saddled him with the responsibility of toting me from place to place, from time to time. Needless to say I was a difficult child to deal with. Today I tease him, saying I am certain that was the reason he never had children of his own. But things happened… and once again my brother was there, waiting for me. His nurturing nature pulled me through one of the darkest times in my life, reminding me of a set of simple facts.

Knowing when to attack is usually the difference between success and failure.
Be mindful of those around you, never make a threat.
Do not fear life or death.
Try to have no enemies, but if you do, do not initiate a fight, avoid them with all you have.
When your enemies attack you, the time to strike will show itself, be patient.
If you strike, do so without warning.
Remember that there is a time and place for everything, so be ye not afraid.

Life has given us two parents beyond our own, they are Mother Nature and Father Time. So, be yourself, be productive, be patient, and be ye not afraid.

OTHER BOOKS
BY Venson Jordan

THE TIMELESS LIFE OF THELONIOUS THE MONK

The Timeless Life of Thelonious, The Monk: is book one in a series of historic fiction novels, by Venson Jordan. The short novels chronicle the fantastic life of the traveler and wise man Thelonious Munkusi. Thelonious is an African man with a genetic defect that slows the process of aging. After his 25th birthday, Thelonious will only age one year every decade. But it never stopped him from living. This story is one of the greatest journeys of all times, an odyssey that spanned the life of a man who lived longer and traveled farther than anyone in recorded history.

His Journey began at the 11th hour on the 11th day of the 11th month of the year 1918. As elder son of a tribal chief, Thelonious was sent on an errand to examine the trade capacity of two foreign merchants. His fortune changed when he was abducted to be sold as a slave at the underground market in Bombay, India. A mysterious Indian woman buys his freedom in exchange for three years' service at her Yacht Club. Eventually she establishes an affection for Thelonious she cannot contain, and the intensity of their friendship makes a drastic change. While in china,

Thelonious accepts the gift of a sacred bird and prepares to travel the world. Full of inspiring situations, and exciting details, the first installment in this series pulls together the early years and unforgettable times in the life of Thelonious; and sets the stage for many adventures to come. In the secret world of academia many people know who Thelonious Munkusi was, but only a small circle of experts knew what he was, or how he lived; until now. Though many of the characters are fictitious much of the history is not, a balanced formula that leaves the reader informed and entertained.

THE CENTRIPETAL NATURE OF TRUTH

This book is informative, entertaining and sometimes emotional.

What is truth?

Venson confronts the question head on and the story surrounding the answer draws the reader into every page. The in-depth discussion between characters is reminiscent of Plato's republic, and the dialogue encourages us to search the things we believe, and consider the things we do not.

Meta Morphic

Venson Jordan's Meta Morphic, is a well-rounded experience for anyone who loves the art of creative writing. His work is thought provoking, his words are vibrant; and his topics are ageless and universally relevant. This fascinating book is a collection of beautifully written poetry, prose and short stories that will delight the senses, touch the heart, nourish the mind and soothe the spirit.

LET MEDITATION BE YOUR MEDICINE

A Healthier Way To Life And Living

I do not think you have what it takes to improve your health. I know you do. The purpose of this book is to help you know it too." For thousands of years, mystics, gurus, imams and priests have taught with a metaphysical certainty that meditation can heal. Somehow, they knew we are more than we can see. That the macromolecular patterns that make us common also make us different; and this difference is an important constituent of growth and a necessary component of success. Whether the energy is believed to be produced by the god of Abraham, or the self-augmenting patterns of the universe; they all appreciate that the core of life is the same.

The human mind has the power to repair the body, and meditation is one of many ways to do it. If your acceptance of new information must be weighed and confirmed by the scientific process, then the institutional data to support meditation as a medicine is growing. Researchers who use it to study the mind are beginning to unlock the creative ways our mind and immune cells interact; because, immune cells have the ability to contribute to the broadcast of chemical messages sent by our brain. Emotions, expectations and other sensations are being transmitted all day, every day. Harnessing the energy that conducts our lives is only a few practice sessions away.

It is also important to understand that meditation is not something you do. It is something you become; and that happens in stages and gets stronger with practice. Let Meditation Be Your Medicine is a book about what happens when an ordinary person discovers the human mind can heal and strengthen the body, and deflect the ailments associated with aging.

□

ABOUT THE AUTHOR

Venson Jordan is the author of four additional books: THE CENTRIPETAL NATURE OF TRUTH: is a book about the ideas that shape and govern the human animal. The center piece of who we are is how we live, how we listen, how we love. When we respect the space and opinions of those with whom we may differ, the road to truth is always clear. (May 9, 2016) META MORPHIC: A collection of beautifully written poetry, prose and short stories that will delight the senses, touch the heart, nourish the mind and soothe the spirit, (December 14, 2015) LET MEDITATION BE YOUR MEDICINE: A non-pharmaceutical way to prevent poor health and maintain good fitness (May 9, 2015) and THE POET IN ME: an anthology of his works (February 1999) Venson is an extensive traveler, he was born in Washington, DC and still resides in America with his family.

Made in United States
North Haven, CT
22 March 2022

17450788R00150